The Time Menders

(A Slipstream Novel)

by
Laine Stambaugh

Also by Laine Stambaugh

The Heart Stone Trilogy:
Raven Wakes the Dawn
Raven in the Runes
The Sea Raven

"And thus the whirligig of time brings in his revenges."
(--*Twelfth Night*, William Shakespeare)

Prologue

Katya
Russia
1918

I'm cursed.

As Katya sat in the small cottage she'd inherited from her mother after her recent death, she tried not to stare at the rain seeping through the roof. Or listen to the sound of it hitting the pails she'd set out to catch the drips as water accumulated in three corners of the cottage Katya had called home for twenty-two years.

Oh yes, she was cursed all right. She shivered and rubbed her arms. Cursed to be born on the day Nicholas II was crowned Czar of all Russia—the day Katya Peshkova's mother gave birth to her on the 30th of May, 1896. As part of the festivities that day, arrangements had been made to serve the peasants food in nearby Khodynka Field, food they hadn't seen since the start of the war with the Bolsheviks. She frowned at the memory and gripped the arms of her chair. Things went horribly wrong from there when someone let the word out that there wouldn't be enough food for the peasants. Parents desperate to obtain nutritious food for their children rushed an area set up for milk, bread, potatoes, and apple distribution. But that person had been right.

"There wasn't enough food," Katya whispered, her throat dry.

Hundreds, maybe thousands of people stampeded the tables set up for the occasion, leaving hundreds injured, and in Katya's father's case, dead. She never even got to see him.

Years later, she asked her mother why the czar had played such a cruel trick on the people, then pretended nothing had happened after the stampede area had been "cleaned up," but her mother had no answers. Year by year, Katya's rage at the nobility grew until she couldn't contain herself any longer. But one didn't stand in St. Basil's Square and curse the czar or declare him an evil man.

"Not if one hopes to keep one's head."

It became routine for Katya to wake up on her birthday and race to the site where it all began, Khodynka Field. Once there, she would cry to her heart's satisfaction. People she knew, like her friend Dima, left her alone the morning of her birthday, if they knew what was good for them.

With the Bolsheviks' murder of the Romanovs two months ago, Katya thought she'd finally get some closure. She wanted to be like ordinary people who celebrated these yearly milestones. Cake and songs. Maybe a small gift.

She picked up a vase with a wilted flower. She'd forgotten all about Dima's surprise birthday daisy. Sometimes he could be so sweet.

The past year had been particularly hard on Katya and her mother. In the last week of April, Katya's mother suddenly became ill. Within days, a fever took her ... and Katya was alone. She'd tried every remedy she could think of to save her mother. She even asked for help from some of her mother's friends who knew a bit about healing, though she was sometimes suspicious of what they suggested.

Katya sniffed, her grief still raw. *What will happen to me?*

In the end, she went with Dima and his gruff aunt, Oksana, to bury her mother in the woods near her home. Now, for the first time in a long time, Katya shoved back the memories and tried to recall some of the good memories she'd experienced with her mother and Dima's family. Memories such as Dima teaching his little sister, Nesya, how to swim the summer before the tragedy. Dima had been so patient with her, so focused. It was a side of him she'd never seen before. This year, she'd been preoccupied. And though her father's death on the day she was born still hurt, it was the first birthday she hadn't raged against the nobility.

She put a hand on the door and pondered whether to visit her mother's grave for the second time that day. *No, I need another distraction, something useful to do until Dima returns.*

So, she picked up a broom and swept, as she considered where she might set up a small altar to remember her mother. The space her mother had made for her father was tiny, with only an old black-and-white photo yellowed with age to remind Katya that although she resembled her mother, she had her father's kind, dark eyes.

She suppressed a sob, refusing to feel sorry for herself. Instead, she vowed not to let the darkness consume her. However, to do that, she must be able to support herself. Her entire life, she'd studied tarot cards, and often sat in on her mother's readings. Not only would the money she earned reading cards for people pay a few creditors, but it would distract her from her grief. Fortunately, Aunt Oksana realized right away that Katya had a sixth sense and natural inclination at telling fortunes, so she set out to teach Katya everything she knew about the history of tarot. With Oksana's help, Katya would assume her mother's role as Madame Peshkova and try to assemble a wealthy clientele. With that encouragement, Katya began dreaming of a modern Moscow apartment, fine clothes, and if she didn't have a husband by then, a loyal little white poodle she'd once seen.

Her thoughts turned to poor Dima. After her mother's death, he had insisted he move in with Katya for her protection, and she had agreed, but only if they each had their own rooms. In exchange for room and board, Dima performed minor repairs around the cottage. She glanced up to see if the hole in the roof near the fireplace had grown bigger from the rain. Even in summer, she felt the cold seep through the cracks and she shivered, as she debated whether to throw on a shawl, despite the humid summer's day. She'd asked Dima to fix the holes long before the rains began. He could be so lazy sometimes, but she didn't criticize. Other than Aunt Oksana, he was all the family she had after her mother died.

"So, where *is* Dima?" she asked the invisible poodle.

She peeked through the frayed curtains and frowned at the condensation that had accumulated on the windowpane on the inside. A variety of small claw marks had chipped away whatever trim used to be on the windowsill. Winters were freezing cold, so she couldn't blame the animals in their eagerness to come inside. As it happened, animals tended to follow Katya whenever she headed for home, as if they knew she was Madame Peshkova's daughter.

"But now, *I* am Madame Peshkova."

At last, the rain subsided, and still, Dima hadn't returned. It was already afternoon, and her day was getting away from her. She glanced at the tarot cards her mother had left on the table before she died, the last reading her mother had done. Prior to this moment, Katya couldn't bring herself to touch them. She walked over to the table and sat down to study them, the back of her throat closing up. She still didn't understand as much as she should, but she saw where her mother had set a card aside and left it face down. She started there and flipped it over.

"For me?" she whispered.

Her mother always pulled one last card for the day, claiming it would guide Katya the next day. She picked up the card, her brow furrowing in question.

"Not the one I would have hoped for."

A young maiden appeared in the foreground, a castle floating in the sky behind her. Her arms were tied around her torso while four swords on each side of her pierced the ground.

Disturbed by the image, Katya walked to the sink and poured a glass of water, contemplating what the card might mean. After a few sips, her throat felt better, as she continued to ponder the message of the Eight of Swords. Normally, the card was meant to indicate an individual feeling trapped, most likely from a credit agreement that left little money for her day-to-day life. She could relate to that. Though normally an optimistic person, it was hard to remain joyful when she had no money. Her mother had owned the cottage outright, but repairs were always adding up, eating away at what little income Katya or Dima could earn. For the last few years Dima had been hounding her to marry him, which would provide her with more security, but the thought of marrying her childhood friend didn't feel quite right.

She would never admit it, but deep down, Katya longed to meet the man who would help her forget her life, shower her with kisses, and keep her from losing her home. However, at times she was glad Dima was around. Whenever she'd had a rough day with a dissatisfied customer or a creditor, she let them believe Dima was her husband, and he would run them off. It was a strange way to live, but she knew no other.

Before she had a chance to consider the other cards scattered on the table in relation to the Eight of Swords, the door crashed open and Dima came strolling in, carrying a package wrapped in brown paper and tied with a string.

Katya glanced down and saw the mud he'd brought in on his shoes. "You filthy pig!" she growled, but he simply held out the package and grinned.

"I had to walk downtown in the rain to pick up your present. Happy Birthday, Katya!"

She shoved him down on a bench and pointed at his shoes. "First, take those off."

"You know, you're not much fun on your birthday," Dima said, sending her a hurt look. "I saved up to buy you something special. Aren't you going to open it?"

What she really wanted to do was yell and scream at the person who'd ended her father's life before she was born. Would her pathetic existence have been different with a father present? Nicholas II was to blame. She'd heard in town that his whole family was to be executed by the Bolsheviks on July 17—in two days' time. She sniffed and swatted at a tear.

"At least the czar will be dead, God rot his soul in hell," she muttered under her breath.

Used to her cursing on this occasion, Dima removed the string from the package and placed the wrap on her lap without a word. "You know, I heard the strangest thing when I was in town today."

"What was that?" She untied the string on the package, and opened it to find a beautiful dress.

"Apparently, the soldiers can't find Anastasia. Eyewitnesses say she didn't travel to Yekaterinburg with her family. She has disappeared."

Katya looked up, fingering the dark red material that felt like satin. "How can she be missing? I thought her entire family was to be killed, then dumped into the same grave. Besides, where would Anastasia be, if not with her family?"

Dima ignored her question and pulled out the material to reveal a stylish evening dress. "What do you think? You look terrific in red."

She suppressed a smile as she noted the stylish V-neck with flutter sleeves, and regarded how beautifully the material draped. Oh, if she only had a special place to wear it.

I can't possibly keep it. She put on her stern face and set it aside. "It's not my style, Dima. And anyway, where in the world would I wear it? It's too impractical. You should know better."

Dima ran a hand through his short, black hair. This time, she could tell he wasn't pretending to be hurt. "That's the other thing. Madame Rudinsky sold this dress to me at a special discount to give to you for your birthday. She said you would need it because you'll be going on a long trip soon. Do you know what she's talking about?"

A chill slithered down Katya's spine as she rose from her chair. She tried not to look at the tarot cards still to be factored into her mother's reading. "You do know Madame Rudinsky is a—"

"Witch?"

For a moment, he paled, as he silently battled his own superstitious demons, but then he pulled himself together and sat up straighter.

"This is the modern age, Katya, not Medieval times. Besides, Madame Rudinsky wanted you to have this for your birthday, and so do I. In the meantime, why don't you try on the dress?"

Katya eyed the feminine fluttery sleeves and her heart began to race. Never had she owned such a grown-up, flirty gown. She tried not to look down at her brown skirt and top meant for work. Hard work. They smelled of sweat and cow's milk. Finally, she relented.

"It's beautiful, Dima. Thank you." She pushed her wavy dark hair back over her shoulders. "I do want to go out and show off this dress, but first, are you hungry? I've heated some soup."

"Yes, thanks. You're the cat's whiskers, Katya." He pulled another small package out of his pocket. "By the way, this goes with the dress. Pavel's wife says it's all the rage."

Katya stopped ladling the thin potato soup to pull aside the wrapping. It revealed a new tube of deep red lipstick which did *indeed* match perfectly. "That's thoughtful, Dima. What's it called?"

"*Sin on Fire*."

"Oh my." She held it under the light, then set it beside her spot at the table.

The tarot cards were completely forgotten for now, as they ate a light dinner. Then she tried on the red dress. She had to admit, Madame Rudinsky was a decent seamstress, because the dress felt custom-made to fit her curves. Next, she applied the red lipstick and twirled around for Dima, who whistled in appreciation. Feeling so much better now, she decided to break the old mold. Everyone else celebrated birthdays. Why not her?

But as she stood to leave, her eyes darted to the cards her mother had placed on the table prior to her death. "Before I go, I need to figure out the cards Mother has left me. I sense she was trying to warn me about something."

"What would she be warning you about?" Dima asked. "Besides, she was so sick at the end, she might not have been thinking straight."

Katya gave him a disgusted look. "You know as well as I do that Mother never missed an opportunity to help us in our lives." She sat at the table and shuffled the cards one last time. Then she drew three cards to indicate past, present, and future. Afterward, she crossed her arms as she contemplated her question. Dima looked over her shoulder, but she could tell he was anxious to leave with the way he kept adjusting his collar.

"So, what's it say?"

She flipped the first card over, and couldn't quite suppress a gasp. Quickly, she flipped it back on its face so Dima wouldn't see the grim skeleton ghost representing Death. "We'll talk about that later. Now, where's that place you wanted to go for a birthday drink?"

To her surprise, Dima snapped up her tarot cards and put them in his pocket as he escorted her out of the cottage. She'd ask the reason later. In the meantime, she wanted a few hours to be young and maybe even learn how to dance.

She pressed her red lips together. "So, where are we going?" she asked again as they started out for the main square in Moscow.

"I heard something really interesting earlier. You know how you've complained about nobles like the Romanovs beating down the peasants? Never mind, don't answer that," he said with a laugh. He put a brotherly arm around her shoulder as a nice-looking man in a suit passed by and gave Katya a wolf whistle.

She turned to Dima who wore a wolfish smile of his own. "Oh, stop that," she said, pretending to be angry by shoving Dima. "Now, what news do you have about the nobility?"

He glanced around them, and when it appeared they were alone, he leaned in. "I met some people who belong to a group that intends to make mischief for the nobility. It has to do with traveling through time, which I admit, I don't understand. But one of their high-placed members plans to be at this party I'm taking you to. You'll get to meet him. Grigori Rasputin."

Katya stopped in the middle of the street. She'd heard things about the charismatic priest who'd saved the tsarevich's life several times. But she'd never heard anything particularly good about him other than that.

She inhaled a deep breath. "He...he died two years ago, didn't he?" she said in a whisper.

"That's what's so interesting about these time travelers. They brought Rasputin forward two years to our time because there was something here he still needed to do."

"Like what? And wh-why would you want me to meet him?"

He smiled his most confident smile, which made her even more nervous. Then he reached into the pocket of his jacket and pulled out her tarot cards.

"Because Grisha, as they call him to avoid alerting the authorities, says Anastasia Romanov is alive. And they want *your* help in drawing out the rich folks who may have information about her. They want *you* to read the tarot cards. You've already developed a reputation with your dazzling style." He tucked a long curl behind her ear. "Besides, this assignment was made for you.

Tonight, we join a group of people who think alike, and aren't afraid to speak up when something goes wrong."

Katya stood in silence, a rush of emotions cascading over her. "Anastasia is alive? What does this group want to do with her? Kill her?" When he didn't answer, she started walking again. "What is this group called?"

"Anti-Time Travel Oversight. ATTO, for short." He put the cards back inside his coat pocket. "We need to get going. I don't want to miss Rasputin and his special guest."

"Who's the special guest?"

His eyes glittered in the setting sun, now that the rain had given everything in its path a shining newness.

"I hear she's an absolutely gorgeous ballet dancer...from the future."

Chapter 1

"It's never too late to begin anew and follow your heart."
(Tarot Card: The Fool)

Dasha
San Francisco
Present Day

A hint of electricity filled the night air at the old opera house. As I gazed across the lobby at all the glitz and glamor that had been dragged out of closets and storage facilities to make a good impression at my mother's annual gala fundraiser for the Heart-Held Women's Shelter, it occurred to me that a certain irony existed among the people of San Francisco. Old money from prominent families. New money from technology industries. And no money for the homeless unless fundraisers like this were successful.

This year, the theme was the Roaring 20s, and some of the ladies looked as if they were born to wear the long-wasted flapper girl dresses in all colors of the rainbow. Their beads and necklaces, made up of sparkly gems, clacked against their chests, their feathers genuine. Altogether, it was an intelligent-looking group.

As I strolled through the crowd in search of my mother, I made certain that everything was running smoothly. I hadn't given my job as the shelter's talent manager much thought prior to accepting the offer, since I considered it a placeholder until the right career fell into my lap. I had only been out of college two years, but time was definitely on my mind as I received one job rejection after another. Fortunately, my mother had seen my worth and hired me. I heard her voice and lifted my head.

Finally, across the room I spotted her, Irisa Marusov, founder and director for the shelter. She insisted I utilize my Russian Studies degree to woo the local Russian enclave. Tonight, my particular job was to keep the vodka flowing. But, I had to admit, based on the laughter that ran into the wee hours of the morning, Mom knew how to throw a great party.

And she knows how to squeeze money out of rich donors' pockets with a smile on her face the entire time.

I glanced toward the stage. My real job was to come up with musical talent so that as the guests sipped their expensive wines, or champagne, or whatever else they drank, they would dole out thousands of dollars to show their benevolence.

I bit my nails and searched the room for Brendon, tonight's entertainment. I wasn't positive these guests would take to an up-and-coming rock band. But, the group was definitely entertaining, and I'd known Brendon from our college partying days, so he was eager for the band's exposure. Meaning they came cheap.

My cell phone vibrated in the pocket of my black-and-green beaded vintage flapper dress. I saw Brendon's name appear, and for a moment, a sense of dread washed through me. Would he cancel?

"Do not panic, Dasha Marusov," I mumbled.

I stepped away from the bright lights so I could better return Brendon's message with a call. My hands turned clammy when he didn't answer until the third ring.

"Brendon, where are you?"

"Dash! We just arrived. We're at the loading dock. Where do we set up?"

A flutter dispersed like confetti over my heart at the familiar voice from years past. We'd had some good times together back in college. B.D.D. Before Dalton died.

"Hey, Brendon. Good to hear your voice. The stage is set up at the bottom of the main staircase. Go ahead and set up and I'll meet you there shortly."

"Cool. See ya, Sunshine."

Brendon had bestowed the nickname on me because of my strawberry blonde hair. But for all I knew, he'd used the same nickname for dozens of girls back then.

Once again, I turned to scan the crowd for my mother, the master timekeeper at these events. I waved to catch her attention as she mingled with those in attendance. It was a balmy summer night in San Francisco. She'd worn a form-fitting beaded gold flapper gown that caught the highlights in her blonde hair, which she brushed back with one hand to reveal a high forehead and sparkling blue eyes that dazzled brighter than the diamond earrings Dad had given her at Christmas.

By now, the room had become crowded, and numerous perfumes got my allergies going. Not the most graceful of creatures, I tried to stifle a huge sneeze, but ended up stepping back and throwing up my arms just as the sneeze exploded. To my embarrassment, I knocked over a full tray of champagne glasses that splintered into a hundred pieces or more.

"Oh, I'm so sorry!" I hated drawing the wrong kind of attention to myself, and immediately began retrieving the pieces of broken glass.

The young waitress apologized in Russian several times as she scrambled to find a trash container to place the broken glass.

"Don't worry. It was my fault," I said, hoping to calm her fears.

The pretty teen had dark curls that bounced when she walked. Her Russian accent sounded as if it was from the countryside rather than Moscow, which made me feel even worse. She probably had a family at home, struggling to make a living while inhabiting a tiny apartment in the Richmond District. It was a Russian enclave for immigrants and those who wished to live among people who shared similar customs and traditions, including language. She wore a name tag that read "Dianna" as she scanned the lobby with eyes that never quite landed on one person. I suspect she thought she was in big trouble.

Just then, my middle sister, Sasha, suddenly appeared with a broom and dustpan so we could quickly dispose of the broken glass.

I signaled a member of the catering staff. Dianna kept her head down as the waiter came rushing over and surveyed the scene. He wore the typical catering staff black pants and tie, with a white shirt. Rather than appear concerned for Dianna, he frowned as he directed his gaze her way.

"How did you manage to break all eight goblets of champagne, Dianna? We're short on goblets, so someone will have to pay for their replacements."

The girl's pale face cast a sickly glow. Seeing that, Sasha reached out and placed a hand on her forearm. "Are you okay? Did you cut yourself on the glass?"

"I am fine," Dianna said in heavily accented English as she tried to politely brush away Sasha's hand.

Sasha, the introvert in the family, said, "Don't worry about broken glasses. My sister, Dasha, will take care of that, won't you, sis?"

I was busy studying the supervisor, whose name tag read "Alex." Something about him seemed old-fashioned, dated. I turned my attention back to my sister.

"You're absolutely right, Sasha. And if our Grandma Tattie were here, she'd say something like 'Glasses are easy to replace. Good workers are not'."

Dianna smiled shyly, as I focused on the spilled wine that had formed a puddle on the floor. The waiter shook his head at Dianna, but wisely said nothing more in front of the sisters.

"I'll get towels to wipe this up," Dianna mumbled, and then hurried off, her dark curls bobbing.

"I apologize, Miss Maruzov. Dianna should have held the tray with a better grip."

For some reason, the waiter's dismissive attitude toward Dianna pushed a button in me. "Say, *Allan*, I bumped into Dianna, not the other way around. Besides, it's crowded and everyone is working hard. However, maybe the wait staff should carry fewer full glasses on a tray. I'm sure my mother—Mrs. Marusova—would agree."

"The name's...Alex."

Sasha's giggle in the background was the cherry on top. I hated rude people.

When Dianna returned, she and I both knelt to mop up the mess, and the floor shined once again. Then Dianna took off to deliver more champagne and Alex returned to his duties. I turned to Sasha, while keeping an eye out for Mom.

My middle sister wore her honey-colored hair in a loose French braid, with wisps of hair cascading down her cheeks to frame her lovely face. Her willowy figure made her the perfect model for the old-fashioned lilac dress she'd found at the vintage clothing store where she worked part-time. Because it was August, the gown was sleeveless, the top of the bodice sheer, the rest lined in a darker lilac and tied artfully just below her slender waist.

"Beautiful color on you," I said, patting her arm.

"Thanks. I couldn't decide between this and the light pink gown I found at the store."

"You made the right choice."

A year ago, Sasha had secured a part-time job at *Araminta's Vintage Clothes* store, and I loved dropping by to see the new window displays. In fact, it had become a new obsession of mine. Most of the gowns from the shop were in fairly good condition, and Sasha was content to repair clothing that needed some TLC. I squeezed her hand. *That's our Sasha. So generous with her time and talents.* I couldn't believe she did those repair jobs for free. Sasha just smiled and said it gave her "peace of mind" to work with those old fabrics.

I'd found a green-and-black beaded band at her shop that wrapped around my forehead, slicked back my hair with Dippity Do, and created exaggerated finger curls at my temple and cheeks, in imitation of old magazine ads. I glanced down at my deep red nails and grinned.

Just then, I spotted my youngest sister, Gigi, across the room, looking self-conscious as she glanced about. It wasn't easy being one of Irisa Marusova's daughters, who was both gorgeous and blonde, and the queen bee of fundraising in the Bay Area.

Gigi squeezed up next to us. "Can you believe all these people? There's, like, a gazillion guests here." At sixteen, Gigi's gown was more modest, showing much less skin than her older sisters. The material was orchid chiffon, and it came in two pieces, a capped-sleeve blouson that fell below her hips, which was then tied to the skirt's flowing scarf. A dark purple, artificial rose finished the look. Like Sasha, Gigi was tall and blonde, a younger version of our mother. Where's Brendon and his band? Is he still a hottie?"

"Gigi!"

She grinned and covered her mouth. "Are you going to ask him out after the concert?"

"I'll wait and see how the evening goes. Not that it's any of your business, Miss Gigi." I tickled her ribs, and was glad she was still young enough to giggle.

Gigi was the nickname I'd given her when our mother decided on the old-fashioned non-Russian name for her youngest. Grace Gabrielle Mazurov. Gigi stuck.

I was about to sip my first glass of champagne when a woman in dark red silk rushed by and bumped my arm. The champagne missed my gown, thank God, but splashed on the floor. The woman stopped, appearing distracted.

"Oh, so sorry!"

Just my luck, the other woman signaled the same waiter—Allan. No, Alex. *Whatever.* By the time he crossed the room and saw the new puddle of champagne on the floor, he wore a distinct frown.

"Are we having a clumsy evening, Miss Maruzov?"

"I...I..." "That's rude," said Gigi with a frown to the waiter. "She didn't spill anything. And my sister is *not* clumsy." She slid an arm around my shoulder.

"Oh, are you Daria Maruzova?" the woman in red asked in surprise.

The first thing I noticed was that her gown wasn't from the Roaring Twenties, but then, what did I know? I'm sure they must have worn more than flapper dresses to work. Teachers. Librarians. Clerks. Until the coming of World War II, jobs for ladies were not as plentiful as one would hope.

The second thing I noticed was her long, wavy dark hair that cascaded down her back, almost to her waist. She wore it loose. The deep red satin fabric of the dress draped beautifully from the bow at the base of the modest v-neck, to a slightly longer waist, then down past her knees. When she put a hand on my arm, I got a close look at her face. I would have guessed her to be in her early twenties. But then, as I tilted my head and frowned, I wondered if she was older than I first believed. She had a "worldliness" I hadn't expected.

"Are you Daria, the eldest daughter of Irisa Maruzova?" she asked, holding her breath.

She used my given name, not the nickname everyone else used. Daria easily transitioned to Dasha. My sister Sasha's given name was Aleksandra, but both the male name Aleksander and the female Aleksandra, were reduced to Sasha, much to my sister's displeasure. Mom didn't like referring to her daughters as Dasha and Sasha. But Grandma Tattie insisted, and as usual, she got her way.

"It sounds like I'm calling two dogs," Dasha's mother once complained.

As a cat person, Sasha was insulted. I thought it was funny.

I gazed back at the woman, wondering what she wanted with me. "Yes, I'm Daria, but people call me Dasha. And you are?"

The woman with hazel eyes broke into a smile, appearing less anxious. "I'm the other entertainment, Madame Peshkova. You called and asked me to come. I tell fortunes with tarot cards." She turned and pointed to a cozy-looking corner of the big hall where a muscular man with dark, slicked-back hair was setting up a partition and arranging chairs beside a round table.

"We'll be ready to go in just a minute." She put a hand on her waist and looked me in the eye.

Her English was accented, but I couldn't place it, while her face was absolutely flawless and mysterious at the same time. Perhaps she was of mixed race, as her skin was light brown, and her eyes were intense, although she seemed awfully young. My immediate response was suspicion.

"Please call me Madame Peshkova. I would be honored to tell your fortune. Please come with me."

I sighed heavily. "Whatever. But you girls have to go next, okay? Brendon's band is setting up. Come get me if they need anything."

Madame Peshkova rushed me along. As I approached the makeshift tarot card table inside the partitions, I noted it had been made into a cozy and private retreat. I tried to recall where I'd seen Madame Peshkova's name on the schedule and who had recommended her. Some people would shun anything resembling the occult or paranormal. Others, like my superstitious grandparents, would have loved it.

Madame Peshkova's assistant cleared his throat to get my attention, then held the chair for me. *Trapped.* I really didn't like that feeling, but I used that moment to study him as he handed Madame Peshkova a deck of colorful tarot cards. I was terrible at guessing people's ages, but I'd say he was in his late twenties or early thirties. He didn't look me in the eye, nor speak, and I wondered if English was his native language.

"Dima, please bring Miss Maruzova a glass of water. Miss Maruzova, you must silently think of one specific question you wish to ask the cards today." She shuffled the cards expertly and then fanned them across the table. I stared at them, not sure what I was supposed to do.

Dima's fingers brushed against mine as I accepted the glass of water. He revealed nothing in those deep brown eyes, so I decided to focus on the cards.

"I know you're in a hurry, Miss Maruzova. But your reading must come first, so we're going to do a four-card spread."

"I go by Maruzov," I said. "My mother decided to name all of us girls using my father's surname. It's simpler, since American names don't use the Russian patronymic system." I shrugged, hoping that didn't feel like a lecture. I brushed back my hair. "Now, what is so important about getting my tarot card reading?"

Madame Peshkova blinked, and gestured that I should take a seat. Nearby, Dima crossed his muscular arms and narrowed his gaze as he watched my every move.

"Why must I go first before the others? My sisters have more time for this."

The young woman gave me a cold stare. "Because that is the order of things. Now, you must prepare the question you seek to have answered today. Do not tell me. Then, you will choose one of these seventy-eight cards. Together, the four cards you select should answer your question." She indicated the deck, and I couldn't help but notice she had little stars and moons decorating her fingernails.

I sat back and decided to go with the flow. I closed my eyes, thought of my question, and chose a card.

"When will I meet the man I will spend my life with?" I handed her the card, and she glanced at it with a nod of her head.

"The Three of Wands suggest expansion, growth, and optimism. Your prospective love interest, or your current love interest, views your relationship with potential. There is momentum here to move forward together."

There is hope, then?

I glanced at Dima and decided if he had a hobby, it had something to do with martial arts. He moved without making a sound, his facial expression stoic and intimidating.

"Please select another card and ask the same question."

I was surprised when she revealed The Moon card. "What does that card mean?"

"It suggests that appearances may be deceiving within your relationship dynamics, indicating a lack of transparency in the situation at hand. And now, a third card."

I quickly picked up another card and handed it to her as if it didn't matter. Then I rubbed my forehead, experiencing the beginning of a bad headache. "Madame Peshkova, I really should be going. I hate to waste your time. I need to deal with a client."

I started to rise, but felt Dima's hands on my shoulders. I settled back into my chair and glared at him.

"We're almost done. This card may be the most important."

I sighed, giving in.

"The King of Wands is a motivated, charming lover who is loyal and has a passion for excitement and the thrill of a challenge. You should expect a sexual adventure with the appearance of the King of Wands."

A sexual adventure?

I shifted in my chair and made the mistake of glancing up at Dima's eyes.

"Are you up for a sexual adventure?" they asked.

I don't think he said that aloud, or at least, Madame Peshkova didn't scold him for embarrassing me, if he did.

"I have to go...and this really is not helping. I've got so much to do tonight." I rose and ducked under Dima's arm.

"Just one more card, and your reading is complete," she pleaded, but I couldn't sacrifice any more time. I needed to dwell in the real world, not one made up of painted cards.

"I don't mean to be rude, but I have to find my mother, Mrs. Maruzova before the musical entertainment starts."

I had made it a practice to always refer to my mother as "Mrs. Maruzova" when I was dealing with foundation business. It had served me well, and I wanted people to treat me as any employee until I earned my stripes, as my father would say.

Madame Peshkova appeared surprised that I was unwilling to hear the whole spiel. She sat up straight, then exchanged glances with Dima. "You will want to hear what I have to say with this last card."

I was just about to ask how one final card could make a difference in a relationship when Gigi came rushing around the corner partition. "Dasha! Brendon says he's ready to go. Mom told me to find you."

That got the woman's attention. Madame Peshkova rose and put a hand on my shoulder. She looked at me strangely, and I wondered if she could see right through me and my half-truths.

"Make a private appointment with me."

"I may not have the time."

When she cupped my cheek, I almost jumped at the feel of her ice-cold hands. The assistant came to stand beside her, his dark eyes intense.

"You are not living the life intended for you," said Madame Peshkova. "This is important. You must hear the rest of the reading so I know you'll be safe."

By that time, I was on to them. It was just another scam. I brushed her hand aside and hurried out into the lobby, looking for Mom in her gold gown, bright enough to light up any room.

I was looking toward the stage when Brendon appeared with his band. Mom seemed relieved when she saw me, and gave me a little shove toward the stage.

"That's cutting it mighty close, Daria."

"Mom, do you know who recommended that tarot card reader, Madame Peshkova?"

Mom appeared anxious, which was unusual for her. She loved to entertain, and she never showed stress. "I don't recall. Is it important?"

"No. I'll figure it out."

The overhead lights of the lobby flickered, and a disembodied voice began to speak. "Ladies and gentlemen, please welcome the wonderful, the talented, Brendon Alessio and All Souls Day!"

Once again, I heard Madame Peshkova in her low, ominous voice. *"You are not living the life intended for you."*

I shivered and crossed my arms.

"Then whose life am I living?" I whispered.

Chapter 2

*"This is a card of illusions and having one's head in
the clouds romantically."*
(Tarot Card: Seven of Cups)

I was still shaking from my encounter with Madame Peshkova as I slid into my seat in the concert area. Brendon said he had a surprise for me, but I had to wait until after the concert. I took a few deep breaths to regain my composure, and felt a chill race up my arms as the lights dimmed and a sudden hush fell over the audience. One lonely electric guitar began to play a slow and bluesy tune as the band members took the stage one by one. Once Brendon had finished introducing each musician and his instrument, I felt as if I was sitting at home in my own living room enjoying a performance from a group of guys from school. Brendon had that folksy touch, and I envied him. His chiseled cheeks and shaggy dark hair, not to mention brown leather designer clothes, pretty much guaranteed the undivided attention of every young girl in the audience, giving the casual impression we all sat in our favorite recliner back home. The volume cranked up as the spotlight jumped around the dark stage, coming to land on Brendon again and again.

The song finished with a flourish, and a disembodied man's voice announced, "Ladies and gentlemen, please give a warm San Francisco welcome to Brendon Alessio and All Souls Day."

Considering this was a fundraising event, a lot of young girls were in attendance with their mothers, as it was a predominantly female audience. Their screams pierced my ears, and I frowned as a group of girls tried to rush the stage. All the while, Brendon remained focused on his guitar, his husky voice reminding me of Bryan Adams or Rod Stewart.

I sighed as he launched into "Girl from Monterey." I could see why he was considered a rising star. He had it all. Looks. Presence. And charisma, as he flirted with girls or young women who sang along as he perched his cowboy boots at the edge of the stage. My heart started pounding. What would Brendon say or do if I approached him after the concert and asked him out for a drink?

By the end of the song, as I watched the audience, I knew the answer. I didn't stand a chance. What was I thinking? I was so *not* a rock star's girlfriend who trailed him everywhere. Perhaps because I had a job that demanded interactions with all kinds of people on a regular basis, I treasured my home alone times. And how would I react when my name started appearing in social media posts?

And yet, I could still admire him from afar. I saw nothing wrong with that.

As the band performed their original tunes, I glanced around at the sold-out concert seats and felt like giving myself a pat on the back. It was true I wouldn't be challenging my mother anytime soon to take over as Queen Bee of fundraising in San Fran, but I could be useful to a lot of causes out there.

A flash of bright blonde hair and a golden gown caught my eye. I could see Mom had finally relaxed a bit, and was tapping her toes to the rhythm of "Wild Child," Brendon's first big hit. The bass player, a quiet guy who bore the unfortunate name of Forest Needleman, looked up into the section where I sat. There must have been a spotlight nearby if he recognized me from that distance, or else he had new glasses, because he gave me a distinct nod as he returned to focusing on his flying fingers.

The song ended and Brendon picked up the microphone. "This next song is new, and is called 'When Seasons Go South'. This goes out to all the lovely ladies of San Francisco, especially those who are staying at the Heart-Held Women's Shelter and need your help."

The audience clapped at that, and I wondered if he was told to say that, or if it came from his heart. Had he been Dalton, I would have known the answer. Dalton had looked tough on the outside, but he was more like a teddy bear on the inside.

Intense screaming a few rows down revealed teenage girls on the edge of their seats, tissues in hand. This reminded me of the year Dalton's wrestling team attracted several fangirls, who followed them wherever they went. To me, it seemed like stalking, but Dalton didn't seem to mind signing autographs and the brief conversations afterward. He was a patient man.

My hands felt clammy as I recalled Madame Peshkova's words. *"This is not the life you were meant to live."* Did she mean I was meant to have spent my life with Dalton?

Damn! Big, those words...like a neon sign in a country bar. What kind of responsible tarot reader said something like that only to let me walk away?

That's right about the time the band finished, and I saw Brendon take his time putting away his guitar. The crowd began to thin as people headed for the exits. Mom was right there, greeting everyone and enthusiastically accepting those last-minute donations. By the time Brendon approached, I was sitting in a folding chair and rubbing my feet. He wore a huge grin and leaned down to kiss my forehead.

"You guys sounded great." I gave him a big smile, saying nothing about those crazy fangirls and their fantasies.

"Thanks, Dash. I'm glad you came. Did you like our new song?"

"It sounded kind of sad. I didn't catch all the lyrics. Those girls—"

"Yeah, they were pretty loud."

He sat down next to me, the circles beneath his eyes revealing he hadn't slept much lately. I tamped down any inclination to push back some of that scruffy hair.

"Maybe you can get a good night's sleep tonight?" I suggested.

He looked down and took my hand. "I was nervous last night. Pent-up energy and all that." He turned my hand over and studied my palm. "You look terrific in that dress, by the way. Is that what flapper girls wore back then?"

"So they say. It's pretty comfortable." I squeezed his hand. "So, you said you had a big surprise to tell me?"

"Oh yeah. The band got a gig on a world tour with a band called Assassin Plan B from Austin. We leave the day after tomorrow. That will be fantastic exposure for the band's new album."

I tamped down my disappointment and forced a smile. "I'm genuinely happy for you, Brendon. I wish you the best." I kissed his cheek, which seemed the thing to do. "You've worked hard, and now your wishes will come true. Good for you."

He smiled, and I realized I meant every word.

Just then, Madame Peshkova waved at me from the foot of the grand staircase to catch my attention, but Brendon touched my bare forearm urging me to ignore the distraction. I'd forgotten how much he liked to touch, and how much I loved his warm fingers.

He rubbed my hand. "You know, I had a thing for you in college. I would have asked you out then, except for—"

"Dalton's accident?"

"Yeah." He dropped my hand and looked over my shoulder. "So, I wondered how long I should wait, you know, etiquette."

I didn't know what to say. Four years. It had been *four years*.

"Time flies really fast," he continued. "I knew you needed lots of time to heal. And I was getting the band whipped into shape. I'm so glad you asked us to perform here. It's a great start."

"Yes, losing Dalton...I haven't...it's been four years." I turned my head so he wouldn't see the lone tear roll down my cheek. I brushed it aside. "Well, thanks so much for performing here."

"Maybe when I return from the tour, we can get together for dinner or something."

I nodded, but I knew I wouldn't see him again. "That would be nice." I glanced at my watch. "I'm sure you're tired and need your rest...for your world tour. Good luck, Brendon." I gave him a quick hug, then rose and left the concert area.

I almost made it out of the theater when a hand with a vice-like grip stopped me as Madame Peshkova's bodyguard blocked my way.

"Madame Peshkova will see you now." Dima indicated I should follow him.

I stopped and glanced toward the door to the parking garage.

"I know I may regret asking this, but why does she need a bodyguard, anyway?"

His eyes pinned mine with a glare. I'd never seen such cold dark eyes before. "That is business between Madame Peshkova and myself."

I tried to step away, but he held tight. I was actually glad to see the tarot reader when she appeared. "Dima, you're frightening Miss Marusova. Why don't you bring the car around?"

He vanished so quickly, I didn't even have time to respond to Madame Peshkova's words.

"That guy moves awfully fast."

"Yes, he does move quickly." Madame Peshkova gave a weary smile and took a step closer.

I guessed her age to be in her early twenties. Like my sister, Sasha, I was good at reading people's intentions, and I saw a hint of desperation in her eyes. She looked as if she'd had a rough night.

"I am so glad I found you again," she said in her distracted, brusque manner. "I must do another reading for you. I fear the first was flawed, and we were not able to finish the reading."

Just what I didn't want.

"That's all right. I'm rather tired tonight. We don't have to finish the reading."

I glanced across the lobby at Brendon and his bandmates, who were laughing and joking, clearly in good moods. They hadn't considered Brendon's news as bombshells the way I had. I wondered where their first stop on the tour was going to be. *No, don't think about that. He's gone. It's just as well.*

"Oh, but we must do a reading. I consulted the cards one more time, and I have more information to give you before you make a huge mistake."

"You know nothing about my life and the decisions I make." I flashed angry eyes at the tarot reader. I hated when people made assumptions. Fortunately, Sasha suddenly appeared at my side, and I allowed my fists to uncurl. Already, Sasha's calm presence made it easier to breathe.

"Dasha, are you okay?"

I gave her a weak smile. "I'm fine." I turned to Madame Peshkova. "Excuse me, Madame, but I really must go now. We can talk some other time. Leave your invoice for your services with Mrs. Marusova and the bill will be taken care of right away. Good night."

Then I made a bee-line for the exit, not even stopping to debrief with Mom. Though not very professional of me, I wasn't able to form a coherent sentence at that point. As the valet brought my car to where I waited at the main entrance, I saw Madame hand her valet ticket to a different, older valet, then glance my way as their car appeared, a black Lexus sedan. Since when did a tarot reader make enough money to afford a luxury car and a combination driver/bodyguard?

28

The mystery kept growing. I had a feeling I would indeed be seeing Madame Peshkova again soon. But, what could she possibly want with *me?*

Chapter 3

"This is a time to think and philosophize; and to become more spiritually aware."
(Tarot Card: The Hierophant)

It was well after midnight when I arrived home. I sat in the car for several minutes, staring up at the outdoor security lights that played across the façade of our home. It was styled after the Victorian homes of London, and built shortly after the San Francisco earthquake of 1906. A house that old had drafts and cold spots, as well as quirks in its design. But it had been our home my entire twenty-four years.

I sighed, not quite ready to forget the strange night.

According to Grandma Tattie, we came from a long line of strong Russian women who'd escaped Communist and Soviet oppression to raise their families in a land free of political whimsy and tyranny. Plus, we lived in a house that I loved. Well, everything except the two ghost ancestors, Nicolai and Vasya, who were killed in the earthquake, or the ghost dog, Tess, a Cavalier King Charles Spaniel, said to resemble a dog belonging to a young Queen Victoria—whose dog was named Dash, which I found humorous.

I looked out the car window and saw a break in the heavy drizzle that had started up, so I grabbed my laptop case and dashed toward the front door to let myself in. The house was quiet, so I removed my strappy pumps and tip-toed up the main staircase to my room. I heard my mom's muted voice down the hall and guessed she was bringing Dad up to speed on the fundraising success. I wondered what it would feel like to always meet or exceed your goals.

I had just changed into my pink silk pajamas when a tap sounded at the door. Without waiting, Gigi barged in and closed the door behind her.

"Why aren't you in bed?" I asked.

Gigi held a flashlight close to her chest, her face as pale as chalk, while her hands shook.

"Gigi, what's wrong?"

She sat on the edge of my bed and hunched down. "They're here. I saw them right after I got home. Grandma Vasya and Grandpa Nicolai."

When Gigi turned six, she told tales of seeing and hearing Grandma Tattie's great-grandparents. They hadn't yet completed the construction of the Mazurov mansion by the day of the earthquake in April of 1906, but Vasya and Nicolai began making appearances as soon as the family moved in.

"I'm telling the truth," Gigi blubbered.

I sat down beside her and put an arm around her slender shoulders.

"You know there's no such thing as ghosts, right?"

"I saw them! They won't leave. Why won't they leave?"

Another light tap on the door brought Sasha tiptoeing into my room in her fluffy cat slippers and nightgown. She closed the door and immediately caught on that Gigi believed she'd seen not one, but *two* ghosts.

"Ah, honey-bunny, are they bothering you again?" Sasha sat on the other side of her and hugged her tight.

"Don't encourage her," I said. "She's sixteen. It's time to let go of ghosts and things that go bump in the night."

"Don't be mean. Tell me you've never noticed this part of the house. It's prone to freezing cold drafts of air at night."

Sasha took Gigi's side in most cases, but I was tired of being the bad guy. Someone had to be the voice of reason. I cleared my throat. "It's just a really old house," I said, reaching for my robe.

Gigi ducked her head and dove for my pillow. "Okay, let's change the subject then. I don't like talking about ghosts."

"Me, neither," I said, rearranging the pillows, then sitting back against the headboard, one sister on each side of me.

"Did you get to talk to Brendon after the concert?" Sasha asked.

I made a face, trying to play it down. "He's leaving on a world tour the day after tomorrow. He says he'll be gone for six months."

"Wow. Didn't see that coming," Sasha commented.

"He's a sweet guy, and I'm really glad he'll finally have a huge success, but..."

"But what?" Gigi poked my side.

I tucked the top of my robe closer, feeling the air suddenly cool. "Earlier tonight, I was sitting there enjoying the music, when it occurred to me that I wanted something not quite so frantic. Easy and calm, like what Dalton and I had. Time to really get to know each other."

"You're still young. You'll meet someone else," Gigi said, as if she had tons of experience. Just then she spotted two slender boxes with the words *Araminta's Vintage Clothing* on the dressing table and pointed at them. One had a red ribbon, and the other, a dark green ribbon. "What are those boxes for?"

I turned to Sasha. "Are those for us?"

Sasha reached for the first box. "Mom's having a small dinner party on Saturday, and she wants us to wear our flapper outfits again. I thought maybe you could use some cheering up tonight, but you'd already gone to the opera house when I came inside your room to check, so I brought this for you. You, too, sweetie," she said to Gigi. "I picked out matching evening gloves for both of you to try on. I think you'll like them."

I was always amazed how Sasha could make any situation turn sunny side up.

I hung onto my funk just a bit longer. "I'm not sure I'll be in the mood. What's the occasion?"

"Just some of Mom's friends celebrating a successful fundraiser. Dad will be out of town for business, so it will be just us girls." Sasha leaned close, like she was telling us a secret. "Mom put new flapper gowns in our closets earlier today, but I peeked inside the plastic covers before I went to work. I wanted the gloves to match."

Gigi opened her box and pulled out a pair of black evening gloves with pink sequins and pearls. Her face lit up. "Oh, these will make me look like a princess!"

"If Mom's okay with it, we'll help you with your makeup," I offered. Gigi was a tomboy, following in my footsteps, so, of course, she agreed eagerly. "Maybe we could take a photo for Mom's Christmas card this year," I added. "That would take our minds off other things for a while."

Gigi bounced on the bed with excitement, and Sasha beamed her approval, so I considered it a fine end to the evening. We said goodnight and retreated to our respective rooms. I took a moment to check the hallway, and seeing no ghosts, I decided I'd done my due diligence.

Before I climbed into my bed, I opened my box to find a pair of black silky-soft evening gloves with emerald green beading on the sleeves. I smiled at Sasha's thoughtfulness, but as I closed up the box, I could swear I smelled the heavy scent of a woman's sweet perfume.

Sasha was our domestic goddess. The next day, she was the first to help Mom and Rosana make incredible appetizers for Mom's party. I decided to go over figures to highlight Mom's next foundation report to the Advisory Board. Gigi chose to spend the day with her best friend, Rani Goldman, but she would be home in plenty of time to deal with hair and makeup for the night's celebration and photo-taking.

For the next half hour, Mom whizzed in and out from the garden to the kitchen, bringing big, bold summer blossoms to arrange in expensive vases. Dahlias, San Francisco's official flower, came in every size and color along with pink and blue classic hydrangeas, exotic bougainvillea in reds and orange, sunny yellow sunflowers, and the reblooming roses. Scented lilies were placed in each bathroom. One would think we were entertaining the Queen of England that night.

Mom had a small repertoire of things she could cook, and for good friends, Spanish paella was her favorite dish. All we could do was stand by and drool. In a matter of hours, Mom's dining room table was transformed into something elegant and Old World. Mom added a crisp chardonnay. The pairing was heavenly. In fact, Sasha and I may have overindulged, because by the time the ladies decided to take our photos for the Christmas card, our cheeks were rosy and our laughter was nonstop. They had us pose in Dad's humongous two-person armchair with me on the right and Sasha on the left. Then Gigi sat on both our laps and kept telling knock-knock jokes, since she hadn't been offered any wine. I felt a bit like a performing seal, but then the huge task of choosing a photo for the card every year would be finished. Phew!

By the time Mom's friends left at about eleven o'clock, Gigi was already fast asleep, and Sasha and I were in my room, admiring our costumes one last time before donning our pajamas.

"Why don't we have a flapper party and invite just *our* friends?" Sasha asked as she turned her glove right-side out. "We could dance, play great music, maybe even indulge in some board games. Have an old-fashioned get-together of people our age."

I squinted as I tried to read a name on a label in my glove. "Sounds fun, Sash. But that's not fair to Gigi. Her friends are too young to invite. And let's get real—I don't have any friends anymore. Not since—"

"Dalton died?"

I looked up. "Well, it's true."

"When do you plan to change that? It's been four years."

I hesitated before answering, thinking about my conversation with Brendon. I never knew what to say anymore. "It's late. I have to get some work done tomorrow."

Sasha shook her head, took her gloves, and started to leave. "It's only going to get worse," she said, then closed my door.

But the door didn't close fully. Instead, when I turned, I heard squeaky hinges and Grandma Tattie was standing there, her eyes glued to the black-and-green beaded evening gloves in my hands. She made a strange sound, kind of like a snake's hiss. Then she stepped forward and knocked the gloves from my hand.

"Where did you get those gloves?"

I picked them up and tossed them on the bed. "A gift from Sasha's store. Why? Is there something wrong with them?"

Grandma Tattie's nose turned up and her eyes grew huge. I stared at her, never having seen that look before. I tightened my bathrobe against the chill, and waited for an explanation.

"Those gloves are cursed," Tattie said in a perfectly calm voice.

Now she was really scaring me. "Don't be silly. There's no such thing as a curse." But my heart was racing as I watched her face take on a bleached-white appearance. She sat on my bed and placed a hand over her heart.

"Grandma Tattie, are you okay?"

She paused to catch her breath, then nodded. "I'm fine, Dashenka. Just surprised. How did these gloves end up here?"

It took a few moments, but her color was definitely returning. I reached for the gloves I'd tossed so casually on the other side of the bed, and examined them closely.

"There's no brand or person's name on the label, so I don't know how Sasha ended up with them." I started to put the glove on my right hand, but Grandma Tattie was quicker this time. She knocked them out of my hands, and they hit the floor again.

"Do you know who wore those gloves last?" she hissed.

My temper rose, but I kept my voice moderate. "No, Grandma Tattie. Who wore them last?"

She gazed across the room, her thoughts clearly elsewhere. I was about to prompt her, when she gave the slightest nod. "Royalty. The last grand duchess—Anastasia Romanov."

Chapter 4

"A time for secrets, wisdom, hidden knowledge and intuition."
(Tarot Card: The High Priestess)

I stared at Grandma Tattie in shock. I'd never seen her eyes so huge or her face so bleached of color as she stood in my room, staring at the gloves Sasha had given me.

A tingling raced up my spine to think she may be headed down the path to dementia. She kept herself in good physical condition, but had she dreamt up this phantom curse idea? This couldn't be healthy.

"Here, let 's sit down for a few minutes and gather our thoughts, okay?"

She sat down in the chair near my bed to catch her breath, while I retrieved the gloves, picking lint and dust off them from the hardwood floor.

"Where did Sasha find those gloves?" Though Grandma Tattie's voice had calmed somewhat, she watched me closely.

I shook one of the gloves, thinking I heard the crinkle of paper inside. "I don't know, but they match the dress I'm wearing to Mom's party tomorrow night." I turned the glove inside out, and a letter dropped to the floor, landing without a sound onto the ornate pink, ivory and gold area rug that had been in the family for decades.

Grandma's mouth fell open. "Don't touch that."

I froze. "Don't touch the glove...or *the note?*"

I reached for the note before Grandma could rise from the chair to claim it. Fortunately for me, although Grandma was still spry at seventy-nine and exercised daily to keep up with her toddler ballet students, I took after her and ran almost every day.

I examined the note as I ran a finger over the textured paper that had once been ivory, but was now yellowed with age. When I sniffed it, I could swear it smelled like patchouli oil. I opened it carefully, and saw the date written in the faded blue ink of an old-fashioned fountain pen.

"This is hard to read, like old European writing." As I turned the page over, something caught my eye. "Interestingly, it's signed by—"

"Oh, Dashenka, I know who penned that note. *Bozhe moi! My God.*"

When I realized what I held, my hands began to shake. "This is signed by...Grigori Rasputin. And what would the note be doing inside a lady's evening glove?"

Grandma indicated I should read the whole letter, but my throat thickened as it always did when I read Russian. I coughed to clear my voice. "My Russian is rusty these days. You should read it out loud, *Bábushka.*"

Sasha and Gigi chose that moment to suddenly appear in my doorway, wearing the latest flapper dresses mother had given them. They offered a welcome distraction. "Don't you both look fabulous in those dresses?" I managed to say, through the tremor in my voice. "Mom is going to go nuts when she sees you." I reshaped the feather on Gigi's band and summoned a smile. "Um, Gigi, I think that band with the feather goes *around* your forehead, not on top of your hair like a tiara."

Gigi laughed and adjusted the band. "How's that?"

"You look ready to dance." Sasha reached out and swirled the long beads around her neck. "And so am I." She then turned to Grandma Tattie. "I'm sorry we interrupted. I heard something about a letter. Where did you find it?"

"Inside this glove," I offered, handing the note to Grandma.

Grandma Tattie turned the short note over to scan the back. Then she flipped it to the beginning, and instead of reading the whole thing, she made a quick translation.

"It's a message dated two years prior to Rasputin's death, when he was still alive. He was well aware his days were numbered, but he warns Nicholas that if he dies at the hands of Nicholas's supporters, the children will also die within two years." Grandma Tattie shuddered and closed her eyes. "He was such an evil man. Rasputin thought he was predicting his own death here, and that the people would fear his powers. But his death was inevitable. It's the deaths of the five children he so casually mentions that break my heart. They were innocent."

Sasha and Gigi both placed a hand over their mouths in horror.

"Two years' time wasn't very long, was it?" Gigi said. "I can't believe that dirty old man had something to do with killing those children. He's a priest, for heaven's sake."

There were times when I loved how sweet and innocent our Gigi could be. Like now. But situations like this made one grow up quickly. Or, at least for the children of the last Russian Czar.

Grandma Tattie appeared troubled as she gazed out the window, while Gigi frowned, still digesting the horrible tragedy that to Dasha felt like it had happened only yesterday. Sasha appeared thoughtful, swirling her beads.

My hand still shook as I took the letter, folded it up, and placed it on my desk. "Okay, enough of mad monks and crazy people. Let's go see if we can help Mom get ready for tomorrow's party. If it's too dull, maybe we can step out in our flapper outfits and cause a ruckus. Maybe go line dancing or sing karaoke. And we're only young once."

"Sounds like a plan," said Sasha.

"But I'm not leaving without tasting Mom's paella," said Gigi, smacking her lips.

I sobered quickly, unable to shake the darkness that had entered the room with the priest's vindictive words. As I looked over my shoulder, I glanced one last time at the letter that had left such a heavy sadness behind, a death sentence etched into the page. A reminder that evil was always right there, peeking over our shoulder. I shuddered and felt thankful for my two sisters. Given a different set of circumstances, that order to kill, in the form of a casual remark by a mad man, could have been for us. It put things in perspective, making my non-date with Brendon seem small in comparison. I inhaled and exhaled, hoping to lift the heaviness.

"*Bábushka*, are you coming with us?"

"In a moment, Dashenka," Grandma Tattie said "You go ahead."

I nodded, not wanting to leave her alone with her memories. After a brief pause, I shut the door and headed downstairs, recalling how her face lit up when I remembered to call her by the Russian word for grandmother. It had been a long time.

Bábushka

Mom had declared Saturday to be Paella Day. Her friends arrived right on time, and their 1920s costumes were flirty, feminine and party-ready. The two older ladies, Jan from Marketing and Lillian, Mom's personal assistant, chose dresses that were blouson-like on top, and looser around the hips. Melinda from Accounting, always the rebel, had a lovely figure and showed it off well in a red-and-black knit flapper dress with hanging tassels for the hem. Mom wore a black sleeveless "dancing frock" of georgette and satin, with a crossed bodice covered with lace flounces. I couldn't help but notice the twinkle in her eyes, and I was so happy for her success.

Grandma Tattie appeared briefly, just long enough to serve herself some paella and to pour herself a generous glass of Verdejo, a white wine from the Rueda region of Spain. Then she disappeared to her upstairs suite. Afterward, we girls got the go-ahead to serve ourselves once the ladies were seated at the long dining table with its heavy dark wood and sturdy chairs. Mom had stayed true to keeping the décor in line with the house's Victorian heritage, although adding a modern touch for convenience here and there.

As soon as we walked into the dining room in our shiny new flapper dresses, the ladies oohed and aahed. Mom liked showing off her three pretty daughters, although, when Melinda asked what I was planning to do with my Russian, I froze. I usually mumbled something incoherent, never quite naming my goal. I needed a solid "elevator pitch"

"Maybe Dasha will go study in St. Petersburg and brush up on her Russian," offered Gigi. "She could be an interpreter at the UN. She's good with people."

Gigi must have heard me discussing that possibility with Sasha, but I had never said anything to Mom, who gave me a heavy sigh, which when interpreted from Mom-Speak meant, "Are you *ever* going to be done with school?" As long as I worked at the foundation, she never mentioned my moving out. But it was lurking there, beneath the surface.

Just then, the doorbell rang. Most of the guests had arrived and were enjoying the wine before dinner, so I didn't think anything unusual was in the works when I opened the door to the latest arrival.

Instead of one of the ladies from the foundation, however, I found myself staring into the eyes of the muscled bodyguard who worked for Madame Peshkova. He crossed his arms and didn't say anything right away, as his eyes roamed over my flapper outfit, which I'd completely forgotten.

"Aren't you...?" I glanced over my shoulder to make sure no one was close enough to hear us.

"Yes, I am Dima. I work for Madame Peshkova. She would like to speak to you...*now.*"

His heavily accented words were the most I'd heard him speak, since I'd met him. Just then, Madame Peshkova stepped out from behind a tree, her brows pinched together in concentration.

"Please. It won't take long. I just need a few minutes to finish the reading I started at the fundraiser." She glanced behind me. "Your house is magnificent, by the way. Surely, we can find a private corner to finish the reading?"

By then, Sasha and Gigi had joined me, and as much as I wanted to shoo the visitors away and shut the door, I knew they'd talk me into this. My hand went to my hair, the way it always did when conflicted. To my consternation, Sasha stopped me from making a complete mess of it by smiling at Dima.

"How long will this take? We're on our way out to sing karaoke."

"Not more than ten minutes or so," Madame replied. "I just need you to pull one more card to connect with the last reading."

Dima's lazy, dark eyes roamed my body, as if caressing every curve, making me feel almost naked in that short, fringed-hem flapper dress. I noticed he didn't regard Sasha or Gigi in the same way.

No. No more Rebound Boys. And especially not Dima. I stepped back and opened the door, wanting to get this over with, as I had a strange feeling these two weren't going to give up easily. "Let's go into the library. You have exactly ten minutes."

It was a mild night, and the bodyguard appeared rumpled in torn clothes with holes in them. He'd rolled up the sleeves of his plaid shirt, giving the impression he came to arm wrestle.

In and out! Ten minutes, max.

"What could possibly require a follow-up reading?" I wondered as I led the way to the library.

For once, Gigi curbed her natural curiosity as she and Sasha followed me silently into the room meant to impress. Dima's and Madame Peshkova's eyes grew wide at the sight of hundreds of books collected by generations of Marusovs. Many were in Russian, including a handful sitting on the end table next to the old Victorian sofa.

"Do you need a table to spread the cards?" I inquired, directing my conversation to Madame and indicating they should sit on the couch.

"No. I will shuffle them by hand. All you have to do is pick one card. This will complete your reading. Do you remember your question from Thursday night?"

Though I nodded and tried not to show how nervous I felt, my hand shook. I never did like sharing personal information in front of others.

"Good. Do not repeat the question out loud." Madame shuffled the cards, her efficient fingers flying. She then fanned them for me to consider. "Silently ask your question once again, being as clear as possible. When you're ready, please choose a card."

I studied the cards for several seconds before I pulled a card and handed it to Madame, who turned it around and smiled.

"Ah, the Wheel of Fortune. This card signifies your luck or fortune is about to change for the better."

"*Slava bogu.* Thank God for that. What about...my romantic life?"

Out of the corner of my eye, I saw Dima looking through one of the books on the table. I knew by the cover and size it was one of my dad's books on Russian architecture. I needn't have been embarrassed about the question posed to me, because Dima didn't appear to be the kind of guy who expressed his deepest feelings easily, let alone discussed the topic of romance when asked. Plus, he was too engrossed with the book to pay attention to our conversation.

Good.

Madame nodded her head. "Your romantic life is undergoing a major change. This card indicates you may meet a love interest during the course of your travels."

"Oh!" exclaimed Gigi. "Maybe you'll meet someone new at the karaoke bar?"

"Let's hope he doesn't know any Johnny Cash," I muttered.

Dima glanced away from his book, his face expressionless. "Who is this Johnny Cash?"

"You work in construction, don't you?" Gigi asked. "Construction guys like country music."

"I don't work in construction. And I hate country music." He frowned and put down the book he'd been perusing on Russian architecture.

"Well, we're finished here," said Madame. "Do you have any further questions?" Her eyes suddenly latched onto the gloves I'd carried with me and set on the side table when I chose a card. Her mouth trembled and her cheeks grew chalky white. "Those gloves... Where did you get them?"

I picked them up, feeling I needed to protect them for some reason. "Why? Do they seem familiar to you?"

Madame shook her long curls and forced a smile. "Oh, I think I saw them at a party...a long time ago. The beading is quite unusual."

Sasha flashed me a warning look not to say too much.

I hadn't seen Grandma Tattie enter the library. She stood motionless, her eyes on the gloves. "That's because they disappeared with the last girl who wore them."

"Wait a minute. *Pridezhitye loshadey*," Dima muttered. "Hold the horses. How do you know the last time they were worn?" His dark eyes narrowed suspiciously.

My facc heated up, and I couldn't help glancing at the gloves, but I was careful not to mention the note I'd found inside of one.

Gigi came to stand at my elbow. She reached out to take the right-hand glove from me and stuck her hand inside. "No, you didn't. It's right here."

Now I could feel the color draining from my cheeks. "That's not possible. I left the note folded up on my desk."

"What's going on here?" Sasha's innocent blue eyes flashed from one person to the next.

Madame Peshkova's eyes grew wide as she sniffed the air. "You feel that cold breeze all of a sudden?" She paused and turned to me. "You may have ghosts interested in your gloves."

I didn't realize how tightly I was hanging on to the one glove, when suddenly, the lights began to flicker. At the same time, a surge of energy pulsed through me, as though I'd become a ghost myself.

I panicked. "What's happening? Grandma Tattie! *Bábushka*, help me!"

Dima lunged forward and tried to grab me by the shoulders, but he ended up with a handful of cold air as I vanished into a cloud of mist.

Chapter 5

*"He is constant and trustworthy, in control of his
emotions, and comfortable with who he is."*
(Tarot Card: The Emperor)

St. Petersburg - 1918

I couldn't see anything through the fog as I hurtled
through space. It reminded me of a roller coaster ride at
Disneyland—except I was afraid this ride would never stop.
Blurred images appeared in my periphery, some familiar from my
youth. Powder Puff softball (I was always the pitcher). Sleepovers
with my girlfriends. My first kiss with Clark Meadows. We both
wore braces at the time, and it took both of us twelve-year-olds
almost a semester to shore up our courage.

My heart pounded in my chest, the sound amplified in my
head as I wondered if and where I would land. When the room
finally stopped spinning, the mounting nausea settled somewhat
as I was deposited in the middle of a ballroom filled with hundreds
of people—all wearing costumes from the 1920s. The piano player
was playing a lively rendition of "the Charleston," and the crowd
was so thick, I had to keep moving my feet or be swept away.

Wait a minute. When did I learn to do the Charleston?

As I did a quick scan of the room, searching for anything or anyone familiar, including my sisters, three things became obvious: this appeared to be someone's home, everyone around me spoke Russian, and my dance partner was a handsome young male with dark hair and dimples. I had never seen him in my life, but he was smiling at me as he executed the Charleston with great enthusiasm.

Was this a Gatsby themed party? If so, how did I get here?

Get it together, Dash. Where are you?

I forced myself to remain calm and focus on the costumes. They all looked authentic. Men wore three-piece suits of all colors, including my dance partner, who was handsome in a European sort of way in his pin-striped emerald green suit. His eyes were as dark as walnuts, and they twinkled, as if he recognized me. Too bad I didn't know his name.

Why couldn't I recall any of this? Was this my mother's party, and I'd just had amnesia for the past twenty-four hours? Had I fallen and hit my head? Perhaps I'd lost consciousness. I looked down at my green-and-black beaded dress but saw no sign of blood or injury. I knew I hadn't been drinking. Besides, I was getting too old to go out drinking and dancing until two in the morning, then get ready for work at 6:00 a.m. It wasn't fun anymore, not when I had a job I couldn't screw up. People counted on me.

Focus!

Where was Grandma Tattie—Mom and the girls? It made me anxious, not knowing why I was at a dance or how I got there. My stomach churned, and my throat burned. There had to be an explanation. Less than 48 hours ago, Brendon told me about his world tour. Perhaps this *was* amnesia—a delayed reaction.

I noticed several people coming and going through a secret door, probably a panel that led to the kitchen. They returned with glasses of wine, champagne, or ale in their hands. No alcohol was set out on the buffet tables, only apple cider and the ubiquitous samovar for preparing tea. Was this Prohibition, or had the alcohol been placed elsewhere? I put my hands to my cheeks, trying to wrap my head around that and what it meant for the time period. They felt as hot as a polyester flapper dress on a hot, sticky summer's night.

"Thank you for this dance, Mademoiselle Marusova," my escort said when the music came to a stop.

Despite the nightmare I seemed to be experiencing, my grandmother's lessons in etiquette kicked in. "*Spasíbo.*" I mumbled a garbled thank you to my dance partner and curtsied awkwardly. As my head came up, I spotted something across the room that I desperately wanted to see.

I excused myself, then practically shoved people out of the way to grab a newspaper lying on a side table. The fact that it was in Russian wouldn't be considered odd for the thousands of Russians who lived in San Francisco and wanted to stay current with events back home. However, the date read March 15, 1918—*the day Nicholas II, Czar of All Russia, abdicated the throne*.

I shivered, strangely cold among the crush of people. To keep myself from fainting, I gripped the back of a chair and watched dancers in sparkling sequins, beads, and silks, head to one corner of the ballroom. Upon closer inspection, I saw that someone had set up a temporary bar at the last minute against the wall where the secret door panel was located to make it easier for servants to carry in all types of liquor. Only one young man was tending bar, and he responded good-naturedly as people yelled at him in Russian. I'd never seen so much vodka sloshing from bottles to tiny glasses before, and the temporary bar was slick with it.

The bartender who approached me looked familiar, but I couldn't trust my memory at the moment. Nothing was as it should be, and I still felt a touch of amnesia. I sighed and clutched the newspaper to my chest.

When the bartender made his way to where I stood, I set the paper on a dry spot of the counter and leaned forward, tapping the newspaper. "Are we in San Francisco?"

He said something I couldn't understand in Russian and shook his head, pausing to serve another customer. Although it was a frantic night for only one bartender, he kept his sense of humor as people yelled and pushed their way to the front of the line. Once he'd served most of the customers in my vicinity, he returned and set a napkin and glass of water in front of me.

"You are American?" he asked quietly, looking each way to be sure no one had heard.

"*Da*. Yes. I'm Daria Masurov. Can you tell me where I am? Whose house is this?"

"I'm Alex, your friendly bartender. As to the house, Lenin's newly-appointed head of secret police, Viktor Borodin, lives here now."

"Oh." I shuddered to think I was in the home of the secret police.

I took a few moments to gawk at the opulence, the luxury. It was as if I were in Paris. Had I been to Paris, or had I seen a photo of this home in a magazine? I ran a finger over my upper lip. Something nagged at my conscience about the sights and smells. I tried again.

"This mansion is old, but well cared for. Who owned the home before Victor Borodin?"

Alex glanced up at the high ceiling of the ballroom. "From what I understand, it used to belong to a Russian businessman who made his fortune in the fledgling technology field. A case of being in the right place at the right time."

"You know a lot about these people." She wanted to ask if he knew Tatiana's parents, John Marusov and the actress, Stella Randolph. If nothing else, they might be willing to temporarily take in a great-granddaughter—if they believed in that time travel stuff. But then again, they might not have been born yet.

I focused on my surroundings once more. Except for the grand scale of the house, it appeared at first glance to be a duplicate floorplan of our house built after the earthquake in 1906, San Francisco. I wished I had more time to explore.

"Do the Borodins entertain a lot? I would think a home like this must be wonderful for entertaining. All this room..."

"Viktor and his wife, Mariana, decided at the last minute to hold a special party to commemorate Nicholas' abdication. I have to say, not many have been invited inside the inner sanctum."

I couldn't help but shiver as I glanced around. "Are the new occupants here now?"

Alex shrugged. "I doubt it. They like to show off the house whenever they can, but his wife doesn't particularly like big crowds. But you never know. They might make an appearance."

My stomach rumbled, and I was relieved the music and dancing covered the sound. Despite the danger I found myself in, my hunger drove me to the delectable aroma of freshly-made piroshkis, small pies made with meat or vegetables. And borscht with homemade bread containing flavorful Gruyère cheese. I also let the aroma lead me to a platter of caviar and blini with smoked salmon. It would all go down nicely with champagne. Even without the champagne, just looking at the spread brought back childhood memories and Grandma Tattie's cooking. But then, there was that little nag sitting on my shoulder with the pointed stick again. How could I possibly enjoy this much rich food when people just outside the doors were starving?

I heaved a sigh. "The food smells wonderful."

"When did you last eat?"

I shrugged. "I have no idea." My stomach rumbled again, and I placed my hand over it then glanced down at the photos on the front page of the newspaper. Famine. War. Cold-blooded politics. "Too bad none of this leftover food can go to the people who are starving outside these walls," I said sadly.

"Excuse me, miss..." The bartender took me by the elbow.

Alarmed, I tried to disengage his hand from my arm as he heaved a sigh and pulled me into a hallway.

"Miss Marusov, listen, I suggest you choose your words more carefully. Times have changed. There are ears everywhere. If you say anything negative about the new government, you may end up in a Siberian prison camp. By the way, they call the city Petrograd now."

"Petrograd? Already?"

"What do you mean by 'already'?"

I could feel the color drain from my cheeks. I didn't argue this time as he pulled me down a hallway and into the kitchen, where he briefly said something to a cook, an older woman with charcoal gray hair gathered into a tight bun. She quickly assembled pirozhkis and bread, and wrapped them in a cloth napkin. The cook gave me a disapproving look as she handed me the bundle.

"Hold onto that. It may be a while until your next meal," Alex said, taking my free hand.

"Where are we going? And must you hold my hand?" Dasha stopped and pulled her hand away. "I don't even know you. Why should I do as you say?"

He sighed and shrugged his shoulders. "Fine, then. You're in a strange town and you don't know anyone. Chances are, you have no money. You have no place to stay. I'll just say goodbye and good luck, and leave you here in the middle of the night."

I swallowed and glanced around furtively. I hated when a man was right. "Who are you, really? It's clear by your accent that you're an American, so explain to me, how did an American wind up tending bar in Saint...Petrograd? I have a feeling you do more than bartending for rich people."

He put a finger to his lips. "Maybe another time I'll explain. Right now, we need to get going before someone in authority starts asking questions. I'll find you someplace safe for tonight. Then, tomorrow, we'll try to find out more about where you came from and how you got here."

I offered my hand to shake, knowing when to give in. "Let's start over. I'm Dasha, and lead me to a shelter, please. I'm tired and I'm hungry."

"Nice to meet you, Dasha. Let's go."

We hurried along a dark passageway with servants coming and going. No one noticed us, though Alex did greet a few people he knew.

It occurred to me his voice sounded different from those who lived in San Francisco. I couldn't help but ask. "You sound like you come from the south or southwest."

"San Antonio, Texas, ma'am." He grinned, dipped a pretend cowboy hat, and grabbed a bottle of vodka from one of the servants walking by, a young woman with blonde curls, who giggled and went back for more vodka.

I cocked my head. "If you don't mind my asking, what are you doing here?"

He used the sleeve of his white linen shirt to wipe the sweat from his brow. "That's a long story. You'll have to wait until we have more time." He adjusted his red suspenders and winked.

The sound of the music faded in the background the further we got from the ballroom. I was operating on fumes, and it was clear I was going to have to take a chance and trust someone. Who else was there? I started to take my cell phone out to add Alex's name to my contact list, when I suddenly realized it wouldn't work here. No cell phone towers or service carriers. I quickly shoved it back inside my purse, hoping it didn't end up causing problems further down the road.

The hall ended, and we entered a conservatory that led to a garden. Once outside, I inhaled deeply, glad for the fresh night air. I hadn't expected the rush of delicate aromas that assaulted my senses—roses, lilies, jasmine, and other summer blooms that filled me with joy, as if I'd arrived home.

"Can we take a moment to look at the garden?"

Alex stole a sidelong glance at me, his lips taut. "Maybe another time. We're not on a site-seeing tour. There are people..."

Right when things seemed better, I felt as though giant waves had come crashing down on me, reminding me that not only was I homeless, I had no control of my life. I was completely at this man's mercy. A queasy lightheadedness settled in, and I gasped for air. I must have turned a shocking shade of white, because Alex urged me toward a bench.

"Here, why don't you sit down for a minute and catch your breath. Things won't seem so hopeless once you have a chance to rest."

I gave a watery giggle, determined not to be *that* girl—the one who fell apart and cried over every little thing.

As I sat down, I blew my nose, then rummaged through my small clutch purse. I found only useless pieces of plastic. I would have been fine using a credit card for a hotel, but that wasn't an option, either.

"You're right, I have no money," I heard myself say. "And I can't rely on you. I don't even know you."

"We'll figure out the details later. Right now, I'm just trying to help a fellow American."

I wanted to argue, but now was not the time. We started out again, and were about halfway through the massive garden when I heard a voice call out, asking me to stop. Before the other man reached me, I leaned over and asked Alex, "Do you know this man's name? Apparently, I've been dancing with him most of the night."

Alex regarded me with an amused smile. "That's Ilya Razinin. *Prince* Ilya Razinin of Caldoran." The cowboy bartender smelled good—sweat and his own unique spice. Almost the same scent as Brendon.

"Be careful of him," Alex warned me in a low voice.

I didn't know Alex well enough to know what he was alluding to, but it did make me consider Prince Ilya with caution, rather than enthusiasm, just because he was born some type of royalty from a country I'd never heard of.

"You didn't say goodbye, Miss Mazurov," said Ilya. "And now you are racing off with this...bartender?"

I glanced at Alex, my emotions like a wall of collapsing dominoes. Then and there, I made a quick decision to keep my mouth shut until I figured all this out. It felt so odd not having Sasha or Gigi there to bounce things off of. I missed them already, but wondered what they would think of my experience so far. In the meantime, I desperately needed to come up with an action plan.

I glanced at the couples walking in the garden on this balmy night as I considered my response to Ilya. The women looked so chic and lively in their flapper dresses dyed in all colors of the rainbow. How ironic that the events taking place outside these walls contrasted so completely with the lavish ball.

A wave of depression swept over me as Grandma Tattie's stories of Russia played out before my eyes. Many of the people in the ballroom I'd just come from wouldn't live to see the turn of the next century, or even the halfway point.

I breathed a sigh, as I finally came up with a reasonable response to the prince, when out of nowhere, Dima appeared with Madame Peshkova on his arm. They were headed straight for me, and not for the first time I wondered what they wanted. But first, I had to get away so I could work out what was happening to me. I needed to go home. I had another fundraiser to organize in two weeks. Now, that job felt like a million lifetimes away.

Priorities.

I was about to fill Alex in on the tarot reader and her bodyguard, when Prince Ilya surprised me by greeting them both as if they were good friends.

I grabbed Alex's hand and pulled him across the lawn, my thoughts jumbled as I repeatedly asked myself who these people were and how they could possibly travel through time?

"I hope you have a good reason for leaving the prince like that," Alex growled. "You don't want him to become suspicious of you. And worse, those two are close friends of Grigori Rasputin. You've heard of *him*, yes?"

"Of course I have! Alex, you have to help me get home."

He stopped and gazed at me like I was mad.

"But first, you said you knew somewhere safe you could take me," I pleaded. "I'll tell you everything I know then. Please? I'm all alone."

I didn't have to fake the tear that rolled down my left cheek. After several moments of hesitation, Alex straightened his shoulders and reached for me. "You'll have to do as I say if you want to stay safe."

"Of course. Anything." I glanced over my shoulder. Dima wasn't far away, and his laser-like eyes had me locked in his sights. "But please, hurry."

I felt like a butterfly pinned to a board.

Alex grabbed my hand and yanked me into the darkness before either the bodyguard or the prince could reach us.

As we raced toward the Neva River, I couldn't stop thinking of how long I'd been gone. I imagined an invisible clock ticking somewhere...just for me, calling me home to San Francisco.

Chapter 6

Grigori Rasputin, or Grisha, as his new friends addressed the priest, heard the two young people racing up the street long before they noticed him at the end of the alley behind his tiny apartment. Waiting. He felt like he'd been waiting a lifetime. The girl was panting as she hung onto the hand of a man dressed in plain black pants, a plain white shirt, and green vest, a typical working man he'd not seen before in the neighborhood. Who was he, and why was he dragging a flapper girl through the streets of Petrograd?

Grisha smiled at the irony and looked up at the sky as full darkness descended upon his dingy building. He sniffed the air for smokestacks. Everything was going as planned.

All his life, he had known that he would die young. At forty-seven, he was considered old by some, but he was still of value when it came to the royal family. No one else, physicians or priests, knew how to alleviate the pain and suffering of the young tsarevich, Aleksei.

No one but me, Rasputin.

Grisha faded into the darkness as the young couple stopped beneath the window of the apartment next door to Grisha's building, and huddled closely as it began to rain. What was taking them so long? A candle sat in the window above them, allowing him to see the girl in silhouette who argued with the well-dressed stranger. Grisha wasn't sure, but he thought they spoke American English.

Da. This was the right girl. Now, if only he could easily dispose of the man. He looked up at his window, confident that he'd prepared well.

The evening gloves had been just the right touch. She had no clue what was to come as his eyes spied the flash of sequins in the pale streetlight.

He smiled again, wider this time, so they would see his rotting teeth and fear him. Now, all he had to do was to wait.

"Just one more block. We'll find shelter soon. I promise."

I held onto Alex's hand and tried to keep up. Rain was falling in thick sheets of water. My dress clung to me, and my head feather kept falling in my face. My feet were soaked, so I wasn't feeling the least bit charitable.

"We're lost, aren't we?"

"No. No. It's right here, close by."

"Who did you say lives here? And how do you know they'll keep us safe?"

He glanced at me from over his shoulder. "Ye of little faith."

We found ourselves at the end of an alley, on either side of old, dilapidated buildings that likely housed entire extended families in one room.

"I don't know about faith, but I sure would like a warm bath and clean clothes." I held onto the tail of his suit coat, afraid to look down for fear of finding dead rats in the filth and mud. "When I get home, I'm going to write a Ph.D. thesis on why men don't ask for directions. You may be a part of that paper, I'll have you know."

"Now, be fair. Give me a moment to get our bearings."

From out of the darkness, a huge hand reached out to stop us, a foul odor assaulting us as a large man grabbed hold of Alex's shirt. I tried to remove his hand, but the man wouldn't budge. He was dressed like the poorest of peasant farmers, and his hair was long and tangled. But what frightened me most were his icy blue eyes. He looked right through me, and then a strange cloud enveloped me, pushing me against Alex.

"Daria, are you alright? Don't look at his eyes."

I clung to Alex's chest and gripped so hard that one of the buttons flew off his vest.

"You must resist him," he whispered in my ear.

"My name is Grisha," the man said. "And you, Mademoiselle Daria Marusova, will do what you are told. I will bring you inside out of the rain where you will be warm, dry, and safe. Come, children."

He opened a door behind him and with a broad sweep of his arms, led us inside, his mesmerizing eyes never leaving ours. Our feet gave us no other option but to follow him...into the bowels of Hell. I had the strange feeling he was hypnotizing us—playing on our weaknesses.

My stomach rumbled, betraying me once more, and then I fainted dead away.

The first thing I noticed when I came to was that Alex was sitting on the floor cross-legged, cradling my head in his lap. As he gazed down at me, his brows formed a deep, worried furrow.

"You're awake?"

"Did I take a nap?"

He removed the feather hairband and set it aside. "No. You fainted."

"This tea will make you feel much stronger," said the stranger with the scraggly beard and fiery eyes.

I shot up and almost knocked over the cup of tea in his hand.

"Rasputin!"

"*Da,* that is my surname. But you can call me Grisha, or Grigori." He set the tea down on a nearby table, then turned to Alex. "And you are?"

Alex appeared nonchalant as he scanned the contents of the tiny apartment, and calmly sipped his tea. He didn't even look at Rasputin when he responded. "Alex McKain."

As I stood before Rasputin, shoulders straight, I couldn't help but wish I could curse him with an eternal pox for his horrific crimes. And though I had to admit, he looked like someone's grandfather, I couldn't possibly trust him, not knowing his history the way I did.

"I take it that in the future the name Rasputin still elicits disgust and misery." He had the nerve to smile and emitted a small laugh.

I bristled. "Your name will go down in history as one of the worst con men of all time. You seduced women, and bullied the tsarevich and his mother. And that's just for starters. I don't know much about your politics, but I have no doubt you played both sides."

"Played both sides? What an interesting turn of phrase."

Does he know I'm not from this time period?

I glanced at Alex, but he looked away, as if not wanting Rasputin to see what his eyes conveyed.

The priest unpacked the food we'd brought from the party, and divided up the pirozhkis into three good-sized portions. On a separate plate, he placed the bread and set it near the fire to warm. The aroma filled the air in no time and made my stomach growl despite my fear.

"It's too bad you didn't bring borscht. I always like a little borscht with my pirozhkis."

I could take or leave borscht, but I remained quiet, not wanting to give away any detail, no matter how small.

On the other side of the tiny room, Grigori Rasputin—Grisha—mumbled something incoherent as he cleaned his long, sharp knife and set it aside. He picked up the plates of pirozhkis and handed one to each of us.

"My new friends, *za mir y za vashe zdorovye!*"

I couldn't believe I was sharing the common Russian toast, "To peace and to your health," with Grigori Rasputin.

I shuddered, wondering if he would feed us first—then use the knife to kill us.

Chapter 7

*"This card signifies difficult decisions, stalemates
and being in denial."
(Tarot Card: The Two of Swords)*

I braced myself for a knife in the heart and closed my eyes. In the background, I heard Alex continuing to tell me not to look into Rasputin's eyes, but it was too late. My mind went numb.

"Dasha! Dasha! Stay with me."

When I regained consciousness, the priest was gone and I was on the floor, tied to the foot of a bed, Alex gagged and bound on the other side. A small fire flickered in the fireplace, sending little warmth or reassurance. I smelled sex and spilled wine coming from the rumpled sheets, and almost gagged as I tried to speak around the rag in my mouth. It would be impossible to breathe Rasputin's name and not recall the truly disgusting stories I'd read about the priest whose seduction of women of all ages inflamed a revolt for an entire nation.

I glanced around the tiny apartment, looking for a means of escape. Alex tried to convey a message through his eyes, though at first I didn't understand what he planned.

Then I peered down at my dress. It no longer sparkled quite so brightly with the damp rain and dirt we'd accumulated in the alleyways as we'd scrambled toward what we had hoped would be a safe roof over our heads. I couldn't wait to pull on my dry sweats once I got home.

Home. I'm so confused.

We'd been struggling with our bonds for about an hour when the door suddenly opened. My stomach dropped, and the terror once again choked me. I'd expected the priest, but instead, a small, curly-haired woman entered, her face hidden in the folds of a bucket-shaped straw hat. She dropped the bag she was carrying, and her hand flew to her mouth when she saw us.

"Bózhe moi!" My God.

My sentiments exactly.

Alex motioned at the ropes and pleaded with his eyes. I didn't know how this woman was connected to Rasputin, but she might be our only chance of escape. She stood bent over, her posture timid and unsure. After considerable attempts to hint that we needed help, Alex finally convinced her to at least take the rags out of our mouths. Once done, she skittered back into the corner.

"Spasíbo. I'm Alex and that's Dasha. We're Americans and we're in a bit of a bind. And you are...?"

"My name is Marya," she said in Russian, pulling the rag from my mouth.

I tossed the rag aside, relieved to have that filthy thing gone, my mouth and throat drier than Death Valley in summertime. Alex held out his wrists, and Marya untied his bonds with trembling hands.

"Water? *Vodá?"* I croaked.

Marya nodded and untied my hands, then poured me a glass of water from a pitcher on the table. For once, I didn't complain that it wasn't the bottled water that cost ten dollars in the hotel mini-bar. It was blessedly cool.

Alex gestured with his chin while Marya finished untying him. "Why are you here, in Grigori Rasputin's apartment?"

She began speaking quickly, but turned to look over her shoulder every few words, as if fearing Rasputin's return. Finally, she stopped talking and looked to Alex to translate, as he seemed to have a calming effect on people.

"Marya cleans Rasputin's apartment once a week. The Russian Orthodox Church has been paying her a monthly salary, but no longer wants to be affiliated with Rasputin. This was supposed to be her last day."

Marya regarded my clothes with curiosity, then turned to Alex, as if he were in charge. She pointed toward the door and rattled off something in Russian.

"She says we should get out while we can. She's right," Alex said to me. Then he turned to Marya and spoke succinctly, gesturing toward the door.

After a few moments of listening to their chatter, anger and frustration boiled up inside of me, and I sucked in a breath. Although I'd studied Russian for six years, I felt utterly useless as I headed for the door.

"Mademoiselle..." Marya faced me, her dark eyes huge in her thin face. "When you leave, it will be dangerous."

"Can you take us someplace where we'll be safe tonight?"

Marya's eyes darted around the apartment. It was obvious she didn't want to get involved, and I couldn't blame her.

Just then, Alex reached into his coat pocket and pulled out a bottle of vodka. What was he planning? This didn't seem like the time to party. In fact, we should be on our way. But then Alex turned his blue-eyed gaze on me, and I caught on. When I nodded, he took Marya's hand and placed the vodka bottle in it.

"*Podárok*, a gift."

Marya shook her head and pushed the bottle back. "*Nyet.*"

"You can sell the vodka for money to buy food...or whatever you need," I said in English.

Alex translated quickly and added, "We've put your life in danger. Consider this a gift...for helping us."

She glanced at the bottle, no doubt mentally calculating how much it could buy in fresh food on the black market, then took it from Alex as if it were a precious gem. She stuffed it into a satchel she'd been carrying.

"Okay," she said in English, a broad smile lighting her face.

Marya gestured for us to follow her as she walked to the door, opened it, and stuck her head out to check the alleyway. "Is clear. We go." She paused to pull an old work coat from a closet and handed it to Dasha. "Is very cold tonight. You take."

Alex helped me into the coat that smelled of fish, the sleeves miles too long, but at least it was dry. I smiled my thanks.

"After you, Mademoiselle Dasha," he said, insisting I go first.

We took off at a brisk pace and kept to the shadows as we criss-crossed through more alleyways. Alex suggested we remain silent, and I was fine with that. The rain had stopped and the temperature had plunged as the early morning hours approached. Workers of all types were still out celebrating the Czar's abdication. They danced in the streets, a few drinking the occasional bottle of wine or beer saved for this occasion. For everyone else, little food was available. I was glad for our *pirozhki* raid at the party, but that had worn off hours ago, so I ignored my complaining stomach once again.

Marya deftly avoided street dancers and troublemakers. The mood was joyful, and yet, I wondered what these people would think when they later realized a 40% decline in the population of the former St. Petersburg due to famine and war.

"We go here." Marya knocked twice on the door of a small cottage attached to a church.

I followed the pair inside, but relaxed when I saw it was empty. "Where is everyone?"

"New provisional government. They send all priests away," Marya said. "But I always use special knock on door—to check first." She perked up immediately. "It looks like we have whole house and church to ourselves. Should be safe. I tell our priest I look after house and cat while he goes away."

It occurred to me that Marya's English had suddenly improved. *Trust is a powerful motivator.* I was glad Alex thought to give her the vodka. Just then, a ginger cat strolled into the kitchen and meowed.

"Sit at table while I feed *Koshka*." She rummaged through the cupboards and set out some cheese and bread. Saying a little prayer of thanks, she then kissed the cat's head.

"*Koshka.*" I remembered the simple word from my studies.

"Means 'cat'. Father Feofan does not believe in giving sentimental names to pets. He says he may have to *eat* them one day." Marya shuddered as she cleansed her hands in a basin of water, then dried them off before slicing cheese and an apple and placing them on the only other clean plate.

"So sorry I do not have more food. I waited in line today for three hours to buy bread."

I focused on the plate, feeling guilty all over again. "But if we eat your bread, you'll be out of food and have to wait in line tomorrow. Won't that seem suspicious, since no one else lives with you?"

She shrugged, as if it were her fate. "Is way of life now. Eat up. Then you must rest. We rise very early and leave with friends and family who take us to safety tomorrow. Is that good?"

Alex hesitated, the veins in his forehead expanding as though trying to make sense of our situation. "Who are your friends, and where are they taking you?"

Marya grinned. "We now have Trans-Siberian Railroad We go east until we want to get off. Rasputin will not think to look for us there." She unwrapped a package that contained a young woman's dress and set it on a chair. "You wear that tomorrow? It belong to my friend...Ana. When I not clean for his Holiness, I work in palace, so have many friends there. Someone will help us get on train."

I had no intention of taking a train to Siberia, but I didn't tell her that as I turned my attention to the white linen gown with a pink sash and flowers scattered around the skirt. If Marya worked at the palace, this dress might belong to Anastasia, so I hesitated to touch it. Especially considering the evening gloves had sent me back in time to when the Romanovs were still alive. If they could do that, what could a whole dress do? But Marya was trying so hard to be helpful that I couldn't turn her down.

"Thank you. *Spasíbo*, Marya." When I looked into her dark brown eyes, I saw terror of the unknown. Would she even be alive tomorrow? I bowed my head. "Our presence is putting you in danger, isn't it?"

"Not to worry. We be safe with cousins and aunts and uncles in countryside." Marya handed us blankets and pillows, then made her own little nest in a corner by the old stove with the cat to help keep her warm as it curled up beside her.

When she mentioned "cousins," I'll admit I felt better. I think Alex did, as well. He got up and checked out the rest of the house then peered in the chapel. By the time he returned, I'd already made my bed on a chaise lounge and stared into the fire, wondering what my sisters were doing at that moment.

It wasn't long before I heard gentle snores indicating Marya had succumbed to sleep. Alex shook out his blanket, searching for the best spot to stretch out. He was of average height, but I imagine being tied up and bound for so long had taxed his muscles so that it was hard to unwind.

"This main room is probably the warmest," he said. "I'll make a bed..." He pointed to the other side of the fireplace. "Over there. Is that far enough away?"

"I appreciate the gesture." Confident Marya slept deeply, I pulled my blanket tighter. "How do you feel about Marya's plan tomorrow? Surely, we're not boarding a train and fleeing to Siberia?"

"I don't know, yet," he said. "In the meantime, tell me more about yourself and your family members."

Alex's voice was low and husky, even as his question about my family threw me for a loop. I laughed nervously to cover the blush warming my cheeks.

I shifted my pillow. "Tell you what, I'll answer your question after you answer mine."

He gave a slow, exaggerated smile. "I'm listening."

"Who are you? Where, no, *when* do you come from? Lastly, how do you know so much about me? And please tell me the truth."

He sat up and gazed at the fire. "Fair enough. I'm Alex McKain. I was born in Texas...in 1886."

"That's impossible! You'd be...you'd be...really old!"

He nodded and looked down at his hands with a smirk. "I take it numbers aren't your strength? I think I look pretty good for a 139-year-old."

In the corner, I heard Marya snoring and glanced over at her. I wished I could fall asleep that easily. I frowned at Alex. "How is that possible?"

"This is all top secret, you understand. Once I tell you, we can't go back."

"Go back where?"

"We can't pretend any of this doesn't exist." He gave me a somber look and moved closer so we could whisper. "When I was twenty-five, I was approached by a government agency that 'fixes' time glitches so that certain events don't happen...or do. Whichever is for the greater good. It's called The Bureau of Time Menders, but operatives are just called Time Menders. We don't change major historical events. But we do correct small errors that influence personal choices and family outcomes."

I stared at him, my mouth open. "That's not possible."

"Oh, but it is, Dasha Marusova."

He sat back, relaxed, confident, his blue eyes meeting mine. Everything about his actions indicated the truth. I took a deep breath to slow my heartbeat. "Let's say, for a moment, that what you said is true. Did you come to that party to meet me on purpose? If so, why?"

He smiled, and darned if he didn't have a dimple in his chin.

"Your grandmother, Tatiana Marusova, claims to be related to Anastasia Romanov in the past. Has she ever told you about that relationship?"

I shifted uncomfortably. "She did always claim she knew her and they were related. But I figured she was going senile. After all, she would have been too old to have known the Grand Duchess. Not to mention Anastasia was seventeen when she and her sisters were killed. That's twenty-eight years before my grandma Tattie was even born in 1946." I plumped my pillow and turned on my side to face him.

"Unless there's such a thing as a parallel universe where we can go to any time and be any age." He winked.

Alex gazed at the fire. "What if I told you, *proved* to you, that your grandma was telling the truth? She was, in fact, a Time Mender. Only due to circumstances beyond her control, last year, she failed in her last mission, and the Romanovs were all murdered, including their entourage of eight staff members. And if we can't get this fixed within the year, your entire family will disappear. There's always a time limit or delayed reaction with these missions."

I swallowed, feeling lightheaded all over again. "What exactly are you telling me?"

"We're sitting on a moment in time that must be 'tweaked', so to speak. Your family is alive and living in San Francisco, after making many choices along the way. It's due to something we call *slipstreaming*. Your physical body can be assigned any age in order to slipstream into a narrow window of time to undo an error that may have consequences for members of your family down the line. Your father's business, for example. He has imported and used precious metals for connectivity in technical instruments for forty years. He was ahead of his peers in that regard. Way ahead." He shifted position and sighed heavily. "He may have made a deal with Rasputin, or his ancestor did, to get where he is today. If you slipstream back to before that deal was made, you may be able to help your father *and* save Anastasia. The government needs you to correct history just long enough to allow Anastasia to escape her fate. It will be a small adjustment. Even if she lives only another few years, Ana could change the course of history by living on so that your parents can be born, and so that *you* can be born. Without that adjustment, there would be no Marusovs in the U.S. or Russia. No Pyotr Marusov and his company, Marusov Technologies. Dasha, you could be a very important Time Mender. That may even be your calling in life."

How could he know how badly I'd struggled all my life with where I fit in? Where I *belonged*. A ferocious headache had returned, and I reached up to rub my temple, hearing Madame Peshkova's words all over again.

When he mentioned my father's name, I felt a churning in my stomach. "What kind of deal would my father make with Rasputin? My father's never done a dishonest thing in his life. What did he do?"

Alex licked his lips and relaxed into his blanket. "I'm not positive."

"Live the life you were meant to live."

I wasn't convinced I could do anything to influence the past. After all, I was no one in the grand scheme of history. But I had to admit, I would enjoy peace and comfort in knowing Grandma Tattie's memory was alive and that my father was still a good man.

I inhaled deeply and let the air out slowly, giving me time to think.

"Okay. Let's go slipstreaming," I said.

Chapter 8

"He represents a state of mind in which you wisely
withdraw and keep your own counsel."
(Tarot Card: The Hermit)

Now that we were no longer captives of Rasputin, I awoke early the next morning without any prompting. I opened the window of Father Feofan's cottage and caught the sun rising in the distance. The air was heavy with smoke, and I stifled a cough so I wouldn't wake Alex and Marya, who were still sleeping. As I closed the window, I recalled that this was the "glorious industrial age" of Petrograd. So much for the glorious part.

Coffee!

I already knew not to expect a Starbucks on the corner in 1918 Russia, and coffee in the stores was hard to come by, at any rate. So, I heated water in a pan and found an herbal tea bag that had hints of blackberry. I yearned for a good cup of coffee somewhere in this dank, dark city.

As I tiptoed around the cottage, I saw Alex shiver in his sleep. I found another blanket and placed it over him, then sat in the priest's rocking chair, sipping my tea. I enjoyed watching the funny expressions on Alex's face while he slept and dreamed. As to his clothing, he'd found an old pair of work pants and a flannel shirt in the priest's wardrobe. Ever mindful of the economic conditions of the common people, he left the waiter's shirt and pants in their place, and I found a note sticking out of a pocket that he'd written to the priest telling him to sell his clothes. He added a ten dollar bill for good measure. Although he'd told Marya what he was doing, in case the priest didn't return anytime soon, she wouldn't hear of taking the money for herself. Poor girl still trusted things to return to normal.

I wasn't sure I would have been so generous with the unknown priest and Marya, but then, I had nothing of value with which to barter. I looked down at the plain gray house dress, the only thing I'd been able to find in the maid's closet, along with sturdy brown shoes. My instincts told me to forego wearing Anastasia's dress until we were in the clear. No use drawing attention to myself, but I would wait until Marya awoke to explain.

When Alex sighed in his sleep, a curl fell across his forehead. Although I'd known him for less than forty-eight hours, my opinion of his motives changed every few minutes. Was he a government agent, or just a master manipulator? Furthermore, could I trust him? I wished Sasha was here. She was so much better at reading people. And much better at listening.

I groaned, unsure what to do next. I was so used to making quick decisions that I didn't like having extra downtime. It allowed for too much reflection.

Alex stretched his arms and yawned. He looked down at the extra blanket, but said nothing. Instead, he folded it neatly and set it aside, then sat up. "You're awake already?"

"I didn't sleep much. Has anyone ever told you that you have the most interesting facial expressions when you sleep?"

His face turned a brilliant shade of red, but he pretended he didn't hear as he finished putting the bedding away. Just when I thought he'd forgotten the question, he rose and stretched, his face turned away.

"Well, now that you mention it, Miss Masurova, you sigh in your sleep, so there."

"I agree!" said Marya with a giggle. "She talks in her sleep, too. I mean, entire conversations." She frowned when she saw what Dasha was wearing and abruptly held her breath. "Why do you not wear Ana's dress? It's beautiful, *da*?"

I hesitated too long, not wanting to hurt her feelings, so Alex jumped in.

"Dasha needs to blend in while we're out and about today. She can save Ana's dress for later. It is indeed beautiful, by the way." He gave Marya a wink.

Marya immediately relaxed, pacified for the moment. "I take bath and dress for the train ride, okay?"

Alex shot me a quick look. "Sure. In the meantime, I'll see what I can come up with for breakfast."

Marya grabbed some clean clothes and hustled to use the priest's old-fashioned shower.

"Thanks for explaining to Marya." I frowned and looked down at my outfit, wishing I'd brought several changes of clothes with me. "What I wouldn't give for my old Stanford sweatshirt and sweatpants, about now. Or jeans and sneakers. I mean, how am I supposed to run around trying to save people from almost certain death in an old gray house dress? *If* I believe what you told me last night."

He straightened and quirked a brow. "You went to Stanford University? Really?"

Dasha's brow furrowed. "Why? You think I'm not smart enough?"

He gazed out the window, as if his mind was a million miles away. "I was just thinking you're a long way from Stanford University. But in the meantime, I'll tell you what you need to know. So, don't worry."

He peered down at the duffle bag he was packing. Consequently, he didn't see the face I made behind his back. *Arrogant, macho, rude!*

"Not just anyone can have a Tree as a team mascot, you know," I stated in my defense.

He laughed, but didn't ask me to explain. That ended that, but the day was still young.

Marya returned a few minutes later, pleased to be clean. She'd washed her hair and let the natural curls air dry. Once she put on fresh clothes, she smiled, ready to go in a crisp pleated navy skirt and white blouse.

"I can't wait for you to meet my friends and family. They be good company on long trip to Siberia."

"About that..." I started to say.

Alex zipped up the small duffel bag he'd found in the closet and faced the young girl. "Dasha and I have something really important to do here in Saint...I mean, Petrograd, in the next few days. We have to move quickly, so we can't go to Siberia with you. Not this time anyway." He exchanged a look with me, and I wondered what he was up to. "But we want to be sure you'll be alright, so we'll go to the train station and meet your friends. Is that okay?"

"That's a great idea, Alex," I said, getting his drift.

I knew as well as Alex that Anastasia was being sent to Siberia where she would face a horrible death. But Marya didn't know that. She naively believed they would be saved by traveling there. It was so innocent on her part. Still, the fact that Alex hadn't taken me into his confidence until after the fact was eating me up inside every time I looked at Marya. But maybe I wasn't giving Alex enough credit. Maybe he simply didn't wish to divulge a plan while Marya was there to eavesdrop.

I frowned, as suddenly it struck me. I knew her, but how? Or perhaps someone just like her?

With a final shrug, I gave up trying to place her. This whole mission seemed so cockamamy to me in the light of day. I knew a little about Russia's future, but I still wished I'd paid more attention to my Russian history lessons.

But I digress. I always do when I'm anxious.

The press of people trying to catch trains to other parts of Russia and Europe to escape the war, famine, and shifting government were like a line of ants trying to make it to a picnic before the food ran out. People shoved and pushed to make it on board in time. Every seat was filled, while some people stood in the aisles.

It took us a while to find Ana's party of six. She and Marya were thrilled to be reunited after almost a month apart. My first glimpse of Anastasia Romanov, if that was indeed her, was of an attractive girl of seventeen with wild reddish-brown hair full of natural curl. She didn't have the more delicate features of her oldest sister, Olga, or the outgoing personalities of the middle sisters, Tatiana and Maria. Instead, Anastasia was the youngest girl, the one most protective of their ill thirteen-year-old brother, Aleksei.

With Marya now safely aboard the train surrounded by friends and relatives, I stayed close to Alex McKain as we scanned the mass of people for a glimpse of Rasputin should he decide to come after the pair. After a while, I turned to him and whispered, "I don't get it. None of the other sisters are here, nor is Aleksei or his parents. Ana is being sent off with servants. Is this how it's supposed to be?"

Alex's brows formed a deep V in his forehead. "I'm not sure. I haven't received any recent intel, but I do need to board the train to speak with one of the men accompanying Ana and Marya. I'll be right back." He set me against the rail office wall. "Don't move. If Rasputin approaches, scream bloody murder."

I didn't need the reminder. As I waited quietly, I wondered what I should do if I did meet Anastasia. Urge her to stay behind, let her go? I still didn't know the plan or what my involvement entailed. Until Alex returned, I was to do nothing. That thought didn't sit well with me as I sank into myself, hoping no one would notice me. Much to my chagrin, however, it wasn't long before Marya came rushing over to me as the train whistle blew, with Ana trailing behind, her hair hidden beneath a large straw hat.

"Oh, Dasha! I not get a chance to introduce you to my friend, Ana, earlier."

I extended a hand. "I'm so happy to make your acquaintance, Ana. Perhaps..." The whistle blew, signalling the final call before departure. What should I do? Make her stay or let her go?

Marya turned to me. "The train is ready to leave station and we can't delay any longer. I'm so glad I have met you, Dasha." She threw her arms around me, squeezing the air out of my lungs. "Say goodbye to Alex, yes?"

Before I could answer, Ana said in a strained voice, "It's time to go. I may be dead if I don't make this train." She fingered the gold cross around her neck.

You may be dead if you do *board this train,* I wanted to say.

But I couldn't tell her that. Instead, I murmured, "May God be with you."

It was all I could think to say in Russian. I was glad when Ana took the initiative and leaned forward to kiss me on each cheek. I was sure there must be a law somewhere about touching a noble without their permission. I wasn't going to fall for that, no matter the circumstance.

The final train whistle blew, and as I watched the two women climb up into the last train car, I had the strangest mix of emotions swirling around inside. An intense wave of sadness overwhelmed me, and my throat constricted as I fought back tears. In two days' time, Anastasia would be dead, and I had done nothing to stop it.

Where is Alex? If he didn't return from the train soon, I'd be here all alone and Ana would be gone, her fate sealed.

For several frantic minutes, I searched for him, but then, out of all the faces in the crowd, I looked into the eyes of Rasputin and my knees began to tremble. I couldn't look away. If Rasputin had his way, the two young ladies would be dead before the end of the day.

Chapter 9

"This card highlights the importance of working together toward shared physical and emotional soul connection."
(Tarot Card: Two of Coins)

Rasputin headed straight for me, his mesmerizing blue eyes holding me in their spell. I tried to look away, but the train station began to spin all around me. Why would he hunt us down? Tears pooled in the corners of my eyes as I searched desperately for Alex. I swiped at them and gave Rasputin a look of warning to stay away.

Fortunately, he stopped halfway between the next arriving train and the Kazansky Station ticket office, where I now stood. He carried no baggage, and an eerie glow circled his head.

"Good girl. You waited for me."

Alex's voice startled me. I turned to the left and saw him strolling casually toward me carrying two duffle bags, one dark gray, the other a lighter dove gray. When I turned back, Rasputin was gone and I could breathe again.

Maybe he was never even there.

I pushed off the wall and headed straight for Alex, ready to give him a piece of my mind. "I didn't know where you were. I thought you left on the train, the same one as—"

Alex placed an arm around my shoulder, pulling me close so he could whisper in my ear. "Ana is okay for the time being, and as for 'our family friend'..." He nodded toward where Rasputin had been standing moments ago. "Play along with me," he whispered. Then, in a louder voice he said, "And how *is* our dear family friend?"

I understood and kept my voice down. "He was staring right at me. Then you came along, and he was gone." I inhaled deeply, forgetting about the smoke from the train, which made me cough. "Something's hinky about Rasputin."

"Hinky?" Alex's right eyebrow lifted while the left brow remained as is. "I'm not familiar with that word. What does it mean?"

Dasha laughed. "It's modern American slang. It means he was acting suspiciously."

Alex frowned. "You're a font of knowledge, Dasha."

"It's nice to know I'm good at something."

"Oh, I'm sure you're good at numerous things."

How had I known he'd say something to make me blush? *Were we flirting just now?*

I looked at the people passing with renewed focus. "How much time do we have before we meet up with the girls?"

Alex pulled out a pocket watch from a silk and wool navy blue vest—which he hadn't been wearing before. The color was stunning with his blue eyes.

"It's nine o'clock. We'll get something to eat, board the train, and then depart at ten. We arrive in Moscow at two a.m. Marya and Ana are scheduled to take the train from Moscow to Siberia shortly after two p.m. With any luck, we'll arrive at the Moscow station in time to stop them from boarding the second train to Siberia."

"Alex, why don't we just take the girls with us now, instead of waiting?"

"Soldiers are everywhere, both Russian and Bolsheviks. One wrong move, and we miss our best chance to make a clean getaway, so no one gets hurt. Besides, I want to know exactly where Rasputin is when we make our move. With both armies looking for us, I'm not sure that's possible here."

I supposed that made sense. And I certainly didn't want anyone to get hurt. I crossed my arms, frustrated by how long things were taking. "How many stops from Moscow to Yekaterinburg?"

"Five." He hesitated and regarded me for a few moments before saying more. "That's what my sources tell me. And about twenty-six hours from Moscow, providing the tracks are clear and the weather good." He pointed me in the direction of the food carts on the station side of the platform. "You look like you could use some nourishment. What are you in the mood for? Potato latkes or...potato pirozhki?" The dimple danced in the center of his chin. "We're lucky the armies allow food at all for civilians on these east-bound trains."

I stuffed my hands in my pockets. How awkward it must be for Alex that I knew things about history that he hadn't experienced yet, whether in books or real life. We should pool our knowledge. After all, I studied the Russian Revolution in college. Surely, it could come in handy.

I'd been so lost in thought that I stumbled over a carpetbag someone had set on the boardwalk.

"I'm so tired." I rubbed my eyes while Alex helped me regain my balance and ushered me to a bench.

"You can sleep on the way to Moscow."

"Thank God." I gave him a quick sidelong glance. "By the way, where did you get the new clothes?"

"I arranged ahead of time for a colleague to bring me some nicer clothes." He showed her the dove gray duffle. "A female staffer picked up a few things for you, as well, in case we get stuck anywhere for long. The bag is a bit heavy, so I'll carry it for now. You can change in our compartment. I suggest the blouse and skirt—always appropriate and feminine. In the meantime, I'm starving. Let's eat."

He stopped in front of one of the carts and eyed the potato pancakes and vegetable pies. He spoke over his shoulder. "Like I said, with the war going on, there aren't many choices."

"It doesn't matter. I'm just hungry," I said, rubbing my stomach to stop its growling. "Oh, wait. Are those turnips? I'm not a turnip fan."

He smiled as if he knew something I didn't. "I think you'll learn to appreciate turnips and beets, and anything else that fills your stomach. Remember where we are."

It felt as if he'd just scolded me. I frowned as I ate one of the vegetable pies. To my surprise, it wasn't half-bad. I carefully wrapped the second pie and the potato pancakes, or *latkes*, as he called them, then placed them where they wouldn't get smashed. Next, we boarded the train. I was relieved to find we had a compartment to ourselves, despite soldiers spilling out of the doors of the passenger cars.

"Did the Bureau arrange a compartment so we don't have to share?" I asked, impressed by their foresight.

He nodded, but his eyes followed the soldiers outside our sliding glass window. "*Da*. I think perhaps we should speak Russian until we get to Moscow. Are you up for it, Miss Dasha?"

I sighed and settled into my window seat, placing the duffle next to me. "Don't say I didn't warn you. I may start an international incident. What was the word for 'potato' again?"

"*Kartófel*."

I repeated the word three times—as if knowing how to say "potato" would save the girls.

"Don't worry, I'll give you lessons, since we'll have a lot of downtime between here and our stop." He grinned and took out a few items from his bag before sitting across from me. "You're a good sport, Miss Marusov."

It wasn't long before a long steam whistle announced the train's departure. I felt the huge iron monster start to chug and pick up speed. Alex was reading a Russian newspaper, and looked like any Russian businessman. We'd left the station far behind when he rose and blocked the compartment window by facing the aisle outside.

"You might want to change now." He turned his back to me and held the newspaper so that it provided a barrier to prevent any peeping toms.

"You won't peek, will you?"

I heard a distinct chuckle and realized I must sound like a schoolgirl. But the truth of the matter kept playing in my head. I barely knew this man. For now, I still needed to watch my back until I knew who I could trust...and who I couldn't. In the meantime, worrying about the lives of those girls was making me sick to my stomach. Or maybe it was the turnips.

I finished dressing in an ivory *crepe de chine* blouse and silk and wool burgundy skirt. Alex had brought a coat for me, so all I could do was hope I didn't end up someplace where I'd really need it, though the black-and-white herringbone tweed *was* gorgeous. I muttered and cursed as I hooked my silk stockings to a garter belt. I had never worn one before, so it took me a while to get them on so the seam down the back of my legs was relatively straight.

I heard a chuckle, followed by, "Need help?"

"Don't you dare turn around!" I cursed a few more times and finally finished. "Crazy ladies wearing garters and nylons. Next time, I'm bringing a package of tights from Walmart."

"Done?"

"Hmph. I suppose it's necessary in 1918, but I want it noted that I *really* don't like these."

"So noted."

At least Alex's staff member at the BTM center had included a pair of black pumps. I stuffed my old gray maid's dress in the duffle bag and placed it on the seat beside me. "You can look now."

Alex's smile showed his appreciation for the transformation. "You look lovely. More like your beautiful self."

I ran my fingers through my hair. "Thanks. It feels good to put on fresh clothes." And yet, despite the new look, it still bothered me that we didn't have a definite plan. I glanced over at Alex, who didn't seem too worried, his blue eyes never missing a thing outside the compartment window.

I jumped up to pace. "So, what's my role during this mission?" I snapped my fingers. "Oh, I know! You're a handsome young businessman, and I'm your..." I gulped. "Mistress?"

"Sounds plausible," he said with a grin.

"Does everyone who can afford it have a mistress here?" I asked, my mouth suddenly dry.

He looked up from the article he was reading. "Not everyone has a mistress. But if that's the role you want to play..."

Heat rushed to my cheeks. "I didn't mean..."

"I was thinking we're more like newlyweds trying to retrieve your wayward niece."

"N-newlyweds?"

He put the newspaper down and smiled with what appeared to be indulgence. "Have you ever been married before? Or engaged, perhaps? Try to draw experience from that."

My breathing grew shallow at the mention of an engagement. For four years, I had been suppressing those memories, hoping no one would bring up that day.

The day Dalton died.

But perhaps this was the day the silence should end, I decided as my face grew warm. The nightmare of that day flooded my mind to overflowing, spilling over to remind me what a charmed life I'd led...until that one moment in time. As if my emotions were locked behind a dam until now, and the spillway had opened, they came gushing out of my mouth all at once, the pain, the sorrow, the guilt that I'd lived with for the past four years.

"There was a man, once," I said with a watery smile. "Back in high school. I was popular then. Head cheerleader, which I loved. Never cared about being crowned homecoming queen or anything related to looks. I played all after-school sports."

Alex set his newspaper aside as if sensing this was important. "Go on."

I released a breath of air to steady myself. "One rainy day, when I was a junior, I happened to run into Dalton Fairfax...one of *the* Fairfaxes of San Francisco. I missed my ride home, and he was so funny and kind. I trusted him almost immediately." A teardrop fell and I swiped at it with my hand. "I never looked back."

"Then what happened?" Alex asked, leaning in.

I forced a smile I didn't feel. "We dated all senior year, and then we both got into Stanford. We liked the same movies, same music, and all sports, of course. Mom adored Dalton." I laughed, despite the pain. "I'm sure it had to do with him being a very rich young man *and* an only child. With Dalton, I felt loved. Protected. He could read my emotions and always knew just what to do."

"You still didn't tell me what happened," Alex prodded, reaching over to take my hand.

That simple touch reminded me so much of Dalton, his kindness, his caring. I caught my breath and continued. "During Christmas break, he'd worked up the courage to ask me to marry him. We were walking in Golden Gate Park at the time. A thick mist covered the bridge behind us. It was magical."

"What was your response?" Alex asked, his knees touching mine.

"I said yes right away." I swiped at another tear.

"Then why aren't you married?" he asked tenderly.

I inhaled and rubbed Alex's hand with my thumb for courage. "First you have to know that Dalton was everything I hoped to find in a man. He was smart, funny, and compassionate. He made me laugh. He always held my hand when I was sad," I said, looking down at Alex's hands, so like Dalton's. "So, the answer to your original question is yes, I was in love and engaged to marry Dalton Fairfax right after college. But he was captain of the wrestling team."

Alex tensed, as though knowing what was coming.

My voice grew more hushed as my mind spooled through the memories. "I was in the audience for an important match against Georgia State. I was watching with our friends, my roommate, Amanda, and her boyfriend, Ben. We'd been talking and laughing about having a Destination Wedding...to Disneyland."

I thought I'd cried myself dry, but I felt fresh tears rolling down my cheeks.

"Dasha, what's wrong? What happened?"

He grasped my hand and pulled me closer. I didn't resist. At that moment, Alex's eyes drew me in with their soulfulness, reminding me of Dalton's. He rubbed my hand with his thumb, as I had done his, just moments before. I saw such compassion in his expression, the same compassion that Dalton had shown me all those years ago. I burst into gasping sobs, the pain so new and raw all over again.

"Tell me, Dasha. Tell me everything. I'm here for you."

Chapter 10

"The Tower hits us with sudden change: the collapse of
an ideal, a dream, an organization, or a relationship."
(Tarot Card: The Tower)

I glanced out the window as the nighttime countryside whizzed by, then swallowed back the pain in my throat and the grief I'd kept hidden for four years. Maybe the time had come to finally get this off my chest, all the pain and heartbreak of that day. The sadness that had wrapped me in its tight grip for months on end. Years of loneliness. *Because I was afraid to get past the memory*. It was easier not to trust anyone.

Alex handed me a gentleman's handkerchief, the small gesture stirring my heart. I licked my lips and squeezed his hand for courage.

"Somehow, Dalton got twisted up, and it snapped his neck. They said it was a freak accident. He died right there on the mat."

"Oh, my God, Dasha! I had no idea. I mean..."

Alex pulled me into his arms and held me, washing away some of the hurt that had haunted me all those years. I could have stayed like that forever, cocooned in his warm embrace, but finally I pulled back, suddenly feeling awkward now that the story was out. I pinned him with a weary gaze.

"That information is probably in a file somewhere, isn't it? A file on *me*?"

Alex shrugged, an apology written into his expression.

"Alex," I said hesitantly, "is there anything I don't know about that incident? Anything that would ease the pain and grief I've felt all these years?" My voice cracked as I fought back fresh tears.

"Four years *is* a long time to carry all that," he murmured as he tucked a strand of my hair behind one ear...just like Dalton used to do.

"Yes. It is," I agreed with a trembling smile. As much as I wanted to know what was in the Bureau of Time Mender files on Dalton...on my family, for that matter, at this point, it wasn't important. I could do nothing about the past, but I could do something about Anastasia Romanov's life here in Russia. That's what mattered now.

Alex scooched over on the train bench and sat with his leg brushing mine as his arm went around my shoulder. "I knew what was in the file. But I couldn't imagine how hard that must have been for you."

"What about you? Have you ever lost someone you loved?" I asked, my voice husky with emotion.

He paused for so long, I was almost afraid he'd decided against revealing his pain. At last, he began to speak, his voice low and subdued. "It was a really long time ago. And not quite the same thing." He scratched his head, appearing uncomfortable.

"So, we've both lost someone we love." I pulled out a bottled water from my duffle bag and took a sip, then set it down. "You don't have to tell me if it's too painful."

He squeezed my hand, the gesture sending a tingle through me that I hadn't felt in a very long time, then he turned to gaze fully into my eyes. "My father died when I was sixteen. That was back in Texas when my parents had a horse ranch. A fire started in the barn." He flinched and looked away. "We lost all the horses. Every last one. Even my personal mount, Crazy Boy. I raised that stinker from a colt. Best darn horse I ever rode, but sure had a mind of his own. My father died trying to save them." He shrugged. "That left me and my mother trying to eke out a living and restore the ranch." He folded the edge of the newspaper. "I was close to my father, and loved those horses. I wanted to breed and sell them, like my father." A familiar sadness dulled his eyes. "But things didn't work out. My mother contracted pneumonia and died a year later. I was an only child, so that left me to figure out what I needed to do."

"Oh, that's terrible. You lost—"

"Everything and everyone."

"Is that when you joined the Time Menders?" I asked, curious.

"Soon after. I was still so young, but I had a good relationship with one of their operatives. A family friend. He got me out of a bad situation and took me in."

I lay my head on his shoulder for several moments. "Thank you for sharing that. I know people experience all kinds of grief every day. It's just...when you're all alone... the night is long."

Alex lay his hand over mine and forced a smile. "You'll find someone to share those tough times with you, Dash. You're twenty-four years-old. Plus, you're beautiful and smarter than you think." He placed a hand on his chest. "Now, I'm no one special. Certainly not perfect. But from what I can tell, I think we make a great team."

Those blue eyes of his seemed to be searching for something inside me. All I knew for certain was that my body hummed when we were together, touching like this.

"So, in all this time, you haven't dated anyone?" he asked, his hands softly caressing my hair.

Again I flushed, but for a different reason. I thought about that for a moment. Is that what he really thought? That I could just jump into the dating pool again?

"Moving on isn't that easy. Dalton was a special person. I haven't met anyone who comes even close." I looked out the window, willing away more tears. "I'm sorry to be such a downer, but there you have it. I haven't dated much since then. It's...too painful." I smiled weakly. "My little sister, Gigi, has a theory that when I do date, I intentionally sabotage potential partners because I don't want anyone to get too close to me again."

"What do you think of that theory?"

His fingers kept in motion, caressing my cheeks, fingering the sleeves of the soft ivory blouse I'd borrowed that was so much more feminine than anything I usually wore to work.

"She may be right. Sometimes, I hear the excuses I come up with, and I know I'm not trying very hard. All I want to do is hide."

"I'm the one who's sorry that happened to you." He pulled me gently to him once again, and I was shocked at how good it felt to be held close. How comforting. He smelled like Grandma Tattie's lemon pie, and I wondered how that was possible. Why didn't he smell like potato latkes? I saw his face draw closer, and I panicked that he would try to kiss me. It was too soon, and I'm sure I must have disappointed him when I gulped and pulled away. We stared awkwardly at each other for several moments, both of us feeling a spark, I felt certain.

He reached out and briefly squeezed my hand. "You can go at your own speed, Dasha. We all have our own timetables to recover from grief. So, I'll do the gentlemanly thing and return to my newspaper, okay?" After a moment, he snapped the page and paused. "Wait a minute. I read somewhere that you were dating that musician at the fundraiser. What about him? Brendon something?"

"Alessio," I said in a raspy voice. "And how did you know about the fundraiser and Brendon?" It suddenly dawned on me, and I snapped my fingers. "Ohmigosh! You're Marya's grumpy supervisor."

"Well, I'm glad you remembered *that* part," he said with a raised brow, "but what about Brendon?"

I breathed a sigh. "I knew Brendon in college when a bunch of us hung out together in between classes. I was seeing Dalton at the time, so I never dated Brendon." I shrugged. "It's been four years since then. It's time for me to grow up and be an adult. But as to dating, that's on the back burner. Anyway, Brendon told me he was leaving on a six-month world tour. He's gone already."

"What a fool for not wanting to spend time with you."

I lowered my head so he wouldn't see the final teardrop fall. When my voice was steady once more, I swiped the tear away and raised my head to face him.

"Before I try to get some rest," I said, giving him a wan smile, then stretching to ease the emotions I had buried until now, "tell me what happens if Ana and Marya are already gone when we arrive? Surely, you have a plan B."

Alex shuffled his feet, appearing uncomfortable.

As I waited for him to say something, I peered out the window at Petrograd's lights, which twinkled far out into the suburbs. "Tell me if I'm wrong, but if we leave Ana and Marya on that train headed to Siberia, Ana's fate will be the same as her family's, right? Can't we stop the train, get Ana and Marya off, and find a safehouse where no one will think to look?"

"Safehouse? I like that expression."

"You'll be using that term a lot, so memorize it," I said with a smile.

He nodded in agreement. "As for the girls, you're correct. If they board the train to Yekaterinburg, they *will* be murdered with the others...in the wee hours, most likely. I'm sure the Bolsheviks want as few witnesses as possible.

Stunned at his words, I sank back onto the bench and picked up a Soviet propaganda magazine that had been placed there before we arrived. I thumbed through it without reading a word as I absorbed the act of violence threatening them.

"Oh, Alex, we have to help them escape."

He raked a hand through his wavy dark hair and sat on the edge of the bench. "You may be surprised to hear this, but I actually *do* have a plan. However, you'll have to leave it to me to execute it when the time comes."

I slapped the magazine down on the table. "Then why did you bring me all the way back to 1918 if I have no say in what's happening?"

He stood and paced. "You'll just have to trust me. So far, we know there are two train stations in Moscow, Yaroslavsky and Kazansky stations, which is where they will begin their Trans-Siberian portion of the journey. We saw them board a passenger car at Kazansky Station."

Alex sat and folded his hands, then stared down at his feet.

"Let's say they take the train all the way to Yekaterinburg, and stay there," I said. "When will they be able to return to Petrograd?" Though I already knew the answer to that question, I had to ask in order to confirm the details.

Alex's eyes met mine. "They can't return. This is no vacation. I thought you knew that."

My head started to spin. I rose, then quickly sat. "Why didn't Anastasia go with her family before now?"

Alex shrugged, then turned to look out the window at the dark countryside. "My colleague, Misha, checked in with the Bureau. He says he wants to marry Ana and keep her tucked away in the English countryside, safe and anonymous, so he talked her into staying behind. But neither England nor France will grant asylum to the Romanovs unless she's married to a citizen of that country. Then they would be forced to accept her. They're afraid of Russia dragging them into the war. Misha is determined to come up with a solution, but for now, Ana has no place to go.

"I feel so bad for her. Do you think she's scared?"

Alex stood, walked over to the compartment door and placed a hand on the doorknob. He looked out into the hallway, making sure no one was close. Then he turned to me. "If she's not scared, then she's not paying attention. This is no game."

That sounded rather harsh, but then he added, "Anastasia Romanova is smarter than you think." He tilted his head. "She reminds me of you. That's why we're going to stay in the shadows as much as possible, because you look a bit like her. I don't want anyone mistaking you for her."

Did I look like her? I'd never thought of it before.

Great. Something else to fear. I look like an ancestor, a famous one at that.

I shifted on the bench and used my duffel for a pillow. "I don't suppose you can wave a magic wand and shorten the four-hour trip to one hour?"

"I wish I could, but in the meantime, hopefully, we can find a way to prevent their train from arriving on time." He pointed to my bag. "For the time being, I had a female aide pick up a few other things you might like. Toothbrush. Toothpaste. Makeup. Perfume."

"I'd say your Bureau friends really went to town for me, Mr. McKain." I batted my eyelashes. "What kind of perfume? Chanel?"

Alex responded with a straight face. "My guess is *eau de potato.*"

I laughed. "*Touché!*"

"I'll be right back. Lock this door behind me. If anyone gives you trouble, brandish this thing," he said, handing me a Swiss Army Knife. Then he waved and stepped out into the corridor.

Brandish? I loved his use of old-fashioned words.

I did as Alex asked, not even questioning his orders as I cleaned up and put on fresh makeup. However, I must have been more tired than I thought, because I took a seat and soon my eyes drifted closed for several moments. But before long, the image of Rasputin filled my dreams, and I bolted upright.

Anxious now, I stood and regarded myself in the mirror near the luggage rack. I turned my head back and forth. Did I really look like Ana? My hair was a lighter blonde color, and straighter, while her hair showed what I assumed were natural curls that cascaded down her back. Something about our noses looked similar, but that's all that seemed evident.

"Oh, Sash. I wish you were here to see all this. You, too, Gigi."

And yet, if they were here in the flesh, wouldn't they be in the same danger I was in? I shook my head of the thought just in time to hear Alex's knock. I released the lock to allow him entry into the compartment, but when he saw me, he took a step back to get the full picture of me in fashionable clothes from 1918.

"You know," he said with a crooked smile. "I believe you were born for this time period. You look smashing in those clothes."

"Thanks. I think. You'll have to thank your colleague, too. She has excellent taste." I patted my hair into place in front of the mirror. "Now, when we arrive in Moscow, what's the first thing we do?"

"The two stations are located on the same square, so not far apart. We'll have to walk to Yaroslavsky terminal just across the square. We'll check the departures signs, find out when the next train to Siberia is scheduled to leave, then search the train for Ana and Marya. If all goes according to plan, they'll experience a delay, which gives us more time to reach them."

"Should I tell her the truth of what's waiting for her in Yekaterinburg? Does she know?"

"Your job is to convince Ana she has a dynasty to save—yours. Say or do whatever you must to convince her. Marya will go along with whatever Ana decides. Here's the plan. We sneak them off the train and onto another train bound for western Europe. I can't tell you more than that."

"And what if they disembarked from the train somewhere between Petrograd and Moscow?"

"We'll find them and follow them no matter where they go."

Several moments passed, then Alex laid a hand on top of mine. "I hate to be crude, but if they die, that means you were never born."

That was certainly a conversation stopper. On that cheery note, I dozed an hour or so, but then I was wide awake the rest of the trip and we spent the rest of it brushing up on my Russian.

As the train approached Moscow, I packed up my things in the gray duffle bag, glad it was cool enough to wear the coat. Once the train pulled into the station, and we disembarked, we rushed to the other platform. My eyes felt gritty from the coal-filled air, but I tried not to rub them. When we arrived at our next destination, we discovered the train to Siberia hadn't arrived yet. Alex checked with the ticket office and returned with a grin.

"Seems they discovered a dead bull on the track outside of Nizhny Novgorod, so their train was delayed...*with* the help of the Bureau." He glanced down at me. "Are you okay? You look worried."

I hesitated a moment as we stood in front of the departures board. Normally, I would have said, "Oh, I'm fine." But I *wasn't* fine. "I'm scared, Alex. I want to go home and be with my sisters. I miss them so much. I feel terrible for Marya and Ana, but—"

He reached into a pocket and produced a bottle of water for me to sip on.

"*Spasíbo*," I said, grateful for the cool drink after such a long train ride.

"I don't blame you for missing them, but if you leave now, they will never be born." He tried to smile, but didn't do a very good job of it. "And if our *family friend* has been sniffing around, I can understand why you're scared. Chances are he's up to no good." He took one of my hands. "I loathe having to ask you this, Dasha, but if we aren't able to save the girls in this time and place, the Bureau is asking us to slipstream back two years to 1916. If we eliminate...*our friend* earlier, several ugly incidents could be avoided. In the meantime, let's see how we do with this mission. I'll provide more information if you say yes, so you won't be going in blindly."

"And this will protect my family?"

Alex smiled, his blue eyes sparkling. "Yes. I can explain everything, once we find Ana and get her to a safe place."

Outside the station, the rain began to fall. While I was digesting what he'd said, two people came to stand beside each of us, one on my side and one on Alex's.

"It *is* her, Dima!"

Madame Peshkova dropped two large carpetbags, her mouth quirked in excitement. "We are here to help you search for the girl."

I felt a cold rush of fear finger down my spine. "Alex, how do they keep finding us? And how did they know where we were going?"

Chapter 11

*"This card brings a speedy development between
you and your love interest based on mutual
attraction, and founded on a love of the challenge
and the chase."*
(Tarot Card: Knight of Wands)

As we stood in front of the train departures sign, I stared at Alex in shock. *What is going on?* I spared a quick glance at Madame Peshkova and Dima, who placed a protective arm around her shoulder as they spoke pleasantly to the soldiers passing by.

When those soldiers began making arrests, I spoke only loud enough to ask, "Are you Time Menders? Is that how you got here?

"Shhh!" Dima put fingers to her lips to shush her. "Not so loud," he warned.

"Hasn't Alex explained anything?" Katya frowned at Alex.

I could feel my temper rising. "He's told me bits and pieces about why I'm here. However, clearly, he didn't say enough."

Dima crossed his bare arms, showing his muscles. All he needed was a black leather jacket that read Hell on Wheels across the back, and he'd have that biker vibe down pat. I wondered how I'd missed that before.

"My dear," said Katya in her condescending Madame Peshkova *persona* as she looked up at the train departures board. "I'm sure you thought the BTM was responsible for the train's tardiness, but lucky for you, my 'misfortune spell' is in good working order. That bull on the train tracks was old and due to meet his maker. It's too bad the railroad driver and the bull's owner ended up in a major fight because of the damage to the rail ties. The passengers had to wait several hours to clear up that mess." She smiled the smile of an angel, her hazel eyes wide. "And here the train comes now. As predicted, though not exactly on time."

"You put a *spell* on the train track?" Alex glared at Katya in disbelief.

Katya just laughed, causing several passengers waiting to board to turn to see where the lovely feminine sound was coming from. It would be impossible for any sane person, male or female, not to notice how gorgeous Madame Peshkova—Katya—was. In fact, I was beginning to understand why Dima was here...guarding her so enthusiastically.

Katya turned to Alex. "I suggest we split up. The four of us can find Ana much quicker that way."

Alex rested his hands on his hips, his lips pressed into a thin line. "Is that what you came here for? To steal my assignments? Because it's not gonna happen."

"Alex," I said, placing my hand on his arm to calm him. "Let's hear them out. We don't have much time."

"The Bureau contacted us for this special assignment. They're rooting for you," Katya explained to Alex. "Please let us help, but we must hurry."

Alex appeared doubtful. Did the Time Mender Bureau really send them to help, I wondered? The seconds ticked away on the train station clock, as we all watched the latest arrivals from Petrograd disembark.

Dima nodded. "Katya is right. Two of us should wait to see who boards the Siberian train in the first five cars. The other two should monitor the last five cars."

Alex faced me, his expression stern. He didn't like it, but what could he do?

"Agreed...though reluctantly. Dasha, you work with Dima, so you can keep an eye on him. I'll work with Katya. That way, no one can accuse the other of kidnapping the girls once we spot them." He pulled out his pocket watch. "The Siberian train arrived so late, it may depart as soon as they re-fuel, to attempt to get back on schedule. Let's go."

"Good plan." Much to my surprise, Dima grabbed my hand and pulled me toward the middle of the train. "You start here and work your way up to the front passenger car. I'll start there and work my way back to the last car."

"And what should I say if I find Ana?"

"Didn't Alex give you *some* idea of...*the problem*?"

I glanced over my shoulder, paranoid that someone might be listening. "Well, yes, but I don't want to scare her when I tell her we're related."

He pulled out a knife and hid it up his sleeve.

"Do you expect trouble?" I asked, alarmed.

"Anytime there's a Romanov in the room, trouble is possible. Let's get going so we can do a thorough job. Don't talk to anyone, if you don't need to."

As I peered down at the train car at the very end, I wondered if we shouldn't stay together, as Alex had advised. However, by the time I turned back to tell Dima what I thought, he'd vanished from sight. Nervous perspiration began to gather on my brow, knowing I was about to confront Ana and maybe Rasputin by myself.

I climbed aboard the first car and scoured each compartment. Many people were still trying to make their connections, and had exited the train already. But others were taking their sweet time. I tried to stay out of their way and hoped no one would start a conversation in Russian. After my long session in Russian with Alex, I decided that my skills were adequate, but could be better. I'd been sent here with no special training in anything from the Time Menders Bureau. The more I thought about it, the angrier I became.

"Tae-Kwando," I mumbled to myself. "I need some kind of self-defense. No way am I carrying a knife or gun around." I checked over my shoulder, relieved no one was there to hear me grumbling.

I had just climbed aboard the seventh car when I noticed two women in the first compartment leaning forward in their seats, whispering. The other passengers were gone already. Both wore large hats—hats I recognized immediately. Marya's knit bucket hat was pulled down low, hiding her dark curls. The other girl wore a straw hat with all of her blondish-brown hair stuffed up inside. They both stood in unison and grabbed their carpetbags from the luggage rack. Marya was the first to recognize me. Initially, her face lit up, then she glanced behind me as if looking for Alex.

"Miss Dasha, you came to see us off?"

Anastasia turned in surprise. "You told this woman where we're headed?"

I sighed in relief, her English surprisingly good.

"Good...morning. I'm glad to see you are both well." I blinked at them, forcing myself to be pleasant in front of royalty on only a few hours' sleep. What I really wanted to do was grab each girl by the hand and run.

Marya's eyes darted around the car, and then she stooped to look out the window. "I would like to visit, but we must go catch our next train."

"Why do you want to go to Siberia?" I asked. "You know what awaits you there?"

Ana's expression turned cloudy. "My family. I want to be with them...to the end."

"And I have only Miss Ana. I will go where she goes...even if it means death."

A man's heavy footsteps on the train's stairs alerted me that Alex knew we were in the seventh car from the front. He boarded the passenger car and raced toward us, then knelt beside the Grand Duchess.

"Ana," Alex said calmly. "What if you had the opportunity to marry and have a family? Misha spoke to the folks in the Bureau. He says he proposed marriage to you. If you escape with him, we can find a safe haven in England or France."

Ana hugged her carpetbag. "I love Misha so much, but...it is my fate to die tomorrow, is it not?"

I leaned in, aware of the ticking clock. "Ana, my grandmother, Tatiana Mazurova, was once a Time Mender. You know what that is?"

She sucked on her lower lip, looking much younger than her seventeen years. "*Da*, I have heard stories of Time Menders. I remember Tatiana Marusova. But she was sixteen. How is that possible if she was your grandmother?" She frowned, and I could detect a stubborn streak in her. Alex glanced my way, and I figured he worried about that stubborn streak, as well.

"We'll have to discuss the mechanics of slipstreaming later, because we're almost out of time. I brought Dasha here to find you, Ana." Alex placed a hand on my shoulder. "Dasha is from the future, born in the year 2001. The problem is, she'll never be born if you don't go with Misha. BTM thinks they may have found a way around the refusal to grant you asylum if you marry him and he stays with you. You will have to live a very quiet life in the countryside and take a new name, but it is possible."

Ana leaned her chin on her carpetbag, thinking.

"I have two younger sisters," I continued, trying to make it personal, therefore, more relatable for the seventeen-year-old. "Sasha is twenty-one, and she wants to start a shelter for homeless cats in our neighborhood. My youngest sister, Gigi, is sixteen. I miss them so much. I miss my parents and grandmother, too. But I can't return to my own time until you're safe. Until *we're* safe."

Ana looked down. "I must be strong...like my family, the Romanovs. I must die with my family."

Tears trickled down her cheeks, and I felt the corners of my eyes begin to well up in sympathy. What a horrible decision. What would I do under the same circumstance? I swiped at my tears and switched my gaze to Alex.

"How safe will she be if she goes to England with Misha?"

He looked away, hesitating, then turned to face her. "I don't know the details for sure, but Misha was born there, so he's a United Kingdom citizen. If they marry as soon as they arrive, it should go smoothly. On the other hand, members of the Romanov family all over the world are targets of hatred these days. She could have a long life with a husband and children, or a few years. I don't think even Madame Peshkova can predict that."

At that moment, Dima boarded the train with Katya. I still wished I knew their intentions, whether they planned to grab the girls and return to Petrograd, or continue on to Siberia. If they nabbed them, I would fight. Fight for the existence of *my* family. Suddenly, I understood why Alex had brought me here. I was the only person who could make Anastasia understand how important it was that she didn't get on that train to Siberia. My very existence depended on Ana's survival.

The sound of military boots on the steps startled me, and when I saw who it was, I gasped. I could tell right away that Alex knew the man, so I had to assume it was his Bureau colleague in disguise—Misha. He was a tall man, perhaps in his mid-twenties, with straight dark hair and a scruffy beard. When Ana's eyes landed on him, she let out a cry of delight and rushed forward to embrace him.

So, this was my Marusov cousin and his fiancee, the Grand Duchess, Anastasia. Who would have ever thought it possible? They gazed at each other, love in their eyes.

"It's about time you got here," said Alex. "Ana has been asked to make a crucial decision—to die with members of her family in Siberia, or escape to England, where she has a chance at a new life and new family." He motioned to Dima. "Watch for any soldiers headed this way."

Dima didn't argue, and immediately went to station himself at the doorway.

"Oh, you don't understand," groaned Ana. "It is more complicated than that. I've been a terrible liability to my family my whole life. For the first time, I can do something to support them in their final hours."

"And what about me, Ana?" Misha asked, appearing tense. "What am I supposed to do the rest of my days knowing you chose death over a life with me?"

I was sweating through my silk blouse, but I refused to give up. "Here's the thing, Ana. If you die with your family, I will cease to exist. A whole bloodline of wonderful people will never be born. My mother and grandmother will never have been born. I'm not trying to be selfish, but I love my family, just like you love yours. Did you know my mother started a foundation to help thousands of abused women? I work with her to make miracles happen every day. If she wasn't born, that foundation wouldn't exist. More women will die, lose their babies from unclean medical procedures, and so on. Women around the world will continue to suffer." I leaned forward in the aisle. "I hate to put pressure on you, but could you live with that?"

A tense silence filled the train. Ana allowed Misha to put an arm around her and comfort her, but the look she sent my way was none too friendly. I really couldn't blame her. Of course I had an agenda, but was it any more selfish than Misha's desire to spend his life with her?

I looked down at the worn carpet, wearing the stains of thousands of passengers each and every day. "Alex says that it's certain your family will die. There's no question about that. What would your parents want for *you*, Ana? To go on living and have a family of your own? Be their legacy, or be buried in the ground, your entire family forgotten?"

"I…"

If only we hadn't taken so long to make Ana understand the importance of the decision to be made, because at that moment, four Bolshevik soldiers quietly yanked Dima out of the doorway and onto the train platform, where he was overpowered and placed in handcuffs.

The dizziness returned and I began to sweat even more as three of the soldiers entered the train car and rushed toward us, shouting and waving their bayonets. I held my head and covered my ears to silence their loud, boastful voices as they forced us to leave the train car. I felt like the worst criminal when they made us sink to our knees and put our hands on our heads. One of the men brandished a photo of a young woman, which he held up and compared to Ana. A disgusting grin bloomed on his lean face.

"We will be awarded a promotion for catching this one." His face was just inches from Ana's. "You have caused us a lot of trouble, Miss Anastasia. Now you will pay for your family's crimes. Guards! Get their names and search for any travel documents, then take all of them to the jail at city hall until further notice. They are under arrest. We'll sort this out later."

I looked up and saw Dima with his hands on his head, yet he didn't appear concerned in the least. *Where is Madame Peshkova?* My heart skipped a beat.

It was as if she'd vanished into the Moscow morning.

Who *was* Madame Peshkova, anyway? I feared the answer.

Chapter 12

*"There may be a necessity to heal from a previous relationship
and find peace. Self-care is required so that you can replenish
yourself in order to give to others."*
(Tarot Card: Four of Swords)

My knees dug into the cement on the train platform while other trains came and went. I didn't dare look up at the soldiers guarding us, nor the curious passersby who craned their necks to see what was happening. Fortunately, my heart had slowed its pounding to a moderate pace, giving me time to think.

Next to me, Alex, also on his knees, gave my hip a nudge. No one else saw it, but that friendly nudge, along with the determined look in his blue eyes, said "trust me." I read about people who say their lives literally passed before their eyes when threatened with death. Sure, it was a cliché, but I couldn't think of anything better at that moment. Nor anyone with whom I'd rather be experiencing such danger.

Two of the soldiers conversed in clipped Russian, their voices rising in volume. Apparently, they disagreed about something, but it gave us a moment to speak.

"Are you alright?" Alex whispered.

"I'm fine. How do we get out of this?"

I glanced at Ana's white face and saw the look of terror in her eyes, then gazed at the platform. Why had no one intervened?

"I guess things like this happen all the time," I heard myself say out loud.

"No one is willing to help us, and you can imagine why," Alex responded, his eyes taking in everything. "We have to save ourselves."

"What happened to Madame Peshkova? She vanished into thin air. How did she do that?"

"I don't know, but I'm guessing she has a Time Mender secret up her sleeve."

Dima knelt off to the side by himself, but he didn't appear worried. Did he know where Katya had gone?

I don't know where it came from, but I had a vision of the Cowardly Lion from the *Wizard of Oz* stuck in my head. Well, why not? I closed my eyes. "There's no place like home. There's no place like home."

Alex leaned toward me. "What are you doing?"

"We're not in Kansas anymore. It's worth a shot." I closed my eyes again, then blinked.

Alex's brows furrowed, as if he thought I'd lost my senses.

"It's a movie reference. *The Wizard of Oz*. A Kansas farm girl discovers if she clicks the heels of her ruby red slippers, she can always return home—"

"Silence!"

I looked up and gasped at the sight of Rasputin. He bent down, his long scraggly beard touching his chest, his mousey brown hair revealing a thin patch on top of his head. For so early in the morning, he reeked of vodka. He trained his mesmerizing blue eyes on me, hands folded over his considerable belly. Then, after a moment, he frowned and waved a hand to the guard.

"This one is trouble. Take her and her friends to our secret location." He paused, hands on stout hips, reminding me that he grew up on a Siberian peasant farm. "We will interrogate them there. Anastasia is to be isolated." He whispered something in the ear of the soldier in charge.

Secret location?

I clenched my hands so hard that my nails dug in, causing my palms to bleed. The soldiers exchanged wary glances and watched Rasputin shuffle across the square in no hurry. Once he was out of sight, the one in charge gritted his back teeth and narrowed his eyes.

"Why must we obey that disgusting pig?" he snarled in Russian. No one had an answer.

If we were smart, we just might be able to use the soldiers' disillusionment with Rasputin's continuing influence, along with the floundering provisional government, to our advantage. I exchanged a look with Alex, and just before I could whisper words of encouragement, the hard butt of a rifle came down on the back of my head, and I crumpled into oblivion.

❖

I awoke with a groan, my hands immediately going to my head. "What in the...?"

Alex appeared with paper towels he'd wetted from his canteen. "Try not to move. You were hit on the head."

He washed the wound and bandaged it with a head scarf from my duffle bag while I took in our surroundings.

"Where are we?"

"Actually, we're in the basement of St. Basil's Cathedral," he said.

"This is the secret interrogation location?"

He nodded. "I don't know why they brought us here."

Alex helped me sit up, and I moaned at the continued throbbing at the back of my head. As I looked around, I winced at the bright sunlight highlighting the gold gilt on paintings and icons all around me, floor to ceiling. "Too bright."

"Don't get up yet. I suspect you may have a concussion."

I waved a hand, already pulling myself up. "I'm fine, although I don't understand why that jerk had to hit me with his gun. They can't do anything to us because we're Americans, right? Where's my passport? I'll let them know this is not the way to welcome tourists to town. In fact..."

I realized I was babbling, which was not unusual, considering the circumstances. Humor had become my way of coping after Dalton's sudden and unexpected death. The grief had been so sharp, so deep, I thought I'd never rise out of that bottomless pit. Humor had kept me in one piece, and now it kept me from shaking apart, knowing what lay in store for us. I rested a hand on Alex's forearm to steady myself.

"Well, let's look on the bright side." I shrugged. "I've always wanted to see this place. It's considered the most visual cultural symbol of Russia. And we got in for free."

"Will you please stop moving around? You're making me nervous."

I glanced at Alex and produced a feeble smile. "Where are the others? If we're not tied up and no one's watching us, I would say let's ske-daddle."

Alex shook his head. "You're a wonder...the words you come up with. Stand still and let me check your wound."

While he checked the bandage on my head, a man wearing a long burgundy priest's robe approached us, his hands stuffed inside huge sleeves. He wore a matching burgundy cap, and the expression on his face remained placid as he addressed me.

"I'm Father Yosef. I understand you've been injured?" He grimaced at the blood on Alex's hands.

"You're kind of late, Father. I don't suppose you have a first-aid kit?" Alex growled.

"There's a hospital a few blocks from here," the priest suggested.

A hospital nearby? I could get my head wound looked at, and then we could slip out unnoticed with all the typical foot traffic and chaos of a major hospital. I glanced at Alex, and he looked down at the bloody scarf, then raised his eyes as if to say it was my call.

Was I willing to leave Ana and Marya? They had no one else.

For a moment, I felt ashamed. This was my family. I had to stay, to fix things and make it right.

"*Spasibo*, Father, but first I need to know if you've seen our friends, Ana and Marya?" To his blank expression, I added, "A young woman with long blondish-brown hair and wearing a straw hat? Her companion is short, with curly dark hair, and about eighteen or twenty years old. We need to find them as soon as possible, as their lives may be in danger."

Alex briefly described his friend, Misha, as well. "I need to find him to confirm our travel arrangements. Have you seen them?"

The priest stroked his chin as he thought for a moment. "I haven't seen the young ladies, although I do recall a man asking questions of Father Vyacheslav a few minutes ago. Shall I fetch him? You two can rest here."

"Thank you, Father," we said in unison.

Alex found a wooden bench that faced south. I settled next to him, awkwardly holding a handkerchief against the wound on my head. The bleeding had slowed, but as I gazed straight ahead, it occurred to me I may be in shock. We were almost out of time. I couldn't ignore the priest's offer of treatment, but chances were good that it would be by a not-so-sympathetic Bolshevik doctor who might think nothing of detaining me or turning me in. No, better to stay put. I focused on the icon across from me and felt a sudden jolt.

"Mmm, Alex?" I pointed at the icon on the wall.

He sat hunched over beside me, alert for anything strange. "What?"

"Just a comment. That icon is famous. It was brought to Moscow in 1555."

Alex craned his head to get a better look. "What's it called?"

"Saint Nicholas from the Velikaya River."

"Huh."

Out of the corner of my eye, I saw Father Yosef approach with an even younger priest than himself. He introduced the other man as Father Vyacheslov, and quickly departed to provide privacy.

Father Vyacheslov answered Alex's questions as well as possible. I wondered how far Alex would be willing to go in revealing our mission to find and stop Anastasia from traveling to Siberia, but as it turned out, I needn't have worried. The young priest easily recalled both the women and Misha escaping, and had provided directions to them from Petrograd.

"When the ladies left the train, they were not brought here. Instead, they went willingly with a man in the direction opposite of you," he said, pointing north. "I only noticed them when I stopped to buy a newspaper for Father Yosef from a vendor. The smaller girl with the hat shaped like a bucket bumped into me, then excused herself when the other girl caught sight of a tall man in a black-and-white striped shirt."

"Did it appear they knew the man?" I asked, trying to quell my anxiety.

"Oh, yes. They hugged, then hurried off. The young ladies were smiling and seemed to go with him willingly."

Alex thanked the priest, then turned to me. "We need to get out of here and see if we can find them without attracting attention. Are you up to walking?"

"I can handle it."

He handed me my duffel bag. "Change into something casual and comfortable, especially the shoes."

I could feel the adrenaline kick in, and I wasn't about to quit because of a knock on the head. I took the duffle bag, then handed him my coat to hold, hoping the aide had thought to put a pair of sneakers inside the bag.

"Let me ask the priest for directions to a restroom," I said, "so I can clean up. Give me five minutes. Then I'll see if the priest can find us a way out of here without the guards suspecting."

The younger priest showed me to a bathroom where I cleaned the blood as best I could. While there, I considered my options. How could we make it out of the basement and to our destination without attracting the authorities? Soldiers and police could spell trouble for us. A Russian guard appeared and stationed himself right across from the ladies restroom, but Father Vyacheslav did a great job of diverting his attention.

I was still running my hands through my hair to get out any residual blood when I met Alex outside the bathroom door. I wanted to hug the aide who'd packed sneakers in my size, along with comfortable walking socks and a small canteen of water. Fortunately, Father Yosef had clued another colleague in on the plan to help us escape, because a novice nun was waiting with a set of keys as Father Yosef kept the guard busy by diverting him away from the door with a loud bang in a nearby room. As they rushed away to see what the commotion was about, I met Alex in the first dark hallway, and we hurried through several more before finally finding an unlocked staff entrance that led to the outside.

"May God keep you safe," the nun whispered in English as she closed the door behind us and then immediately retreated inside.

The air had never smelled so good, smoke or no smoke. We hiked for a considerable time before we felt we could slow down and take the time to pick up some food. While Alex was paying for more latkes, or, *draniki,* as the Russians called them, I spotted a small kiosk selling hats of all kinds. Even though the humidity masked a dazzling sun, it still hurt my eyes. The broad-brimmed straw hat that I purchased helped.That is, until the thought of

Rasputin popped into my head while I was biting into a latke. I made a quick scan of the square, but fortunately saw no sign of him...for now. When Alex returned, he was already biting into the last latke. I turned around and quickly modeled my straw hat with most of my hair tucked inside before taking to the streets.

"Do I remind you of someone in this hat?" I asked as we hurried away in case the guard had discovered our ruse by now.

Alex chewed and gave me his full attention as we raced down one alleyway after another. "Mmm. Not really. Why?"

I stopped only long enough to swat him on the arm. "Look again." I made a couple of model poses from different angles, and finally, I saw it dawn on him. He paused in the darkened alleyway before taking another bite.

"Wasn't Ana wearing a straw hat like that?"

"Yes! And our hair is almost the same color—blondish-brown from the sun. She has more curls, and her hair is a bit darker from being inside, but if I wear it up, people who know her might not notice. I can be a decoy so she can board whatever train or bus she needs to in order to reach a safe port."

He shoved the last bite of latke into his mouth. "You do realize you may be putting the two of us in more danger by posing as Ana?"

For once, I remained silent, and gazed back at him, hopeful. He gave me his last bite, then cleaned off his hands with a napkin and tossed it into the trash he found behind a restaurant.

When he saw my determined expression, he said, "Okay. You win. Let's go."

We walked briskly toward the closest train station. Next to it was a bus terminal. Alex was calling all the shots, so the first thing he did was to get a locker. He stuffed my long coat inside and handed me a key to retrieve it later.

"What if we have to leave suddenly? Or, I forget about the coat?"

"The Bureau paid for it. They'll retrieve it, if needed."

"I find it odd a government bureau would pay for so many luxury items, and not demand reimbursement."

Alex turned his head to peer out a window onto the square. "It's not a regular government bureau. It has its own funding."

"Not a regular government agency? Tell me more."

He patted my arm to hurry me along, which annoyed the heck out of me.

"I'll explain when we have more time. In the meantime, we need to keep searching for Ana and Marya. We know they came this way. Look for a sign that directs us north. And I don't know what Katya is up to, but keep an eye out for her and Dima, Rasputin, as well."

The cool morning had turned into a hot, humid afternoon, and soon, my feet hurt and my head throbbed. I seldom got sick or suffered injuries. However, my energy was depleted, and I was dripping with sweat. I was about to suggest we sit, have a nice cold drink and call it quits, when something gave me pause and my heart leaped into my throat.

"See those three people headed for the entrance to the museum across the square? I think that's Misha in the black-and-white striped shirt."

"How many men in Moscow are wearing black-and-white striped shirts? Maybe a dozen in Red Square alone," Alex countered, but he held up the binoculars to check.

"My, you're grouchy today. No more latkes for you." I took the last latke from him, needing some energy. "But see how tall he is, and how he carries himself? And I'm pretty sure that's Ana in her straw hat following him. She and Marya are both wearing their school uniforms."

"Wait a minute. What the—" Alex muttered, raising his binoculars again. His eyes narrowed. Two busloads of students pulled up, and as they exited the bus, a schoolteacher handed each student a straw hat with a wide brim, just like Ana's. Boys and girls combined, I counted almost thirty students in the pre-teenage group, the majority of them girls. I turned to Alex, eyebrows raised in question at the hats that weren't normally part of a schoolgirl's uniform.

"Cover, no doubt, provided by the Bureau. Ana will be harder to spot that way."

"This could be to our advantage to gain us some time." Again I searched for Ana in her straw hat, but to no avail. I worried that Rasputin would slip by us and reach her first. "Let's hurry and get ahead of the crowd. I'm afraid we'll lose sight of Ana and Marya among so many girls with straw hats."

At that moment, I glanced over my shoulder in time to see Rasputin charging through the entrance, his henchmen not far behind. My hand went to my mouth.

"*Bózhe moy!* That piggy priest moves fast for a big man." I tried to keep it light, but I was already feeling anxious and exhausted, plus my head throbbed. What I wouldn't give for a couple of Excedrin tablets.

Alex must have seen the fearful expression on my face, because he intentionally tripped the first man headed for us. What followed was a cascade of men tripping and falling over each other, like a bunch of clowns in a circus. That gave us time to race through the entrance to part of the first exhibit. We reached the staircase ahead of Rasputin who had stopped at one of the counters to ask a harried-looking young clerk if she'd seen the duchess.

"I'm afraid to ask what you're thinking of doing," Alex groaned, breathing hard.

Without thinking, I took hold of his hand and smiled. He turned and regarded me as if I were some mysterious beast with two heads. I dropped his hand, but kept my smile.

"We have to hurry. There! I see Misha by that window. Where are the girls?"

For a moment, I panicked as I lost sight of the two young women. But then I glimpsed the large straw hat Ana had donned. I quickly scanned the room for Marya. Most of the young people still clutched their straw hats, polite enough not to wear them inside. What we needed were a bunch of impolite kids.

Two girls slowly headed to the only ladies room, and it gave me an idea.

"I'll create confusion and buy us some time," I whispered to Alex.

"Then hurry. We're running out of time."

I grabbed my duffel bag. "I'll be back in five minutes. I'm going to change out of these 1920s secretary clothes and put on something more casual." I glanced at him over my shoulder. "I'm going to make a friend or two while I'm at it, hopefully, friends with hats."

I changed quickly, and was still pondering the question as to why Misha had brought the two girls to this museum when a killer was after them. Were he and Alex supposed to meet there to exchange Bureau information, or had the Bureau planned an escape route through the museum? But, why risk endangering Ana and Marya, not to mention a whole lot of teenagers?

I was checking my scarf bandage to make sure it was still intact when two young girls came out of the stalls to find me in front of the bathroom mirror. My BTM aide had packed a pair of blue jeans, a watermelon-pink V-neck shirt and a good pair of running shoes in my size. I hoped the outfit didn't scream "I'm from the future!"

"That's a pretty-colored shirt," said the taller brunette in Russian.

"*Spasibo*," I answered, biding my time.

A third girl in school uniform entered the bathroom, and they all primped in front of the mirror, doing what girls around the world did—gossip. She was waving her hat around, and appeared upset by something. She spoke Russian so fast that I didn't quite catch it all, but I did recognize "Rasputin" and the word for pig, *sveenyá.*

I put a few things into my duffle bag and was getting ready to leave, or pretend to leave, when the brunette turned to me.

"You are American?"

"Yes." With luck, these girls wouldn't get pulled into our mess. To ease my fears, I complimented them on their hats, but they only nodded. Carefully, I placed my hat on my head to cover the wound, and decided to jump in.

"I'm trying to find a friend. I think she came to the museum this afternoon. She's wearing a hat like this. Have you seen her?"

The brunette seemed to be the ringleader, because she immediately placed her hat on her head. "I am Svetlana. We have not seen your friend." She gestured toward my wound. "Rasputin?"

"One of his men," I responded, not sure where this conversation was going.

The three began whispering quickly, and I felt the woozy feeling returning. I refilled my canteen and took a small drink to make myself more alert.

"Rasputin is pig priest. He treats all girls and women bad. My mother said so."

The smaller blonde spoke a bit more English, and for that I was glad because I didn't want to make a horrible mistake when communicating with her. She turned to Svetlana and asked her something. The brunette nodded.

"We can help you stay clear of Rasputin. Give us a few minutes."

I didn't ask what they had in mind. "There's a handsome gentleman standing outside the door named Alex. Can you please tell him I'll be out in another few minutes?"

"Oooo, a handsome man," the three girls said in unison with enthusiastic giggles, making me blush.

"Does he speak Russian?" Svetlana asked with a grin.

"Better than I can. Thank you so much for doing this. Every little bit helps, believe me."

Svetlana held out her hand. "*Spasibo*. Our Russia needs your help."

I shook her hand with a somber nod as they donned their straw hats at a jaunty angle. Then they hurried out into the exhibit hall. It seemed that in a matter of minutes, forty young people had been asked to do their part and defy Rasputin by wearing straw hats. I poked my head out and waved to Alex, who gestured for me and my hat to get going.

Rasputin, who had been searching for Ana, rushed from one child to the next, ripping off hats and tossing them on the ground. Svetlana and friends kept retrieving the hats and putting them back on. When we finally saw Misha and the girls go through a door marked "Street Exit", I felt some of the tension roll off my shoulders.

"Where do you think Misha will take the girls?" I asked as we set out across Red Square.

"I'd rather not speculate. How are you doing?"

"I'm...okay. Where are we going?"

"You're going home to America to get medical treatment and to rest."

"Wait a minute. I want to talk to Ana one last time." When I stopped, I realized I actually liked all the intrigue of being on the run. Not hunted down by a psychotic priest, of course, but I would remember that sea of straw hats the rest of my life.

"I want to put her mind at ease for a future free of Rasputin."

Alex nodded. "That's kind of you. If we're lucky, and Misha didn't run into any trouble, he may have the girls somewhere safe by now. And I know just where to find them."

I smiled, believing we were home free, so to speak.

Sometimes, I could be so naïve.

Chapter 13

*"This is a time for determination and focus as you
travel in a new direction."*
(Tarot Card: The Chariot)

With Rasputin in the vicinity, we had to hurry. Consequently, we moved quickly on our way to the safehouse, Alex all-business since we left the state historical museum behind.

As we walked briskly through the streets, listening to the many languages spoken there, I now had mixed feelings about returning home. On the one hand, I could see Grandma Tattie and my sisters and fill them in on what I'd learned. And, I had a *lot* of questions for my grandmother. On the other hand, something almost magical had happened when Alex and I shared our grief in the train car. It's as if a part of me I had kept closed for a very long time had broken open, allowing all the raw pain to come flooding out. I was relatively certain Alex felt the same. Still, it was too soon to give into emotions. We had so much to accomplish first. All I knew was that I felt secure and protected standing next to him.

We'd been walking about fifteen minutes or so when I began to pay more attention to my surroundings. I noted the tall, modern buildings on each corner, interspersed with Russian businesses: banks, bakeries, hotels, deli shops, and restaurants. All the comforts of home. Moscow looked like any other major city in the world experiencing industrialization at a rapid pace.

As we neared the safehouse, I finally summoned the courage to ask where we were going."

"We're almost there. Another block."

Alex wasn't very talkative after that, other than issuing terse orders to stay away from the front window, as we entered what appeared to be a relatively new six-story hotel. The lobby featured dozens of framed black-and-white photos taken of World War I. I remembered reading that photography came into its own about that time, and not just in Russia. While the faces of the dying, the destitute, and the haunted were not exactly uplifting, I felt compelled to look closer at those who'd given up hope. It was enough to make any sentimental person weep, but then, that was war. So, how in the world did I end up traveling through time to witness the Russian Revolution?

Alex exchanged a few words with a young man in a neatly trimmed beard standing behind a marble and walnut counter. He and Alex spoke in low, tense voices, and I wondered how well they knew each other. His nametag said "Yuri," and as he slid a message to Alex he nodded politely at me.

"Let's go." Alex put a proprietary hand on the small of my back and escorted me to an elevator, which I eyed askance. Alex merely smiled and held the elevator gate open. "It will get us to our floor...eventually."

We stopped on the fifth floor, then walked to the end of the hall. Alex fitted an old-fashioned brass key into the door, and then shoved it open with his foot as he scanned the room for potential danger. By a large window with a view of Moscow, I was surprised to find Misha waiting, Ana and Marya asleep on the couch. The room had the appearance of an office, rather than a hotel room. In fact, a queen bed lay hidden away behind a bamboo screen, the walnut desk and file drawers facing the window taking center stage. Framed in a plain black metal frame, the photo of a giant elephant ear leaf dominated the wall, with smaller similar botanical subjects surrounding it. A rich, Art Deco-themed tapestry in deep rose, midnight blue, and dark green hung next to the botanical frames. In my opinion, that piece brought the room together and gave it a unique personality.

"Whose room is this?" I asked.

"Mine," Misha said.

For the first time, I got a really good look at Misha as he turned to face us...my distant cousin. To me, he had that "preppie" look of a clean-cut, conservative guy. He wore his dark hair short, and was dressed in a suit and tie. On a nearby table lay an open briefcase. His severe expression made me wonder if marrying Anastasia, and then disappearing, was what he really wanted. But when he put a finger to his lips and glanced over at Ana sleeping, his expression softened. That look answered my question.

The silence was broken when the telephone jangled. Alex picked it up and listened briefly, then hung up. "Girls, time to wake up and pack your things," Alex said, scanning through the paperwork in the briefcase. "That was Yuri. We've got five minutes before Rasputin catches up to us."

"Rasputin is on his way here?" I felt like I had been caged in the old elevator while it plummeted to the ground.

Ana rubbed her eyes and woke Marya. "You said we'd be safe here and that I could sleep all day," she told Misha, her lips forming a pout. She then noticed Alex and me. "Oh, it's you. Marya's friend."

I don't know why that hurt, but it did. We'd risked our safety to find Ana and say goodbye one last time, but Ana could clearly care less. Yet despite her less-than-enthusiastic response, I was thankful Alex had given me this opportunity to say goodbye.

I decided to mask my hurt feelings and be an adult. Alex pulled Misha aside, and they talked quietly as Marya refolded the things they'd taken out of their carpetbags. While the others were busy, I sank down on the couch next to Ana.

"I'm returning home...to the future, so I can get medical help for my head wound. I plan to discuss this trip with my grandma, Tattie, and my sister, Sasha. Maybe they'll have some ideas to help us get rid of Rasputin for good."

"May I see?" Ana asked, indicating my head wound.

I removed my hat and scarf. Gently, she parted my hair, then sat back. "This happened because of Rasputin? Because of us?"

"He knew Alex and I were trying to help you, so I guess he thought he'd try to get us out of his way." I smiled, but my heart was breaking at the thought that Grand Duchess Anastasia Nicolaevna Romanov may die soon if we couldn't save her and Marya.

"Two minutes, Dasha." Misha handed Alex the briefcase from the desk. The two time travelers hugged briefly.

"See you in the next life," Alex said, slapping him on the back. It must have been an old saying he referred to often, because he smiled and stepped back.

I stood and opened my arms to Anastasia. "I know it's hard to believe, but someday, a long time from now, I will be your great-great granddaughter. However, you must do what Misha says. He'll take care of you and Marya, so you can trust him." I kissed both cheeks and felt my throat ache. "You will do great things, wherever you go, *if* you remember the past and the lessons you've learned." Then I turned to Misha. "I hope to get to know you, cousin...someday."

"I hope for the same thing, Dasha." He turned and addressed his charges. "Time's up. Come on, girls." A loud pounding stopped them. The girls froze, clutching their carpetbags and looking to Misha for escape.

Alex remained calm as he crossed the room. He lifted the Art Deco tapestry to reveal not a wall, but a hidden door. Opening that door, he urged the three travelers down a staircase that appeared to lead outside. In mere seconds, they quietly disappeared, then Alex dropped the tapestry back in place and grabbed my hand.

Confused, I frowned. "I thought I was going home."

He squeezed my hand and looked me in the eyes. "This will be one last sacrifice to buy them time. Please forgive me, Dasha."

The door crashed open, and Rasputin hurtled into the room with eight men in search of their prey.

Rasputin snapped his fingers at the soldiers. "Search every nook and cranny in this room, then every room on this floor. We know Anastasia Nicolaevna and the others were here. They could not have escaped me this time."

He turned those mysterious, mesmerizing blue eyes on me, and I felt my whole body quiver.

"And as for you, Miss Marusova, you've gone too far this time. You will be arrested, tortured, and murdered. Just like I plan for your new friends, Anastasia Nicolaevna and Marya." He laughed. "I will soon have someone on their trail, *konechna.*"

Of course.

Chapter 14

"It is time to get a situation – or individual – under control."
(Tarot Card: Strength)

"Not so brave now, are you?" Rasputin said in a calm, almost soothing voice. He then barked orders at his soldiers to form a protective ring around us to prevent us from slipping out of his hands again.

"You will call me Grisha," he said, leaning close enough for me to smell garlic and vodka on his breath.

His pale eyes glistened, and his pupils were dilated. Had he taken some kind of drug?

Grisha nodded toward the guard in charge. "Take them to our secret location. If they try to escape, shoot them. And gag the woman."

The next thing I knew, I felt a pinch from a needle, and in moments, I crumpled to the ground.

I awoke, hours later, to a prison cell and the sound of fists on bone. Although Rasputin had threatened me with torture earlier, I rubbed my eyes to discover it was Alex his men had worked over. I only needed a glance to see who was winning this fight.

"Please, leave him alone," I begged, tears rolling down my cheeks as I sat up, trying to shake off the effects of whatever drug he'd given me. "He's bleeding, and I need to treat his wounds." But the soldier ignored my pleas.

Alex, who lay on the ground of our remote prison cell, licked the blood from the corner of his mouth and smiled at me, acting as though it was all a game.

"Is that all you've got?" he taunted the soldier.

If one were to judge Alex by his looks, one would think he was a "pretty boy" with that handsome face, neat clothes, and well-groomed, yet athletic body. But I had learned that he had a core of steel, and that's what drove him to do whatever it took to get us free so we could complete our assignment. Did Alex know when to call it quits to protect himself?

For the next twenty-four hours, they took turns working him over. Tears hadn't moved Rasputin when they'd taken Alex for questioning, so each time he was returned to the cell, I would bathe his wounds and put him back together. At times he was barely awake, but I whispered in his ear to keep him alert and aware of his surroundings.

Soon, I was removed from the cell, as well, so that Rasputin could interrogate me as promised. When I returned from my cell after a second thirty-minute session, Alex waited for the guard to leave us alone before speaking to me. I was beginning to lose track of whether it was day or night, and my head hurt. We'd been moved to a prison in some kind of public building that had only four cells in its basement. The second and third cells each held one prisoner, leaving the fourth cell empty. A quick scan revealed that neither Ana nor Marya were occupying those prison cells. I wanted to believe they'd escaped and were safe with Misha.

I must have whimpered as I tried to sit, because Alex responded on the other side of the cell across from me.

"Dasha, are you alright? Are you hurt?"

"I should be asking you the same question." I shuffled over to where he lay on a thin mattress filled with straw and knelt beside him. No one had bothered to wipe up the blood on his face. I looked for a cloth and clean water, hoping that the soldier had taken pity on me and brought what I asked, but Alex waved his hand.

"We can worry about that later." He checked his nose gingerly and winced. "Am I still that handsome guy you like?"

"What makes you think I like you?"

He grinned crookedly. "Mmm, no reason."

He chuckled, despite the obvious pain, then sat up just as the sound of booted soldiers and the jangle of a brass keyring announced Rasputin's presence. He stopped in front of our cell and put a hand on the iron bars.

"I have a fun evening in store for you two."

I was so exhausted that normally, I could have cared less what that man had to say about anything, but I knew what his words entailed now, so fear turned my legs to jelly. I sank gratefully onto the bench.

"I'm American, and my father has a lot of influence back home. Let us go or you'll pay for this." I'd been repeating those words for two days now without success, hoping he'd finally take notice, so I decided on a new tack. "He can offer you mo-ney." I enunciated, just in case it wasn't clear. "*Moi otyets* has lots of *Amerikanski dollars*." My grammar was off, my pronunciation stunk, but I kept trying.

Alex looked up. "Is that true?"

I narrowed my eyes to slits. "Why? You want money, too?"

Alex laughed softly and watched Rasputin exit their cell and speak quietly with the head guard. "Dash, I know about as much as I need to about you and your family. Money doesn't matter. Not to me, and not to...our *friend*, Grisha."

"Seriously? Then, what *does* he want?"

Alex got to his feet and stretched. "I would think it's obvious, based on his not so stellar reputation."

I snorted. "You mean the ladies?"

He stepped over to the door and held on to the door handle. "What else?"

To my surprise, Grisha must have been listening in on our conversation because he said, "It's more than just young ladies." His hooded eyes narrowed as he shook his head, his strange blue eyes never blinking. "This is what power is in Russia. I can do whatever needs doing and by any means." He settled his strange gaze on me. "We're going to be such great friends, you and I, Miss Marusov. And as I said earlier, I insist you call me Grisha. I shall, of course, call you Dasha—like your Grandmother Tatiana does. How is she, by the way?"

Rasputin knows Grandma Tattie?

Bile inched up my throat.

Rasputin...*Grisha*, leaned so close to me, I could see the pulse of his forehead, smell the rot of his breath, and feel my own heart race like a Kamchatka bear escaping a wildfire—the Kamchatka bear being one of the largest bears in the world and native to Russia.

Beside me, Alex growled his frustration. "Remember, Dasha, don't look at his eyes. You don't have to tell him anything."

"As I recall, your grandmother was a spirited woman, much like you."

Although Grisha's smile sent a shiver down my spine, I couldn't look away.

"I always had a soft spot for Tatiana Ivanovna."

"How could you possibly know her? She hasn't been born yet. Not until 1946."

Rasputin—Grisha just wouldn't stick—smiled. "Ah, Dasha, you should know by now that not everything is as it seems. We have so much more to discover together, you and I."

I shuddered and closed my eyes, my head aching with the effort it took to be so alert all day as I struggled to remember Russian after such a long break from it. As I stood there, I willed him not to talk about Grandma Tattie or anyone else in my family for that matter.

"Should I tell you what interfered with your grandmother's goal to be a teacher?"

With considerable effort, I straightened my shoulders and launched into a barrage of words. "No, you filthy beast. You may *not* talk about my grandmother. You are despicable and evil!" I knelt by Alex's cot and chewed the bottom of my lip at the bruising and blood I saw on him. "Bring me a bowl of fresh, clean water, and clean rags. *Now*." I feared that Alex might have a concussion after all the beatings, as he appeared to be drifting into a deep sleep, a soft snore sounding escaping his mouth. "Bring those to me, and hurry, do you hear?"

Grisha's scraggly gray brows rose on his high forehead at my demands. "I will not let you go, you know. Never. In fact, tonight I have something special planned for you two lovebirds. You won't need to clean up the blood until then." At that, he laughed like the madman he was, and then shuffled out.

It didn't take a genius to figure out that Rasputin—Grisha, that is—insisted on controlling every aspect of our demise. After two days in the cell and two days of interrogation, I grew weary of his games. Fortunately, Alex had awakened and we were allowed to tend to our needs for a few minutes at a time, but I was getting discouraged. The room was barely large enough to pace, and the only furniture was two straw mats and a filthy blanket for each pallet. I used my duffel bag as a pillow, greatly missing the luxurious down pillows on my own bed at home.

When Alex thought I wasn't looking his way, he watched me closely for symptoms of a head injury, just as I had done with him earlier, not that we could do anything about it now. At home, I'd always been the strong sister, the one who stood up to anyone who bullied my sisters. But as I looked around at the filthy cell floor strewn with dirt and straw, I had the horrible feeling I would never get out of this place. I'd been raised Russian Orthodox, and it had been a long time since I'd attended church. But on that day, in that horrible place, I began to pray. Pray that I'd get through this nightmare. Pray that Misha and the girls were safe in England, or wherever they ended up.

I don't know how much time passed, but I was awakened much later by the sound of a tin cup banging against the bars of our prison cell. When I looked up, I saw several men in uniform, along with Grisha, wearing his food-stained priest's robe.

The soldier in charge unlocked the cell and stepped inside with a second soldier to deliver a tray of food, our first since the day before. They also left a bowl of clean water and some clean rags.

Alex was awake and had propped himself up against the bars of our cell, watching everything around him. Grisha pointed at the bowl of water with a long-nailed index finger.

"I bring what you ask. Now, tell me where Anastasia Nicolaevna has run off to with that dark-haired young man."

"I don't know where they are." I glanced at Alex, who appeared pale and exhausted. "I can't tell you what I don't know."

"You have come a long way and endured considerable inconvenience. Why? What is Anastasia Nicolaevna to you?"

I was about to blurt out the whole story when I felt Alex take my hand and squeeze.

"No need to explain." He inhaled a tired breath and glanced from me to Grisha. "Our agency helps runaway minors, particularly young ladies in need, whose parents can pay us adequately for our services."

I was stunned to hear those words coming from Alex's mouth. How had I missed that?

Grisha appeared angry, but he responded in a calm voice. "That's a start, but you must be convinced to reveal all. I *will* know, you understand?"

Grisha gestured for the two guards to grab hold of Alex and drag him out of the cell. I jumped up and wrapped my hands around the bars. "Where are you taking him?"

His beautiful face was already bruised and beaten, and his upper torso looked no better beneath a torn shirt. How much more could he withstand? As he passed slowly by the third cell, I saw him take a good look at whoever was inside. If he recognized anyone, he gave nothing away. He was so good at deceiving people when it suited him. I needed to remember that. When it came right down to it, I was all alone here in this time and place. And I could trust no one.

Chapter 15

As Katya sat in the jail cell, listening to the clang of the doors opening and shutting, she recalled the day she was glad she'd become a Time Mender. The day she'd received the message. She didn't trust the words written in the note she carried. Supposedly, Grigori Rasputin's wife had something to give her. Katya had never met her, and wasn't looking forward to it. Since Rasputin lost his royal influence with Nicholas and Alexandra, his living quarters had been moved several times, each apartment a bit further from court, each a bit shabbier than the previous. It could have been worse, Katya reminded herself. Rasputin grew up in Siberia, and traveling there would have required several days' journey out and back, maybe even weeks, depending on weather and road conditions.

I don't have to do this.

But she'd promised long ago she would look into all leads regarding her father's death.

As she walked slowly down the cobbled road that led to the house of Rasputin's family, she was glad she'd brought Dima. He was smiling and pleasant, and she supposed it had to do with getting a free day to do whatever they wanted. That, and the fact that they both preferred being back in their own time.

Katya had been thinking lately that perhaps it was time to settle down and raise a family. Although she was only twenty-two, her days were seldom her own—not since she'd joined the Time Menders. She'd only joined to learn more details about how her father died, but Dima loved the adventures and assignments that took them all over the world. However, Katya knew she would be fine on her own, relying on Madame Peshkova's talents, and owning her own home to decorate however she liked. Recently, she'd changed her mind and considered living in St. Petersburg, for a fresh start. Dima wouldn't like her leaving him behind, but it couldn't be helped.

She glanced over at him and hoped he'd behave himself. She'd heard rumors about Rasputin's wife, Praskovia Fedorovna. She wasn't the most pleasant conversationalist, and was known to be semi-illiterate. But apparently, she'd found a way to send a note to Katya to inform her that she had discovered her husband's diary of the past two years' events at court, and had it in her possession. She'd seen Katya's father's name mentioned in the diary several times, and must have assumed her husband considered her father important. Enough so that she decided to contact Katya and offer her the diary.

"I'll bet she expects a reward for the information," Katya muttered as they drew closer.

Dima grew serious and wiped dried mud from his one good coat. "Just remember to look at it first, to make sure it's authentic. If she tries blackmail, don't let her get away with it."

"I know, I know." Katya was growing tired of his constant nagging. She'd like to meet someone new. Someone more mature and ready to settle down.

They stopped in front of apartment number five, a brick building that had seen better days. They exchanged looks. Dima knocked firmly on the wooden door, and they stepped back and waited.

It took several moments before they heard someone shuffle to the door and unlock it. A pale young girl on the other side barely held the door open as she peered out at them. "What do you want?"

Katya held up the note. "I believe your mother sent me this note and asked me to come. Is she here?"

The girl took the note and glanced at it. "Oh, I see. Please, come in."

She showed them two chairs, as an older girl with straight dark hair and deep brown eyes was already boiling water for tea while eyeing them both with suspicion.

"I'm Varvara," said the first girl with curlier hair, a mousy brown in color. "And that's my sister, Maria. I believe Maria wrote that note for our mother."

"That depends. Who are you?" Maria asked with a glare.

Katya girded herself and blinked at Maria's sullen attitude. "I'm Madame Peshkova. Katya Peshkova. The note said your mother had something to give to me. Is she home?"

The younger girl moved slowly and had the appearance of a child often sick. Maria, on the other hand, had a shrewd look in her eyes, as if waiting for her next big opportunity. She held her hand out for the note and glanced at it quickly before setting it on the table.

"Mother is on her way home from a neighbor's house. She should be here any minute." She eyed Dima's muscular physique with interest. "And you are?"

"I am—"

"Dima is a friend who agreed to escort me today."

He gave her a strange look, as if wondering why she didn't let him say "bodyguard" for once.

Just as Varvara set the teapot on the table, Maria rummaged in a cupboard, but shrugged, emerging empty-handed. "Sorry. We have no cake or cookies to offer."

"What about that tin of English biscuits Father brought last month?"

Varvara brushed past her taller sister and pulled out a tin from the pantry. When she opened the tin, only three biscuits remained, but she smiled and placed them on a plate. "There, that's better. Please sit."

The apartment was a shambles, and it looked as if they were in the process of moving. Katya wondered if they were being thrown out because of that man. Rasputin. She and Dima sat and waited.

"Oh, show her the diary," Maria said in exasperation. "I want to know what it's worth."

"But Mother said—"

A cough in the doorway caught their attention. "I said be careful with it," came an older woman's raspy voice.

She shuffled forward and held out her hand. Katya felt her limp handshake, and wondered when she'd slept last.

"I am Praskovia Fedorovna, Rasputin's wife. What do you two want?

Katya pulled out the note and showed her. "We won't take much of your time, madame."

The woman's dress appeared old and frayed, the material faded, more gray than black, with an ivory collar that buttoned up her neck. Her long, gray hair was held back by a leather strip, while long loose ends escaped to float about her face. Her complexion was dough-like, her eyes pale, reminding Katya of Rasputin's hypnotic gaze.

"I am Katya Peshkova, also known as Madame Peshkova. This is my friend, Dima. I saw your note, and came to see what you had for me."

Praskovia Fedorovna had a plain demeanor, no flare, no fanfare. She appeared dead on her feet, more than anything.

Katya thought she'd never feel pity for Rasputin's wife, but she heard herself say, "I'm sorry things have been so hard for you, madame. You look like you've had a long day. We'll be on our way just as soon as you show me the diary you think might interest me.

You said my father's name is mentioned several times in the diary? Stepan Peshkov?"

"Ah, yes. Stepan." She walked over and opened a drawer, then pulled out a black leather diary. She ran her hand over the cover and sniffed, as if she could smell and feel her husband's presence. She hesitated a moment, before handing the diary over, and glanced at Maria almost regretfully.

Maria stepped in. "How much will you pay us for that diary?"

Madame blushed and looked away. "I am giving this freely to Madame Peshkova. I owed her mother for a card reading I had, anyway.

"Don't be like that," said Varvara. "Mother wanted to give it to her. So, give it to her."

Reluctantly, Madame Rasputin held out the diary with two hands, her chin lifting at Maria's scowl.

Katya accepted the diary and felt an immediate chill. She needed to get outside so she could breathe. Reading the diary could wait. Besides, she wanted to go through it in private. She graciously finished her tea, thanked her hostess, and readied to leave.

Not quite as graciously, Dima scooped up the untouched English biscuits and shoved them in his coat pocket before leaving. Katya gave him a dark look and quickly put several coins on the table.

"I'm sorry I don't have more. If this diary can help me know my father better, I will be forever grateful."

Maria started to say something, but Varvara pinched her arm, eliciting a grunt. Katya nodded politely and turned to the door, held open by Rasputin's weary widow. The day was nearing its end as they set out for the bus stop. Katya put the diary in her bag before climbing aboard their bus, and patted her bag as if it were a baby.

"Can I see it? I want to see for myself what all the mystery is about," said Dima, reaching for Katya's travel bag.

Katya pulled the bag away from him, her hazel eyes flashing a warning. "I want to read this when I am alone. If I see something that concerns you, I will let you know."

They didn't speak on the bus ride home. For the first time in her life, Katya felt like it was a tiny moment of independence from Dima—maybe for the first time in her life. But now, as she sat in the jail cell, she discovered maybe she did need him, after all.

Chapter 16

"This is a time of fast and deep transformation and an opportunity to let go of whatever you no longer need."
(Tarot Card: Death)

With dread, I watched as the guards dragged Alex from our prison cell out into the hallway. What would they do to him? I shuddered to think. My imagination worked overtime, coming up with all kinds of scenarios for torture. I worried that they'd cut off a finger or an ear, scar his precious face, or do something equally hideous and cruel. I had to focus on something else or I would go crazy with worry. Tears welled up inside me as I listened to them drag him away.

Oh, Alex. How can I help you?

I wanted to shout down the hallway to demand that Rasputin leave Alex alone. But the words wouldn't come. Besides, it was too late. He wouldn't hear me now, as an outer door slammed shut with a metallic clink. Alex was gone.

Please, please, keep him safe and let him return to me.

I ground my teeth together, but refused to dwell on the evil plans Rasputin had up his filthy sleeves, so I turned my thoughts to resolving my current situation. With the guards gone, I felt instant relief. No one to watch my every move...except when Alex was here. But he was different. It was true I didn't know him well, but I was stunned by my sense of loss, even if only temporary. I'd become used to his warm presence, his thoughtfulness. That silly crooked grin when he teased me.

He has to be okay.

I heard a faint rustle in the cell across the room, and turned to see one of the prisoners standing at the bars of his cell. Dressed in a black coat and matching pants, the prisoner wore a midnight blue shirt that made his dark eyes flash in the gloom that surrounded us. I wondered how he could seem so familiar to me, and yet, I wasn't acquainted with anyone in 1918 Moscow.

And then a woman's voice called softly, "Dasha, is that you?"

The woman wore a hooded cloak and came to stand where one corner of her cell met the corner of the cell next to hers. That was when the man in black joined her. For the briefest moment, his fingers touched her hand.

"Oh, my gosh! Is that you, Katya?" I called out.

"It's about time you figured out we were here," said Dima, his disapproving growl recognizable even in these dark quarters.

"I've been waiting for a chance to talk to you without those soldiers around, and that horrid man who brought you here." Katya trembled. "Alex contacted me last night. He said he needed help getting you back home to a hospital. Are you badly injured?"

"Alex worries too much."

Oh, how I lie.

Not only was my wound probably infected, I now had Alex to worry about. Plus, hospitals in this age were still questionable. That fact scared me more than Grisha's torture. *Almost.*

My mind grew fuzzier by the minute, as I'd pushed myself nonstop since I arrived here. Up until now, Alex had kept me safe every step of the way, except for the gun butt to the back of my head. But that wasn't his fault.

Please, God. Don't let Grisha harm him.

What would Grandma Tattie do?

I could hear her voice. *"Chicken soup. It cures everything."*

I sat down on the chair beside the table at the center of the cell, and rested my head on my arms. If I could rest for just a minute...

"Dasha? Are you awake? Try to stay awake." Katya's voice wobbled, and I heard the fear.

I was a stranger to her. Why would she care? Perhaps Alex had ordered her to take care of me. Silly man. "I'm...not...goin' anywhere," I mumbled, my speech slurring.

My eyes closed of their own volition, then through my lids, a flash of light lit up the dark prison cell. When I opened my eyes, Katya stood there in my *locked* cell. I blinked. "How...how did you do that?"

"Someone must have left the door open." She helped me into a sitting position and pulled out a piece of blank paper and a pen. "I'm going to send you home so you can get that head looked at. I'm not sure when they'll bring Alex back, so I advise you to write a note for him in case he panics when you're not here."

"Can't have that," I mumbled.

"Do you trust Alex?" Katya pushed back a strand of my strawberry-blonde hair. She smiled as she placed the pen on top of the paper and pushed it in front of me.

"Sometimes. Usually." I sipped some water left on the table.

"More than most men?"

"I guess." I looked up, thought about it for two seconds, pen poised in my hand. "Yes. I do trust him."

"Tell him what that means to you. This is the perfect time. But hurry. I don't want to run into Rasputin again."

I pictured Alex's big blue eyes, and how the ends of his dark hair curled around the collar of his tuxedo. And how the natural warm and spicy scent of his skin tickled my nose when he leaned close. I bent my head and began to write.

Dear Alex,
Katya is sending me home to get my head wound
checked out. If you're able to read this, please
know I didn't run away from you, or from my
responsibilities to my family. I'll be back, and...if you
need some TLC (tender loving care), I can help with
that as well. Whatever comes next, I want you to
know I trust you. Completely.
Perhaps we can share a latke on the run for "old
time's sake".

Dasha

That finished, Katya rummaged through her bag until she came across what she was seeking. The green sequined evening gloves.

I folded my message in half and looked up. "Katya, how did you get those evening gloves?"

"Your family ghosts told me where to search." She chuckled at my startled expression. "Your ghosts are quite pleasant. You should converse with them more often, especially the dog. She is wonderfully well-behaved and wise. I think her name is Tessa?"

I shook my head gently, shivering at the thought she was acquainted with ghosts. "And now you want *me* to converse with ghosts? Who *are* you, really?"

Katya chuckled and picked up the gloves. "I'm a simple tarot reader...with a bit of gypsy magic in my blood." She closed her bag. "Once you put on the right-hand glove, it will start the Time Menders' timer. You will have seven days to seek medical help and take care of business with your family in San Francisco. After that, Alex will pick you up if he can. Pack a change of clothes. Don't wear anything that screams 21st century. If, for whatever reason, he can't travel to the future, the Bureau will send someone else to guide you and explain the mission. You *must* finish this assignment." She closed her bag and held out the glove. "Any questions?"

I sat up and took the glove, feeling a bit more alert. "Let's say the mission is accomplished. How do I get back to my own time? *Permanently.* Just reverse those steps?"

"That's a bit more complicated. Alex will have to explain."

"He won't be able to explain if he's not here or...or recuperating from Grisha's torture." My mouth went dry. I hated even saying that word.

Katya held up a hand, as if to ward off any more questions. "He's a strong man. I'm only telling you this for your own information."

She snapped her fingers, and once again the bright light appeared. Dima opened my cell door, and walked outside to wait for Katya, I assumed. I stood, feeling less woozy as I glanced at Katya.

"Will I see you again?"

Katya smiled, but didn't answer me directly. "Just remember my tarot readings. By the end of this mission, you will understand which life you are meant to live. You must be sure to ask the relevant questions along the way. Tatiana Marusov is key."

My grandmother?

Of course she would be at the heart of it all.

Katya gestured for me to put on the glove.

"I think this makes me considerably overdressed. What do you think?"

But before Katya could answer, the light around me took on a rosy glow, and I felt myself sucked into a vortex of cool air and bright light.

I should have asked hundreds of questions before allowing myself to be ripped through time. It proved a quick process, but it wasn't without its speed bumps. For a brief moment, the air seemed to pull from my lungs, and I thought I would never catch another breath again. After spinning in place for several revolutions, the unseen tornado dropped me unceremoniously on the floor of our attic.

I peeked through my fingers to be sure of my destination, and when the dizziness subsided, I slowly got up. I shuffled toward the window at the pitch of the roof and peeked through the curtains. It was still night out, which explained why it was so quiet.

When I turned back to the room, there, in the corner, were the dolls my sisters and I played with growing up. Their clothes were a bit ragged from the wear and tear of being dragged everywhere, and several of them had thin hair from Sasha shampooing them a few too many times. Then I saw the *Matryoshkas*, or Russian nesting dolls. Whenever Mom and Dad went on business trips to Russia, Mom brought back gifts like these for each of us. They came in so many sets: images from fairy tales, politics, pop culture, dolls that featured animals, both domestic and wild, and so on. Dad had put up several bookshelves to hold all the dolls, and as I reacquainted myself, I picked up an exquisitely painted girl with blonde hair, and wearing a blue, white and pink dress, holding a white cat in her arms. That had been Sasha's favorite. Mine had been a set of five that looked just like the Beatles during their Sergeant Pepper phase. Gigi's favorite was whatever caught her eye that day. When Mom wasn't looking, we sometimes played "adventure" with them, so visible scratches could be found on their small wooden bodies.

I wasn't paying attention to my landing spot, but I knew I was home safe. Consequently, when something bumped into a nearby stack of books, knocking it onto the floor, I stopped breathing for several seconds. Moonlight filtered in, and I found myself staring into the ghostly eyes of a dog. I'd seen so many photos of Tessa, I recognized her right away, but it took a few more moments for my heart to return to normal. According to Grandma, Tessa had been the perfect companion for an introverted young girl obsessed with ballet, who loved to read light romances in between the Russian classics her parents insisted she read during school terms. As the only child of John William Marusov and Stella Randolph, she'd had the opportunity to attend college, and majored in literature, then planned to become a high school teacher. And yet, something had thwarted that goal. Something, I suspected, I'd got caught in the middle of, as well—The Time Menders.

I cocked my head, listening for sounds in the darkness. I figured it was early morning, rather than late at night, so I was hesitant to wake up my sisters or grandmother, even though I had little time to waste. I removed my straw sun hat and set it aside. The throbbing had increased, and I held my head in my hands for several moments until it calmed down. Tessa's ghost took a step closer, the little stump of a tail wagging in greeting. She seemed friendly enough, so I held out my hand and let her sniff it. She was a sweet dog and loving companion...who had died in 1963. Grandma Tattie had just turned seventeen—-the same age as Anastasia.

I moved around the attic slowly, trying not to make any noise. Mom had refurbished the attic several years back, hoping to create a room where all three of us would enjoy studying and hanging out, and where we could keep the noise to a minimum. She'd sorted out the stuff our family no longer needed, and called the junk man. With more space, she'd painted the walls a refreshing shade of white with blue trim at the window. I chose a fancy and comfortable moon pod chair in rose quartz for ultimate relaxation. Gigi went for a simple microsuede chair in hot pink. And animal lover, Sasha, had ordered a big white shaggy polar bear, with paws serving as arms. Mom had refinished two desks, so we could do homework there. One of the round oriental rugs replaced elsewhere in the house did a good job of highlighting the pinks and blues we'd selected. After I started college, however, Sasha and Gigi visited this room only rarely, especially with Gigi swearing she'd experienced several ghost sightings.

When I walked over to the desk, which was now finished in a distressed gray-blue, I could hear the ticking of a china clock on the desk, and checked the time: 4:30 a.m. Fortunately, I was no longer feeling quite so woozy, though it occurred to me that I could ask Sasha to drive me to the nearest hospital at this early hour. I just didn't know how I was going to explain the wound to my parents or to Grandma. Even more troublesome, how was I going to explain my absence?

As I stood pondering these questions, I heard the floorboards creak outside the door. I froze and saw the ghost dog, Tessa, vanish just as the door opened and Sasha entered, her phone flashlight in hand.

"Is anyone here?"

"Sasha?"

"Dasha? Is that you?"

"Yes! I'm back."

Sasha turned off the phone flashlight and switched on the lightswitch.

"You'll wake Mom and Dad," I said.

"They went to Monterey for the weekend."

I let that sink in, my balloon burst. "They didn't even know I was gone? How?"

"Well..."

I didn't wait for an answer as I grabbed Sasha by the shoulders and gave her a big hug. "I missed you so much. How long was I gone?"

Sasha hugged me back, then rubbed her eyes. "Three days. Grandma Tattie said not to worry, and that you were doing something very important. Say, where *did* you go? Grandma Tattie seemed very upset. I think she even closed her door and cried, thinking that whatever happened was her fault."

"We should talk right away. I don't have much time to complete my assignment, and you all need to hear this."

Sasha glanced out the window. "Do you want me to wake everyone up so you can tell them your story?"

"Where did you tell them I went?"

"I suggested that maybe you went on a short trip with your girlfriends."

"You did *what*?"

Sasha waved her hand, like it was nothing. "I thought it was just as good a guess as Gigi's suggesting you were taking time out to do an *Eat, Pray, Love* project."

I reached up, wanting to tear my hair out. Instead, I yelped at the reminder.

"What's wrong with your head?"

"A Russian soldier hit me with his bayonet. In 1918 Moscow."

"Oh, my." Sasha stared at me in shock, her expression one of disbelief.

But then she must have thought better of it, since Grandma Tattie had told tales of time travel as far back as they could recall. Up until now, the three of us had chalked it up to old age, and perhaps the onset of dementia.

"I want to hear all about your travels, but this room gives me the creeps, thanks to Gigi and those pesky ghosts." Sasha took a quick look at my wound, then placed her hand on my forehead. "No raging fever, but we should still get you treated at a hospital, then you can tell us the whole story from the beginning. I'll make some coffee and wake up the others. She sniffed and made a face. "You should take a shower and put on clean clothes before we go. Let me know if you need help."

I looked down at the dirt and blood clinging to my clothes. "You're probably right about the shower. Although, just for the record, this isn't my blood. It's Alex's."

"Is he okay?"

I thought for a moment about how to put it. "I don't know," I said, truthfully. "But I do know that he's probably the most amazing man I've ever met. And the most aggravating."

"Then, where is he?"

"I don't know, Sasha. Last I remember, he was taken to an interrogation room...by Grigori Rasputin."

Sasha's face drained of all color, and she grabbed onto the desk. "That can't be! Rasputin died a long time ago!"

How wrong she was.

Chapter 17

*"A good time to nurture your creative endeavors,
your business, and the relationships you value."*
(Tarot Card: The Sun)

Sasha threw open the attic door and let the light from the hallway shine in as we headed down the stairs. "What do you mean Alex is with Grigori Rasputin? That's not possible."

Sasha's normally calm personality changed to downright cranky whenever something frightened her. And yes, she *should* fear Grigori Rasputin. My throat tightened at the memory. As much as I was elated and relieved to be back home, and to be free of that man, anyone who could beat a good man like Alex didn't deserve to live, in my book. Now, I had to use this time at home to figure out how I could free Alex before it was too late. I bit my lip, fighting back tears.

"Come here, Sasha," I said, wrapping her in a bear hug. "I'll tell you absolutely everything, but after I shower. Meanwhile, if you could make some strong black coffee and get me a bowl of cereal, I have a lot to tell you." I started walking downstairs to my room. "Is Grandma Tattie here?"

"I'll explain later. I'm dying for a shower, then some strong hot coffee and breakfast, in that order."

"Don't wash your hair. You might start the wound bleeding again," Sasha advised. "I'll see if Grandma Tattie is up."

She didn't appear too pleased to postpone the conversation as she headed downstairs, but I was nowhere near ready to deal with the illogical reality that I was a time traveller just yet.

Before my abrupt arrival in the attic, home was always the place where I smelled Rosana's cooking as soon as I walked through the door. And true to form, as I gathered my things for the shower, I smelled the heavenly aroma of her French toast, accompanied by coffee, my favorite breakfast. Did she know I'd been gone?

Before I entered the shower, Gigi appeared in my bedroom, shrieked, and asked about a hundred questions. I gave her a big hug. "I'll answer questions after my coffee, Gigi."

"You promise?"

"Of course, sweetie." I closed the bathroom door behind me, then turned on the shower. I laid out my towel and body lotion on the white marble counter. Then I attached my terry robe to the hook on the door, my thoughts flooding back. According to Sasha, I'd only been gone three days. How was that possible? It felt more like a week, at the least. Maybe time was measured differently in parallel worlds. Or maybe I'd seen too many sci-fi flicks. Did parallel worlds even exist? I was the one who stayed up late and watched old classic movies into the wee hours with my dad. It was the only "us" time I'd ever experienced with Pete Marusov, CEO of Marusov Technologies. At least, I knew we had one thing in common, small though it was.

I gathered my hair into a large shower cap, then lathered up the sponge with my favorite jasmine and vanilla body wash. It felt so good to be clean and in my own bathroom. I groaned at the decadent scent that made me feel like a pampered princess, but it was inevitable that my thoughts turned to Alex. I had so much left to process. Fortunately, he had an uncanny way of avoiding permanent injury. Thinking of that made me feel guilty, now that I knew Alex was more than just a pretty face, though I'd had my doubts at the beginning. And yet, he'd proven himself by putting his life on the line for women he didn't even know time and time again. My heart told me he was a good man. Somehow, I wished I could protect him from any future pain or injury, but I was helpless to do so at the present. Frustrated, I rinsed off the body soap until I felt soft and clean once again.

At first, I'd believed he was just a well-dressed, part-time bartender hired to work at my mother's fundraiser. I knew my mother typically used the same catering company and their staff, so perhaps Alex was a recent hire, like Marya.

Marya. That made me think of Anastasia Nicolaevna. I wanted to imagine the former Grand Duchess living someplace like Wales or Ireland on a farm with Misha.

I was standing with my face under the sprayer when I heard pounding on the door. I opened the shower door a smidgen.

"Dasha," Gigi said in her loud bossy voice. "I told Grandma Tattie about your head, and she says to get out of that shower and get dressed for the hospital, pronto!" She says you have ten minutes, or she's dragging you out, wet or not."

I smiled. Gigi loved it when she could tell me what to do. For that matter, so did Grandma Tattie, which explains where it originated. I turned off the shower. "Alright. I'll be there in ten. Tell Grandma to hold on to her reindeer."

"What? Why would she do that? She doesn't have a reindeer." Gigi sounded confused on the other side of the door.

"It's an old Christmas classic, Gigi. It's called 'Grandma got run over by a reindeer'." I was met with silence and shook my head. "I'll explain later." Not everyone got my sense of humor, unfortunately.

The fact that I still had a sense of humor was a miracle. I stepped out into a steamy bathroom and turned on the fan before toweling down and removing my shower cap. I quickly added body and face lotion, but skipped the makeup. My room was empty when I exited the bathroom. I could still smell Rosana's French toast in the air, and would sorely regret missing out on that.

I dressed in loose jeans and a light green summer sweater, then reached for my favorite sneakers. I ran a brush through my hair—or most of it. It would probably be a long wait at the hospital, but it had to be done. I wrapped a clean scarf around my head, hoping that hid most of the wound. I took one last look in the mirror and headed downstairs.

"Rosana—"

"I save you French toast!" she called from the kitchen. "You take good care."

"*Gracias!*"

Grandma Tattie was indeed waiting in her black luxury SUV driven by Marcos, Rosana's son, home from Afghanistan. We all piled in, like so many times before. On the way to the hospital, my concern for Alex left me feeling breathless and wishing I knew his fate without having to return to 1918 Russia. Usually, I was the staid one, but to my surprise, tears welled up in my eyes for a second time, and I angrily brushed them away. That was so not me. At least until recently, but a lot had changed in my life.

It took thirty minutes to see the ER doctor, but then we waited in a row of chairs in the hall for the CT Scan results. Gigi kept the conversation going, which was no surprise.

"What happened? We looked everywhere for you. Sasha said you ran off with your girlfriends to pout because Brendon left town."

I turned my grin to my middle sister. "Sasha said that, did she? Well, the last few days *were* pretty amazing."

"Start with the amazing Alex," Sasha suggested with a sly grin.

"Wait until we get home," Grandma Tattie suggested, her eagle eye on Gigi.

All of us girls fell into an awkward silence. A few minutes clicked by on the large wall clock, when Grandma started rummaging through her purse.

"Who wants to bring their *bábushka* a cup of that stuff they call coffee from a machine?"

"We'll both go," said Sasha, taking her grandmother's coins. "Come on, Gigi." She looked over her shoulder as she headed down the hallway.

Once they were gone, Tattie turned to me and said, "Now, how did you get your head wound, *vnúchka*, granddaughter? What really happened?"

In the past, I would have tried to make myself invisible, but all I could think about was Alex and my aching head. This time, I decided to tell the truth. "It was from the butt of a Russian soldier's bayonet in St. Petersburg. In 1918. I can't tell the doctor that, can I?"

Grandma Tattie appeared shocked, but folded her hands in her lap just the same. "This is one of those situations where, perhaps, you tell the part of the truth the person can handle. Don't worry about the rest. You'll come up with a plausible story."

A few minutes later, Sasha and Gigi returned with a coffee for each of us. I grimaced at the taste, but at least it had caffeine. We'd waited in the outer room for ten minutes when the ER doctor on call appeared with results from my CT scan.

"I was attending a historical reenactment, and accidentally got in the way of someone's bayo—um, rifle butt."

"In the middle of the night?"

I squirmed in my chair. "It happened around dinnertime...at the camp."

Dr. Beacham turned his disapproving gaze to Grandma Tattie. "Would you come with me, and you, as well, Ms. Marusov."

My hands broke into a clammy sweat. Did he find a brain tumor or something? Was I going to die?He closed the door of his office and indicated we should sit. "I was concerned there might be bleeding on the brain, so I took a CT when Ms. Marusov first arrived. Just to be sure, I took a second scan before I considered discharging her."

I grabbed Grandma Tattie's hands. "What is it? Am I dying?"

The doctor glanced back at the second CT scan of the brain...and smiled. "No. Quite the opposite. In fact, that area is totally healed and sealed." He pointed it out on a screen.

I pulled off my scarf and felt for myself. Grandma Tattie's hands trembled as she checked the same spot. After a few moments, she sat back and exhaled. "He's right, Dasha. It's completely healed. You'd never know a wound was there."

"Did you eat or drink anything unusual that could have aided the healing?" Dr. Beacham appeared dumbfounded.

All I could think was that I'd dodged a bullet, or a bayonet, and never wanted to see one of those weapons in person again.

"No, nothing other than ibuprofen," I said. I rose quickly and helped Grandma Tattie stand. "You must be an amazing healer, Dr. Beacham. We should let you go deal with sick and injured people. Thank you so much!"

"This doesn't mean you can disregard a concussion. Please take it easy for three days or so and get plenty of rest."

"Absolutely. I'll do that."

He raised a hand as if to make another point, but I was intent on getting us out of there and not having to answer questions for which I had no answers. My hand firmly on Grandma Tattie's arm, I hustled her out of the ER, where we met Gigi and Sasha.

"Don't ask till we get home," I whispered to my sisters and got us loaded back in the SUV and on our way home in record time.

Marco had us home in five minutes. Then Grandma hurried us inside in one big bundle, as if we were her precious ballet babies.

We settled at the dining table, and Rosana must be psychic, as she had a full breakfast ready with strong hot coffee. I held out my empty mug, and after taking several exploratory sips for temperature, I sat back and tossed my scarf onto a couch behind us, finally ready to relax.

Grandma Tattie insisted I start at the beginning, so that's what I did. I left nothing out. Sasha and Gigi wanted to know every little detail about the flapper's ball. I was telling them about the costumes worn by both male and female guests when a lightbulb went on inside my head.

"I was dancing the Charleston in a mansion twice the size as ours. My dance partner was..." I turned to Gigi. "You're going to love this part, Gigi. His name was Ilya Razinin, and he was the prince of a place I've never heard of."

Gigi squealed, her exuberance contagious. "A *real* prince?"

"Oh, yes. He came to St. Petersburg in search of a wealthy woman to marry in exchange for a title." I turned to Sasha, who had picked up a pad of paper and pen to take notes, as if she were the assigned secretary. I noticed she did that a lot to avoid conversation.

"Here's the really weird part," I said, jumping to the end of my story.

"They're *all* weird parts, Dash," mumbled Sasha as she doodled.

"After I arrived at the hospital, the doctor took a CT Scan. It showed the wound, bright as day. But a short-time later, he took another scan, and it was clear. Nada. The wound healed itself."

"How is that possible?" Sasha asked.

"That is so cool." Gigi beamed. "And time travel brought you right back to us, all better."

Grandma Tattie didn't appear impressed. "The wound may have healed, but remember what Dr. Beacham told you. You have a mild concussion, so you need to rest up a few days. That means no racing around or watching TV or spending too much time on the computer."

I nodded, but said nothing. If Alex appeared and was alright to travel, I was out of there.

"After all that chasing around St. Petersburg and Moscow, did you finally get to meet Anastasia Romanov?" Grandma asked quietly.

"Anastasia? Didn't she die a long time ago, Grandma Tattie?" asked Gigi.

I switched places on the couch with Gigi, then Tillie, who had chosen to curl up on my lap, for some reason. "That's true. However, through Alex and the Time Menders, I met her. She ended up running off with a man she'd fallen in love with. But before we talked her into escaping, Anastasia still wanted to take the train to Siberia and die with her family to atone for the trouble she caused them. She was quite the firecracker, from what I could tell."

"Yes, she was that." Grandma Tattie took my hand. "But you talked her out of going to her death so our family could exist? I mean, we're sitting here, aren't we?"

I nodded slowly. "It took a few conversations. It turns out, she fell in love with Misha Marusov—a distant cousin of ours. He works for an agency called the Bureau of Time Menders. It's their job as operatives to travel through time to fix little mistakes that can affect their descendants." I looked directly at Grandma Tattie. "You had a mission with them, didn't you?"

Instead of answering, Grandma Tattie looked down at her hands. "Why were *you* chosen to be a Time Mender, Dasha? Did they tell you that?"

"They already had a file on me. I suppose they chose me for my Russian background and language ability. My work history. All the stuff that makes me who I am." I shrugged. "I didn't think I was good enough, but Alex encouraged me and trusted me. In the end, he believed I was the only one who understood what Anastasia was going through with her family. So, I convinced her they'd want her to have a happy life, even after their deaths, wherever she chose to live with her new family."

"Where did she end up?" asked Sasha.

"I don't know. There have been theories floating around for decades because, supposedly, her body was buried with her brother, Alexei, and found separate from the rest of her family. Write that question down, Sash. Let's see if anything has changed since I got back. There should be something on the internet, I would think."

"So, she must have lived and had children," said Gigi in conclusion. "Or we wouldn't be here, right, Grandma Tattie?"

By the rules of the Time Menders, we *shouldn't* exist. I wanted to ask Grandma Tattie how that could have happened. But I wasn't sure I wanted to hear the answer just yet.

"If it's true that Anastasia is alive, then she'll have a son," Grandma Tattie said, to our surprise. "His name will be John William Marusov. Maybe you can start with that."

I wanted to ask how she knew that, but I had a feeling there was a lot I didn't know about her, so I returned to the matter at hand.

"The link that binds us is Grandma Tattie," I said. "We should be able to uncover that information in some resource that Anastasia married Misha Marusov and had a son, who married and was Grandma Tattie's father. We'll have to find family records, although, if she and Misha were living quietly in the countryside somewhere, they may not have registered the child's birth." I frowned, thinking. "But then again, Anastasia probably changed both her first and her last name, so finding her would be extremely difficult, if not impossible."

"You could always start with my birth in 1946, and go backwards from there," Grandma Tattie said in an unusually calm voice.

"Good idea!" I said, perking up. "Sasha, find a couple of those ancestry websites and make that a priority."

"If she wanted to stay hidden from the Russians, we may never find any information. Not everyone posts on social media," said Sasha. "And we'd have to join and pay. But I'll write it down and check what's out there."

"That's good thinking. I'd hate to get our hopes up." I regarded Sasha with new respect. It's like she was engaging in the world after a long sleep. It made me wonder if I'd changed in some positive way, as well.

After all, a lot could happen in three days. I should know.

Chapter 18

*"Relationship betrayal can denote affairs or
disloyalty in other life areas, such as work
relationships and business dealings. Self-care is
required so that you can replenish yourself in order
to give to others."*
(Tarot Card: Four of Swords)

For the next two days, I waited, but Alex still didn't appear. Nor did he materialize in the next four days. The sixth day, a Saturday, brought the rain. Drops slid gently down the windows and made the living room seem gloomier, colder. To counter it, I cranked up the heat and zipped up my sweatshirt as I sank onto the comfortable ivory leather couch. Tillie, the pampered house cat, had found her spot in the laundry room, so as a substitute for a warm furry body, I held a bright orange pillow to my stomach and gazed out the window at the rain.

Five days, and still no word. I couldn't decide if I was angry or relieved not to have to leave my home in the same fashion as before. I glanced around the comfortable modern living room. Would Alex appear out of thin air? Would I vanish, like I did before? Was he even alive? I prayed that he was okay.

If he *was* alive, he said I would have the choice of either working with him or remaining in my own time period after we completed our next mission, but I still felt wary. And after we were done with our mission, if Alex returned to his own time period, would I ever see him again? Did I *want* to see him again? Or did I really want to just forget this entire episode, this crazy dream.

Gigi sat across from me, reading a thick historical romance novel, but she didn't seem to be making much progress, while Sasha sat at the family computer, doing ancestry research that might shed some light on Anastasia's whereabouts. Grandma Tattie had been relatively quiet since we left the hospital, and was now focused on her knitting project.

After a long period of silence, I closed my eyes and mulled over what Alex had asked of me—to follow a complete stranger who had lived over a hundred years ago. It would require a *strong* reason to take that leap of faith once, let alone twice. I opened my eyes and let out a sigh. I still couldn't quite believe what I'd seen and experienced.

"Grandma Tattie," Gigi called out, breaking the silence as she looked up from her romance novel.

"Yes, dear?"

"You said when you were younger, you wanted to be a schoolteacher. Why didn't you follow through?"

Grandma Tattie's face fell, and she set down her knitting. "Ah. Life gets in the way, but I'd rather not think about things I can't change." She picked up her knitting project again and pasted on a smile. "You, *moya lyubimaya,* my pet, could be a wonderful teacher with that curious mind of yours."

Gigi grinned. "I want to be a marine biologist and talk to whales and dolphins."

"Guess that means you'll have to get over your seasickness when we go whale watching." Sasha smirked, but didn't look up.

"Now, Sasha, don't discourage Gigi. Besides, you only have one year of college left. What are *your* plans?"

That wiped the smirk off Sasha's face, as she gazed out the window. "Something to do with animals."

"Hmm. Good for you." Grandma opened her mouth to speak to me, but must have thought better of it, because her lips pressed into a thin line as she examined her knitting project.

It was obvious I was floundering with my career, though I was embarrassed to admit it. Grandma Tattie understood that, even if my mother didn't.

I was just about to head to the kitchen for a diet soda when the doorbell rang. It was one of those long, elaborate rings that allowed me time to make it to the door just as it ended. I looked through the peephole and saw a man wearing an HVAC technician's uniform. His face was turned to the street. I paused for a moment, trying to recall if Mom or Grandma Tattie had scheduled service for the air conditioner or heater. I was typically the last person in the loop, so I opened the door.

When the man turned to face me, I almost had a heart attack.

"Alex!"

"Hey, Dasha. I didn't want to scare you." He held a clipboard in one hand as he waited for a response.

I stepped outside, closing the door behind us. "What are you doing here? Are you okay?"

The porch roof kept the rain off, but it wasn't particularly comfortable outside as the temperature had dropped a good twenty degrees since the day before. I indicated a spot on the porch swing, since it was sheltered from the rain.

"How have—"

"You look—"

I leaned forward and studied his face. Any bruises and bumps had disappeared, and stubble had accumulated on his lower jaw. "Is that new? The beard?"

I'd only been gone a few days, but about a week's growth was visible. It was disconcerting to think there was more than one universe, more than one plane of existence for those who traveled through time. Too tired to ponder the time-travel thing, I wanted to reach out and touch the neatly trimmed beard and that beautiful face I'd grown to love. I shook my head and pulled back my hand. Love? What was I thinking?

"I see you got back alright. Did you get your head wound checked?" he asked in a husky voice.

"The wound is all healed. The ER doctor couldn't explain it. I guess this time traveling thing speeds things up?"

He looked down. "You're right, but we can discuss that more in depth later. I wanted to check and see if Katya helped you get back okay. Did everything go smoothly?"

"Yes. Fine." I furrowed my brow. "Alex, who *is* Katya? I can't put my finger on it, but something about her bothers me."

He rose and walked to the porch railing, stopping to set a small wind chime in motion. The chimes created a gentle, tranquil sound, then died abruptly. "I should explain some things, *if* you're considering going back with me. We need to clean up a few loose ends with Anastasia's relocation."

I walked over and stood next to him, crossing my arms. "About that. I admit I was kind of hoping you wouldn't return, and I wouldn't have to make such a difficult decision. Alex, these people mean business."

He set down his clipboard and took my hands. "You're right."

"Alex, who's the power behind the scenes?"

He hesitated a moment and squeezed my hands. "I told you I work for an organization called the Bureau of Time Menders, or BTM for short. But there's another secret organization that tries to stop us any way they can, claiming we have no right to manipulate time, even if more people benefit from our work. And in fact, they manipulate time themselves, which is why we got into the business in the first place, to counter the messes they make. They call themselves Anti-Time Travelers Oversight, ATTO. It originally was just called TTO—Time Travelers Oversight, before we began opposing them. They have clandestine sites all over the world, as does the BTM."

"And what does that have to do with Katya?"

He grimaced. "Maybe it will shed some light if we examine her backstory." He put the palm of his hand on the smooth railing and looked out at the early evening gloom.

Alex filled me in on what had happened at Khodynka Field the day of the stampede that killed thousands. "Katya's father, Stepan, was one of those in attendance. Dima was about five, and lost his little sister that same day as well. His family was friends with Katya's family, so as he grew older, he began to look after Katya and later, vowed to always take care of her. I think I mentioned earlier that Katya's mother died of a sudden fever the year before last." He gazed out at the street, wet with rain and smelling fresh. "We just learned that Katya was going through her mother's things after the funeral a year ago. She found a note from Rasputin's wife, suggesting she had a diary Katya might be interested in. Rasputin kept detailed accounts of court matters that took place for the past few years. He mentioned Katya's father's name several times."

"Why would he be concerned with a peasant farmer?"

Alex turned and faced her. "Apparently, Stepan Peshkov was a community leader, and didn't hesitate to question the local officials when he thought something wasn't right." He shrugged. "Like so many other peasant families, he was most concerned about the lack of food for the village children. Rasputin wrote that Katya's father made some kind of deal with local officials from an early version of the BTM to distribute food at the festival in honor of Nicholas' largesse. But clearly, something went wrong. Only half the food promised was delivered, and that's what started the stampede."

Alex sat on the porch swing. "I haven't seen the diary myself, but I'd like to make sure that it's Rasputin's handwriting. He could easily have written a lie to gain cooperation from Katya.

She was desperate to learn the truth. That's why she and Dima joined Time Menders in the first place, to try and learn more details about that particular event and to fight the aristocracy and Nicholas' narrow-minded thinking. But Nicholas never budged on the sovereign rule issue. And few secrets ever escape the lips of a Time Mender's agent, so Katya has had to bide her time. I'm thinking this diary she discovered fired her up again because she has been acting strangely. Rasputin's wife could read only bits and pieces, so didn't know what it entailed. But she did recognize Stepan's name. She figured Katya would want the diary and left her a note to come get it."

"What was in the diary?" Dasha asked.

"Katya read about a father she didn't really know, except through her mother. She had no clue he was a rabble-rouser who stood up for his community, in addition to his family. We don't know what else was in the diary, though we're trying to find out, but whatever it was, it seems to have had a profound effect on Katya. I wouldn't even be surprised if she's a double agent and is working for ATTO on the sly as a result of what she's found. And Dima sometimes reacts a bit dangerously, because he wants what Katya wants. On top of that, she has certain powers that make her...a challenge."

A niggle of fear inched down my spine. "What kind of powers?"

Alex worked his jaw. "Her mother taught Katya everything she knows about reading tarot cards, and from what I've been told, she's *very* accurate in those readings. After her mother died, Katya assumed her mother's business name, 'Madame Peshkova.'" He brushed a piece of lint from his sleeve. "Not all Time Menders have the ability to travel through time and space, but somehow, she's tapped into the way Time Menders travel. We never know when and where she'll show up. She must have an unusual and rare type of talisman that takes her anywhere in time. It's become a real problem."

"Using the name 'Madame' assumes she's married, doesn't it?"

He shrugged and gazed over the neighborhood that had begun to encroach on Masurov land. "She's twenty-two and Dima's twenty-seven. He steps in whenever necessary, and will claim to be her husband, if it gets her out of trouble."

I fingered the pocket of his HVAC shirt with the name "Alex" embroidered on it. "So, do you think Katya wants revenge on the Time Menders because she believes they were somehow responsible for her father's death?"

Alex hesitated and very slowly removed my hand from his pocket. "Here's where things get murky. It seems that Nicholas ignored the stampede and the dead bodies that had been picked up and disposed of, and went ahead and attended a gala event that same night without acknowledging the tragic beginning to his reign. As you know, Russians can be very superstitious in their beliefs and religion. Many said Nicholas' reign was cursed. We have reason to believe that Katya may think that the BTM could have prevented the tragedy and didn't. That, and the diary, may have caused a sudden change of heart about the bureau, and why we suspect that she may have joined ATTO, but first we need proof."

"Wow! Okay, but you said she had powers. Was it just the tarot cards?"

Alex chewed his lip. "Katya readily admits to learning basic witchcraft over the years from relatives and neighbors. Enough to know how to make potions, charms, *and*...perform curses."

"She's a witch? Oh my." I slowly exhaled, shocked that she would admit to it. "But the Bolsheviks had already killed Nicholas. She got what she wanted," I argued, wondering why he'd removed my hand, and trying not to feel hurt. I sat back on the porch swing.

Talk about your unavailable man.

"What do you think she'll try to do next?"

Alex looked up at the sunset, then zeroed in on the problem at hand. "I'm not sure, but ATTO has been trying to eliminate Time Mender agents. Maybe even the whole bureau. Katya may wind up helping them."

His eyes narrowed, and I spotted exhaustion for the first time.

I was so focused on Alex, I didn't hear the front door open and close softly. Sasha stepped onto the porch and looked in my direction.

"Gigi was asking why you're having such a long conversation with the HVAC man." She had a beautiful smile when she bothered, and she turned it on Alex, causing a twinge of jealousy to rear its ugly head. "Hi, I'm Dasha's sister, Sasha. And you must be...?"

Alex took a step forward and held out his hand. "Alex McKain. Pleased to meet you, Sasha." Odd. His Texas twang was suddenly audible, something he'd played down during our recent partnership.

Sasha glanced from Alex to me, and quietly let go of his hand. "You're not the AC man, are you?"

"And you're just as beautiful and smart as your sister." Alex chuckled and indicated his uniform. "I didn't want to just materialize and scare everyone."

"So, what do you really do?"

He hesitated, once more turning to me, his eyes asking if I'd told my sister anything about the Time Menders.

I shrugged, exhausted by our current topic of conversation. "She knows what she needs to know. Now, give me a good reason why I shouldn't stay right here, where it's comfortable, and where no one tries to hit me in the back of the head with a bayonet?"

Sasha stood behind me with her hands on my shoulders. "Pardon my sister. She gets a bit cranky when she's tired and hungry. It might be best if you leave."

I was ashamed to say she was right. I wondered if my head injury had made me crazy. I turned my gaze back to the sunset.

"Rest up, Dasha. I'll be in touch, one way or another. Hopefully, I'll have more details next time." Alex turned away and headed down the steps to the street. He never glanced back, yet I couldn't help but wonder what he thought *I* could possibly do about all this.

I saw something flutter onto the porch. "What's that?"

Sasha reached down and retrieved a business card. "I guess Alex left this for you as a way to get in touch with him should you change your mind."

"I won't change my mind." I had graduated from cranky to grumpy. Who did Alex McKain think he was, anyway? A good-looking stranger. Alright. A *very* good-looking stranger who used his looks to manipulate unsuspecting, vulnerable women like me.

"Damn."

Sasha went inside and closed the door, but as she did, I caught that knowing smirk.

Chapter 19

"This card suggests that work is required for the relationship to thrive. It underscores the necessity of labor and dedication in nurturing love or potential connections."
(Tarot Card: Eight of Coins)

After Alex's visit, I fumed like a teenager. I didn't have much time to decide whether to accompany him or not on his next venture, and I didn't appreciate the pressure. The following day, I was in my room, working on my computer, when I received a text message, asking me to meet Alex. He chose a coffee shop that overlooked the bay, so I took a taxi, not wanting to compete with all the tourists attempting to find a place to park.

The recent rain had washed away the dust and dirt, making everything seem new and clean again. As I stepped inside the coffee shop called Pop-po's Lattes, I saw Alex seated at a table with a view of the bay. I approached and pulled out a chair, pleased to see that the cafe wasn't packed, as most places were during summer. Though the shop wasn't as new and clean as a Starbucks, they had the best coffee in town, with an aroma that could lure serious coffee drinkers from a mile away. Alex looked up as I removed my messenger bag and placed it on the chair next to me.

"So, how did you find my cell number to text me?" I asked.

A lazy smile greeted me, then he looked down and stirred his Coffee Americano. "I'm a detective. I have my ways."

Although I was careful not to show it, I was relieved he had no visible wounds or bruises. Had they disappeared just as mine had? And was this a weird side effect of time travel? I didn't know but I aimed to find out.

In the meantime, I turned my attention to his sapphire silk shirt. It made his eyes stand out, while his black suit appeared expensive. If I were seeing him for the first time, I would have guessed him to be a male model for Calvin Klein. Even from across the table, I detected a faint masculine cologne that reminded me of someplace warm and sunny, like Greece.

"Do you have any idea how worried I was?" I groused, feeling like a petulant child, but then decided now was as good as any time to pop the question. "You don't look like a man who's been tortured."

He gave a lopsided grin. "That's a good thing, isn't it? Did you miss me?"

I pretended to hit him and sighed. "You Time Menders must have developed a super advanced healing technology."

"Now, that would be a miracle, wouldn't it? I'll pass that along to the powers that be." He gave me a mischievous smile, clearly evading the issue.

I watched as he wrapped his hands around his almost empty cup. Across the room, a young blonde waitress had been eyeing our table since I entered, and she finally came over with menus. Even Mother Teresa would have noticed the hungry look in the woman's eyes when she addressed Alex.

"May I refill your coffee...sir?"

"A refill would be great." Alex held out his cup and reached for the cream.

"Can I get you anything else? A scone? Croissant? Muffin?"

He smiled politely, and gestured toward me. "What would you like? Have you eaten?"

I sat back in my chair and studied the menu, suddenly no longer hungry. "I'll just have coffee. Black is fine."

Alex took a sip of his Americano and smiled, half turning to the waitress. "By any chance, do you have something made from potatoes?"

I choked on my first sip, but caught myself from spitting it all over Alex.

The waitress appeared confused. "Potatoes? You mean, like, french fries?"

"Never mind. He's joking," I said, waving her off.

As the waitress took the menus and retreated, I wrapped my hands around my warm mug. "It's probably a good idea you picked an out-of-the-way place like this instead of a Starbucks where we were more likely to be spotted."

"My thoughts as well. You didn't like my potato joke?"

I inhaled and leaned in. "Let's get to the point. I have a foundation project proposal due by 5:00 p.m., which I'm doing from home."

He nodded and sat back in his chair, showing no surprise. "That suits my schedule, as well."

"For starters, what's the next mission?"

He set his coffee aside and folded his hands on the table. "We were right to believe that Katya's a double agent." His blue eyes locked with mine. "We have it on good authority that she's made it known she wants to close down the BTM and get rid of every agent."

"*Boshe moi!*" I exclaimed. "Or as Grandma Tattie would say, 'My God'. She's just a young, flighty girl. What could she have learned from the diary that made her think of something so drastic? And why not talk to a BTM member about the stampede, first? Do you have any idea what she and Dima are planning?"

Alex glanced around the room as though uncomfortable. "We don't know the details. It could be a bomb that takes out our headquarters, or the kidnapping of an agent. Over the course of her job, she's met a lot of people from all walks of life, and unfortunately, now she knows the inner workings of The Time Menders. So, the sky's the limit."

"Is your director watching out for you agents?"

"A special task force has been assembled to deal with it. They're fact-gathering at the moment. We need to do some background checks before we come up with a solid plan."

"What about Ana and Misha? Are they safe?"

Alex watched the waitress deal with a disgruntled customer, then turned his eyes back to the ocean view. "All reports indicate they entered Finland, and are temporarily renting a cottage while they prepare to come to the U.S. by ship, for the time being, until they can work things out. Marya will be their housekeeper."

"I'm so glad they're all okay. Are those preparations the 'loose ends' you mentioned earlier?"

"Partly. We still need to gather small details for the files. As for Misha—that's just his Russian code name, by the way—he's gone back to using his BTM name, Michael Morgan. For Ana's safety, he won't be using the name Marusov. As you know already, he's your distant cousin with a link to your grandmother, Tatiana. Anastasia changed her name to something more American: Annie Marist. They filled out marriage documents, so that's in the works now, while agents reported they've booked passage on a ship leaving Helsinki and arriving in Boston in two weeks. Apparently, they have cousins they will stay with while deciding where they want to live. All in all, it couldn't have turned out better, once we got Rasputin off their trail."

I thought about that, a feeling of accomplishment stirring inside. "And Rasputin is...dead?"

Alex shifted in his chair. "We have to wait for a copy of the autopsy report. Officially, he died of a gunshot wound to the forehead on the 30th of December, 1916. A BTM colleague said he was an abnormally strong man who took his own sweet time to die. But, yes, he's gone from our lives for now."

Worried we'd be overheard, I glanced around so I could see where our waitress was located. I spotted her putting fresh coffee beans into a grinder so figured that would take a few minutes.

"When you dropped by my house, I got the feeling you were distancing yourself—pushing me away. Was I wrong?" I ventured to ask.

Alex cupped my hands in his, waiting. "I'm sorry about that. I was worried sick that you were okay. When I'm separated from you, I tend to...get distracted." He let go of my hands. "That's not good when we may have future assignments together. You can ask for a different agent to partner with, if it makes you feel better."

Feel better? I'd lost five pounds in the past few days, holed up in my room while reading the news on the internet. I had never felt more miserable. "I don't think we need to do that. Let's see how the next assignment goes. Do the Time Menders want me to work with them?"

At that moment, Alex's cell phone buzzed, and he looked down to read a message. Then he heaved a sigh and ended the call. "You keep resting." He paused and looked into my eyes. "Please eat something and take care of yourself, Dash. It took me longer than anticipated to jump forward, and I was hoping you would be strong and ready to go.

"Katya told me I only had seven days to deal with my business here. Does that mean I'll be whisked away?" I rose and reached for my messenger bag, preparing to pay for the coffee as the waitress approached.

Alex waved me off, seeming distracted. "Don't worry about that. It's my fault. I'll fix the time clock." He pulled out a credit card from a beat-up leather wallet and handed the card to the waitress. "I'll get this."

While the waitress ran the card at the cash register, Alex leaned in and whispered, "It would seem time marches on a bit quicker in the time corridor we occupy. Apparently, Annie and

Michael Morgan are leaving right now on a ship to America. They'll be arriving in Boston in one to two weeks."

When he slipped into his suit jacket, butterflies took flight in my stomach. Afterward, he threw me a reassuring smile, left a generous tip, and then headed for the entrance, drawing every female eye in the shop.

As we walked out the door, I faced the ocean and felt my body hum, which I'd discovered it did whenever I stood next to Alex. "I'm so happy for Ana...I mean Annie and Mi...Cousin Michael."

"There's an extra complication—not my typical assignment. But it's not impossible to resolve." He reached for my hand and we started walking.

I glanced down at our hands entwined, then decided I liked the feel of it. Dalton had loved to touch and to hug. Brendon didn't like to hold hands. He said it made his hands sweaty, and then he'd mess up on his guitar.

"What complication?"

Alex squeezed my hand and gazed into my eyes for a long moment. "The time continuum has speeded up. Annie is already pregnant and planning to give birth here in the States in three months." He smiled warmly. "Dasha, the BTM Director has asked that you be named the child's godmother."

Chapter 20

Pleased to be back at her own cottage, Katya sipped tea and settled on an outdoor bench that overlooked her herb garden. Dima was joining two male friends for a night out to discuss job possibilities. Oh, she knew they would secure illegal vodka somewhere, but Dima always made it home.

Evening came softly as she fingered the outside of the diary, as she had done so long ago, the day she'd first received it. Even then, she was sure the diary would change everything, and she had been right. Her thoughts returned to the day she'd first read it. Rasputin had written his initials at the front of the diary, rather than his full name. Not that it mattered, because his sprawling cursive handwriting was quite unique. What Katya wanted to explore were the dates included. She'd been led to believe the diary covered the last two years of Nicholas' reign, but, instead, it started with his coronation. When Katya rested her hand on that date, she felt a shiver work its way all the way down to her toes.

"Thirtieth of May, 1896," she'd read out loud. "My birthday." She set the diary aside for a moment, pausing to take a deep breath. When she felt composed, she picked it up and continued to read. "Today is the day Nicholas II becomes Czar of all Russia. I, Grigori Rasputin, am a peasant farmer, living in Siberia. I do not know him, nor do I expect I ever will, but I must put this in writing:

I predict his reign will be cursed because of an event that occurred on this date."

A noise made Katya look up. A young boy and girl were trying to make a broken swing work on the other side of their dirt lane. Though still quite young, they seemed to believe an adult should have fixed it. "Don't you know? Everything in Russia is broken," Katya called out to them. They just stared at her, saying nothing. She shrugged, but offered some consolation. "I'll tell my friend to come fix this tomorrow morning. Is that alright?"

They nodded solemnly as a young woman arrived, a sweater wrapped around her thin shoulders. She called their names, and they trailed after her without a fuss.

Katya wanted no more interruptions, so she rose from the bench and headed for another quiet place. Oddly enough, she chose the cheese cellar on her property, knowing Dima wouldn't think to look for her there. It was dark and a bit damp, with only a little light streaming in through a street-level transom window. But once she lit a fresh candle, she could make out the words of the diary just fine.

A long time passed before she lifted her head and peered through the small window that led to the street. Dima was probably home now and wondering where his dinner was, but then, they had so little food, he should be able to figure out a simple meal for himself, one would think.

As usual, she felt guilty for taking time for herself. She was just starting to get up when her eyes fell on one sentence toward the end of the diary. She froze and located the date. Rasputin's dates shifted around, often revisiting one particular day if more facts were learned later. Katya's birthday was one such day.

"Stepan Peshkov, a leader in our peasant community, took the initiative to provide food for our peasant families by making arrangements with an organization called BTM (members shall not be named due to strong opinions and emotions at this time). It seems many people brought their families early, and by noon, claimed there wasn't enough food. That caused a stampede, and thousands were injured or killed. Among the dead, Stepan Peshkov." Katya gasped, but read on. "It was later learned that BTM sold half the food on the black market to fund their organization."

Tears rolled down Katya's cheeks to learn that this all could have been prevented. "What a mess!" she whispered. "How could they do something so cruel?"

Dima must have heard her voice through the thin walls when he went outside to look for her. He pushed on the stuck door and brushed off the cobwebs. "I've been looking everywhere for you. What are you doing here?"

She sat quietly, a hand covering the lettering on the outside of the diary.

"I wanted someplace where I could read the diary and not be disturbed. But I see you found me."

"It's late. I was worried sick."

"Did you find something to eat?"

"Well, yes, but I'm still hungry. Why didn't you tell me about the diary? Is there something in it you wish to keep secret?"

Katya rose and pulled her sweater tight. "I didn't have time to finish it, so I'll do that tomorrow. We'll talk once I know everything Rasputin wrote. Oh, before I forget, the swing is broken again at the park across the way. I told two little children you would fix it tomorrow."

Dima appeared disappointed about the diary, but he nodded and led the way up the cellar steps.

Once she was back in the house, Katya found an apple to eat and then went to bed. She'd actually almost finished the diary, but didn't want to deal with a petulant Dima that night. Soon, the house was silent, and she felt confident Dima had dropped off to sleep in his own room. She lit another candle, and she read to the end.

Her eyelids drooped, and sleep was not far off now. She set the diary on the nightstand, her heart heavy as the first day she'd read it. In two days' time, she would leave for the United States. She must remember to pack warm clothes. And then, once and for all, take care of the people who had killed her father, the Romanov nobles.

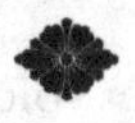

Grisha couldn't help but note the expensive-looking suit Alex wore when he arrived by taxi at the coffee shop earlier in the day. He had watched as Alex smiled, then lifted his nose in appreciation of the aroma of coffee wafting over him. Grisha had to admit, these Americans knew how to brew a good cup of coffee.

As he stepped into the shadows of the building opposite the coffeehouse, he narrowed his eyes to get a better look at Alex, whose dark blue shirt must have been silk, the threads shiny in the sunlight. Even his shoes glittered in the sun. Grisha stiffened as Alex looked up and down the sidewalk then straightened his black-and-silver tie before stepping inside the upscale coffee shop. Grisha knew enough about surveilling a target to know his life just might depend on one missed detail.

As Grisha made himself comfortable on the hard bench across the street, he felt confident both the Anti-Time Travelers Oversight and its nemesis organization, the Bureau of Time Menders, had no clue he had not only cheated death, he had gained a new ability to travel to whatever time he desired whenever he wanted. He had discovered this new ability quite by accident, and he planned to use it to outrun the law as long as possible.

He thought about his diary, a masterpiece of lies, if he did say so himself. He'd been the one to make the arrangements to get it in Katya's hands through his wife. It was his way of getting back at Nicholas, who'd turned on him in the end. As he thought about the Romanovs, he wondered what pretty little Katya would do as a result of his diary, now that she had it in her possession. Had it been enough to push her over the edge?

At times, he was amazed by the lies that came so easily to him as a priest. He barked in laughter, catching the eyes of a few passersby.

But then a metallic taste filled his mouth, and he frowned. Katya's behavior had changed this past month. It was almost as if she thought *she* was the time traveler with true power. Grisha snorted and folded his arms across his chest while he mulled over her actions. They seemed almost frantic, as if she knew she was running out of time. Emotional women made him nervous when he had no control over them. She may appear simple and sweet on the outside, but inside, she was a smart woman in a world still catering to men. Grisha's daughter, Maria, was like that. She, too, was an outgoing girl. And Katya most definitely hated to be ignored or delegated to sit out a mission in which she'd invested so much time in the endeavor.

Grisha growled as a city bus whizzed by, stirring up a wave of dust that made him cough. As a peasant, his family had been poor, illiterate, and susceptible to the usual diseases. He had hated men like Alex, who'd had everything handed to them. And still Grisha had risen to power at the highest levels of *his* Russia, using his unique talents. Who needed fancy clothes to impress?

He chuckled as he listened to the inane chatter of all types of customers seated at tables outside the coffee shop. *Mongrels, these Americans.*

With that assessment, his thoughts returned to his time in Russia. If not for the czar's little boy, Alexei, being born with hemophilia, and a few select introductions to a Romanov widow or two, he might never have made it to power. But he'd saved the boy, and he'd never let them forget it.

He laughed out loud at the irony, just as a passing woman appeared intrigued by his appearance. He trained his hypnotic eyes on her, then nodded, just as he had done with countless women at the palace court. He had a knack for hypnosis, and he used it every chance he got, especially with women. Nicholas and Alexandra were putty in his hands, as well, allowing him to work his magic on Alexei with ease.

But then the woman looked down at his disguise, an old, faded Mexican poncho, paired with well-worn men's jeans with holes in the knees, and she moved on. He sighed at the lost opportunity. But there would be more. Women here appeared easy to attract, which made him grin as he waited for Dasha.

He had to admit he was beginning to admire her. She would definitely be a challenge, but no woman was immune to his supernatural charms. He looked down and regarded his "hobo" attire. He particularly enjoyed the feel of the worn flip-flops by moving his bare toes, then he adjusted his sunglasses. He'd need to find a shiny, expensive suit like Alex's, at least for a short time.

The minutes ticked by, but then a taxi pulled up and a smile formed on his lips when he saw Dasha step out. She said something that made the taxi driver laugh and then waved as she turned to face the coffee shop.

Grisha noticed the details of Dasha's striking outfit, just like he had with Alex. Dasha looked every bit the California girl in a pair of fashionable wide-leg white jeans with blue and purple flowers embellishing the lower leg. It was turning into a warm summer day, and she'd thrown a denim jacket over her white top to catch any cool breezes coming her way. She and Alex appeared to have opposite tastes in clothing.

Why would she want to date a stuck-up, arrogant man with a chip on his shoulder like Alex McKain, anyway? Grisha cursed, muttering to himself. Those BTM boys were all the same. A bunch of rich mama's boys playing spy games.

As Grisha leaned into the shadows, Dasha entered the coffee shop. She would come around to his way of thinking. And if she didn't, he'd make sure she disappeared during the execution of his plan with Katya that came directly from his superiors at ATTO.

Not pleased to be kept waiting, Grisha rubbed his eyes. Alex and Dasha conversed for about thirty minutes, and then emerged outside on the sidewalk. They talked for a few more minutes, oblivious to his presence across the street.

Grisha put his sunglasses back on and tugged at his long brownish-gray ponytail, then followed at a discreet distance. He admired how the two conversed so easily in this big city. Grisha blinked at the traffic lights and cars racing by, trying to clear an intersection before a light turned red. Larger vehicles tried to fit into tiny parking spots, horns blared, people shouted The vibrations coming from the city of San Francisco sent shivers of delight racing through him.

I could live here.

For one brief moment, he panicked as he nearly lost Dasha and Alex, who quickly joined the flow of pedestrians crossing the street and then entered a circular driveway in front of a fancy hotel. Grisha hurried to catch up as Alex stepped forward and said something to a bellhop, who indicated a short line of taxis.

From a distance, Grisha admired Dasha's tall, slender figure. She was a spitfire, all right. He liked that. But Alex didn't seem to notice. *Poor dumb bastard is in love with his job.* He figured Alex was too much of a gentleman to take Dasha up to a room with its fancy down-filled bed.

He groused, his mercurial mood changing quickly, like the gathering storm clouds. The Time Menders thought he'd died that dark December night in 1916. Little did they know a beautiful stranger from ATTO had pulled him from the Neva and revived him. Since then, he'd bounced around a few times and places. He chuckled, drawing stares from a couple passing by who shook their heads. Had he been talking to himself again? People in this day and age made quick judgments about homeless people. They assumed the homeless were mentally deficient. He suppressed a laugh. If they only knew a fraction of what he did about how easy people were to manipulate, they'd be bowing down to him.

Before he could dwell on it further, Alex and Dasha shared a taxi and took off, entering the whirl of a city that had literally risen from the ashes, from what he'd read about the earthquake and subsequent fires. He paused for a moment, noting the taxi cab had headed west. Soon, it disappeared over a hill.

The rain had stopped and the sun had come out. It was a perfect day to explore his new favorite city. Grisha smiled to himself as he headed toward a sign that pointed to Fisherman's Wharf. As he continued walking, he wondered if Katya knew what she held in her hands. Maybe the most important question was, had his lies been enough to stir ATTO into taking action against the BTM? If so, those devious, over-educated, well-dressed BTM agents would soon vanish overnight, leaving the Anti-Time Travelers Oversight to step in and take control...unchallenged.

The streets suddenly seemed more crowded as Grisha ducked and dodged through openings, occasionally bumping into people. A rumbling came from deep within his chest.

Maybe he was overthinking this, and needed to just let things flow. But then Grisha snapped his fingers with excitement because he knew what would motivate Katya to eliminate Ana and her child. With both of Katya's parents deceased, she would have many debts and could use a little extra cash. Yes, that should do nicely. ATTO would back him up with additional funds, he felt certain. Once Katya had some extra money in hand and her bills were paid off, she just might be willing to help them bring down BTM as well. As an insider, she would know the inner workings of BTM. He rubbed his hands together in anticipation of the glorious annihilation of the Bureau of Time Travel. Good riddance.

He was heading toward Fisherman's Wharf when he saw an advertisement for a restaurant on Pier 39. "Bubba Gump Shrimp," he read. "It captures the charm and American spirit that made *Forrest Gump* a smash hit." He scratched his head. "What is this *Forrest Gump?*"

"Awesome movie!" said a young man whizzing by on a board with wheels attached, pointing to the words on his pink Bubba Gump Shrimp Company T-shirt.

A moving picture with fish? Grisha had never tasted shrimp. He thought maybe he should take this opportunity and give it a try. He waved his thanks to the young man and picked up the pace.

These Americans were surprisingly generous.

Grisha could smell the fish and shellfish caught locally, and it made him suddenly ravenous. A full stomach and a wide open evening should help him decide on a plan to convince Katya to join his side, if she hadn't already. Grisha pulled open the restaurant door and stepped inside Bubba Gump's with a big smile on his face.

Chapter 21

"The traditional meaning is a crisis of faith and a period of emotional vulnerability. You have a decision to make, and to choose wisely, you need to rely on your senses rather than logic."
(Tarot Card: The Sun)

My family sat around the dining room table eating in silence, the tension in the air thick. Mom and Dad must have fought over something on the way back from Monterey, and although Rosana did her best to lighten the mood, food just wasn't enough to smooth things over this time.

"Gigi, did you finish your homework for this week?" Mom asked.

For the next twenty minutes, my little sister talked about mathematics in a way that made my head spin. Fortunately, I had learned to tune her out, but I don't know what Sasha did to survive, because she was the least scholarly of us all. I suspected she may be feeding Tillie under the table, but I wouldn't swear to it. I decided to go along with the family vignette as long as someone didn't: a) ask me when I was going to see Brendon again; b) beg me to get a *real* job using my language skills; and the ubiquitous c) demand that I get married and have some babies. The last came from Mom, of course. She'd suddenly become obsessed with babies, and although I knew without a doubt that she'd enjoyed our babyhood, once we'd become toddlers, she turned us loose like wild animals to raise ourselves. Our only stop-check since our early teens was Grandma Tattie, who now asked Rosana to bring our desserts to keep us entertained as she had countless times throughout our childhood. Mom had asked Dad to stop at a bakery in Monterey before they left, and we devoured our strawberry cheesecakes like the good little piglets we were.

Afterward, I decided to swim some laps in the indoor pool, not wanting to go to bed with that heavy feeling. Sasha joined me, but that didn't last long. By 10:00 p.m., everyone else had tired and gone to sleep. Relieved to finally have the place to myself, I draped my arms over the sides of the pool and closed my eyes, thinking about Alex and the news about Anastasia's baby. I'd felt a wonderful sense of pride that we'd completed our mission, even though I still wasn't sure how it would all turn out.

I opened my eyes and floated my hand on the water. The last thing Alex had said was that I'd be a godmother. "Now, how did he know that?" I muttered into the darkness. "Besides, I can't be godmother to someone's child born in 1919. After all, I don't exist yet, and I don't even know her mother that well."

I shivered as I climbed the steps to exit the pool, then reached for a towel. A breeze blew in from off the ocean. It whisked through the open window and sent a chill down my back as I dried off and wrapped the towel around my hips. I entered a sliding door toward the back of the house and headed for the main staircase. At the foot of the elaborate staircase, I set my hand on the bottom newel, then paused to listen to the grandfather clock in the foyer that chimed away the hour, an old habit of mine. Once it was done chiming, I padded up the stairs and entered my room. I pulled my pajamas from the dresser drawer, all the while thinking of Alex. He was so different from any man I'd met, including Dalton. My fiancé had been predictable, and as I thought about all the changes I was experiencing at the time, I guess predictable was what I needed. On the other hand, I seemed to be in an experimental phase now. Perhaps "lost" was a better term for my state of mind. Sometimes I thought it was Dalton encouraging me to try new things from his spot in the Great Beyond. Speaking of which, I'd been sitting on the bed for only a few minutes or so when I felt the temperature drop suddenly. It made the hairs on the back of my neck stand up, and I shivered.

"Anybody out there? *Bábushka* Vasya? *Dédushka* Nicolai? Dalton, is that you?"

When none of my dearly departed answered, I remembered our ghost dog, Tessa. One time, Gigi asked me if Tessa was lonely, because she was closest to Grandma Tattie. Grandma Tattie had just turned seventeen in 1959, and she'd told me how broken-hearted she'd been when Tessa died. She hadn't bought another pet until Tillie showed up and adopted every one of us, but mostly Sasha.

Speaking of loneliness, I thought about calling Alex, but I didn't want to seem like one of those clingy women. For all I knew, he was in the Himalayas in the 1800s, finding a cure for some rare disease. He'd tell me when I needed to know something about a new mission.

I put on my black-and-pink satin pajamas and crawled under the covers. After a minute, the covers rustled, and I pulled them back. "Tessa? Is that you?"

She tried to nuzzle me, but it only wrinkled the covers. Now would have been a good time to sink my fingers into her long coat for some pet therapy, as Sasha called it. But she wasn't really there, so I forced my imagination to settle down.

You're not hallucinating, Dasha, so relax and go to sleep.

I sighed into the dark and rearranged the quilt. My thoughts kept returning to Alex, and I wondered if all his wounds had truly healed, especially his emotional wounds. For some reason that was important to me.

Before, I hadn't been sure about volunteering for the second half of the mission. But now, I decided I might. I had a few things yet to discover before I could move on emotionally.

It wasn't long before I drifted off to sleep, but I kept waking every hour or so, listening to the old house moan and groan. I heard a dog bark faintly from another room and whispered, "Goodnight, Tessa."

Then, I slept the sleep of the dead.

Katya awoke, her head throbbing, eyes dry from reading the diary late into the night yet again. She'd fallen asleep in the early morning hours, and sat up now to peer out her bedroom window to gauge the time. It appeared to be mid-morning, and she muttered a curse as a knock sounded on the door. It reminded her of the day after she'd discovered the diary. Her mind scrolled back to that time, when it had been Dima at the door of the cheese seller.

"*Blin!*" she swore, stubbing her toe as she reached for her robe.

"*Dobroye utro*, Katya! Are you alright in there? It is a beautiful day, and I have brought some breakfast for you."

"I'm fine, Dima. My toe's not happy," she said with a huge yawn. "I was meaning to stand in line today for bread."

She opened the door and found Dima holding a tray—a measly breakfast of tea and unappealing, slightly burnt toast.

"I could stand in line for you," he offered, setting down the tray on her nightstand. "Besides, you look kind of pale today."

She finished tying the belt to her robe and hesitated. She wanted to read through parts of the diary one more time, while she was awake, in hope that the words would tell her what to do with this information. She picked up a mug of strong hot tea and took a sip.

"I *could* really use the time to finish dealing with Mother's belongings. I promised to give what dresses don't fit me to the relief center today."

She hoped Dima would focus on that, because she still wasn't ready to discuss the contents of the diary with him.

"I'll be glad to wait in line for you," Dima said. "Besides, I'll probably run into Pavel and Kolya, and it's always good to catch up."

"Have either of them found jobs yet?"

Dima shrugged. "I can ask. Maybe they know who's hiring."

Katya silently ground her back teeth, wondering when he was going to grow up and accept adult responsibility. "Kolya's wife is due to have her baby any day now. Kolya needs to try harder to find a job, and not be so proud."

Dima shoved his hands into his pockets and glanced around her room. "He'll find the right job as soon as all of the Russian nobles are gone from Moscow."

Katya sucked in her breath. "Don't say those things out loud, Dima. Now, go clean up and see if we have any bread left in our pantry for supper. And don't forget to fix that swing! It's the same one we used to play on as children."

"All right. But only for you."

"Nyet. For the *dyeti*, Dima. For the children."

He shrugged and finished his tea. "Why is it your job to make children happy?"

"Because there is no one else."

Katya wondered how her mother and Dima's aunt were able to coax the best out of Dima when her mother was alive. He was becoming more belligerent every day, and lazier.

"I didn't agree to raise this man-child," she muttered, as she washed her face and dressed.

Once she heard the front door open and close, she took her tea and toast out to the dining table, the diary tucked under her arm. Every encounter with Dima made her that much more convinced it was time for her to live on her own and stretch her wings. She had no female friends, unfortunately.

She finished breakfast, poured more hot tea, and took out her tarot deck to place next to the diary. She opened the book to a passage about her mother having two miscarriages many years ago. She'd forgotten about that, and for some reason, felt ashamed that her mother had confided in Rasputin, or at the very least, his wife. Katya suspected he'd put her under hypnosis to elicit that kind of emotional reaction at a woman's lowest point. Her mother's life had been so much harder than her own. Zoya's face didn't possess the delicate feminine features that Katya had nor did her body possess the gentle curves. But she always saw the positive side of a situation and demonstrated a healthy sense of humor when it was warranted. And, as Madame Peshkova, she never gave a bad tarot reading, of which she was most proud.

Katya shuffled the cards, closed her eyes, and asked her question. "Is Rasputin lying?" She then pulled a card. When she turned it over, she gasped.

The Tower. Sudden change. Collapse of a dream, an organization, or a relationship.

Now, what could that *mean, and how does it apply to me?*

She bit her lip and turned to gaze down at the diary, then back at the card and its meaning: *A secret comes to light, which may be shocking. It is time to let go of past patterns of relating.*

Well, that's no help at all.

Dima, her partner through thick and thin, wasn't going to be able to help her connect the dots between her tarot reading and Rasputin's diary. There must be someone who could help her figure out what was true and what was false. Katya brushed aside a lone tear, stopped trembling, and straightened her shoulders. Who *did* she trust?

With a spark of excitement, she recalled the vibrant woman with amber eyes she'd met on her birthday. Dima had introduced them, but when he'd crossed the room to speak with Rasputin alone, the woman, Sin Ryland, had leaned close to Katya and said, "I would be happy to mentor you into ATTO, Katya. Just say the word. You won't be alone."

Even though Katya didn't really know Sin Ryland well, she'd heard good things about her at the gathering. Sin even complimented Katya on her new red dress and lipstick. Not used to compliments of that sort, Katya felt her cheeks blush as red as her dress, but Sin *seemed* sincere.

Her mind made up, Katya grabbed a carpetbag from under her bed, and stuffed a few clean items of clothing inside, her mind racing ahead. She scribbled a note and put it smack in the middle of the table, where Dima would be sure to find it.

"Dima, don't come after me. I need some answers. I'll be fine. Katya."

Carefully, she set the diary in the bag, then grabbed a small container of liquid with a simple handwritten label reading "Time Elixir." Rasputin kept one of those vials while she'd been taken for questioning at the jail cell, and he was clearly using it liberally, because he seemed to show up willy-nilly, in past and present. So far, Katya had told neither ATTO nor the BTM about the discovery she'd found among her mother's belongings. It came with a note titled "Time Emergencies Only!" Katya put that in the bag as well. She'd have to read the warnings later.

She closed the bag, grabbed her coat, and headed for the park she'd visited last night. She didn't know why, but it was as if her mind was telling her what to do and in what order, and her feet obeyed. And she wasn't feeling the least bit like herself when she arrived and sat on a wall surrounding the small children's play area.

"What am I waiting for?" she said under her breath, eyes alert. "Sin Ryland," she said, louder now, "we need to talk."

It was indeed a clear day, and upon saying those words out loud, a golden cloud appeared before her, and in seconds, a vision appeared. Suddenly, the image materialized into a solid form, becoming a female with a dark bob in her late forties. Katya recognized the woman. She'd know those deep amber eyes anywhere.

Sin Ryland smiled and held out her hand. "Madame Peshkova, what perfect timing. I have a proposal for you."

Chapter 22

I sat on the cushion in the bay window of my bedroom, Tillie purring contentedly in my lap. Outside, the fog obscured any view of the Golden Gate Bridge and anything else, for that matter.

Four days had passed with no contact from Alex, and I began to wonder if waiting on pins and needles was part of a psychological test for BTM employment, like the kind I'd read about in the military or the CIA. In the meantime, I had plenty of time to go over what I knew about the mission. I had no burning desire to burst in on Misha and Anastasia or Annie or whatever she went by now, and upend their lives, especially with a new baby and a new-ish husband.

As the week passed, I came and went from work at the foundation, when one day I found myself staring at the office phone, willing it to ring. "How ridiculous. I'm a grown woman," I muttered as I sat at my desk.

"Did you decide to join us for lunch?" a colleague asked, thinking I was addressing her.

I shook my head, then typed a sentence of gibberish onto the computer. "No. Thank you, but—"

The phone rang, and I grabbed it, answering on the first ring.

"Daria Marusov," I said, proud of myself for not blurting out Alex's name and remembering to use my formal name instead.

"Dasha, this is your grandmother. I was wondering if you'd join me for lunch today. I have something to speak to you about, so I've made a reservation for 12:00 at the Samovar."

My mouth began salivating at the memories made at that restaurant. "I haven't been there in ages."

"I thought that might be the case. I'll send Marcos to pick you up in front of your building."

"*Spasibo, bábushka!*"

With something delicious to look forward to, that should keep my mind off of Alex...for a while. But what could Grandma Tattie possibly have to tell me that she couldn't tell me at home? I would need to be patient. Minutes later, I walked into the Samovar Restaurant, which was run by a good friend of Grandma Tattie's and felt like "home," at least for a few pleasant hours.

Russian restaurants tended to have the heat turned high, even in summer, and that, mixed with the exotic aromas coming from the kitchen, made it a special place. Over in the corner, a man dressed like a Cossack began to sing a familiar folk song while strumming his odd, triangular balalaika. Nearby, a waiter poured black tea from an elaborate samovar placed on an ornate buffet table, for which the restaurant was named.

"Kind of brings back old memories, doesn't it?" Grandma Tattie started the conversation. "When you were a little girl, you always wanted to sing along with the musicians."

"Oh, how embarrassing."

"You were so cute, *Dasha moia.*"

I couldn't help but chuckle. After a long moment of silence, I looked up to see a shadow cross my grandmother's face, but she quickly recovered.

"Grandma Tattie, what is it? You said you wanted to speak to me about something."

Before she could begin, the waiter took our order, and I went with a tried-and-true favorite, Russian *borscht* accompanied by *pirozhki*—small pastry pockets filled with meat. Secretly, I wondered if it might taste different from the ones we'd eaten in 1918 Moscow during their great famine. And yet, Alex always made our dining experience fun, rarely complaining about the food, although I couldn't blame him for bringing up the potato pancakes constantly.

Across from me, Grandmother sipped tea from a china cup delicate enough to have belonged to Tsarina Alexandra. I never noticed before how impeccable Tattie's manners were, but then she was a classy lady, even when running after her tiny ballet babies.

"I heard through the grapevine you are considering taking a trip with Alex. What do your parents think of that? Do they approve of him?"

I set down my tea. "Oh, you misunderstand. We're not traveling *together*." I laughed, planning to explain it was just business, only not the usual kind. I couldn't give away too much, and yet, Grandma Tattie was familiar with the Time Menders. Should I just blurt it out and deal with even more questions? Even better, I could pivot...fast.

"Grandma Tattie, you've never told me much about your time at the Time Menders."

Grandmother filled her teacup again and signaled the waiter to bring another hot teapot. She smiled and cocked her head. "You're changing the subject, aren't you? Well, before I answer you, do you still have the green evening gloves?"

I tried to remember where I'd hidden them, but I also didn't want to give her a chance to go through my messy closet. "Yes, they're someplace safe. Why do you ask?"

"People have different methods for becoming involved in time travel. You must remember to use the same object to travel and return. Something that ties you to your home and place. Clothes and jewelry are favorable conductors. Alex knows all this, and should be a good guide."

"When's the last time you time-traveled? And how come we never knew about it before now?"

"The ability to time travel has always been with us. The organization and management of time and space, not so much." She leaned down and took several sips of her borscht, then dabbed her lips with a cloth napkin. "The Bureau of Time Menders was established to monitor procedures and practices for our permanent agents so they may correct and monitor ATTO, our competitor, which has a bad tendency to make things worse for those affected by tweaks in history. Our agents know our first priority is to keep them safe, and they are paid well so their loyalty is never in question."

I wondered how much Alex earned, not that it mattered or was any of my business. It could certainly answer questions about his lack of concern for funding. The appropriate clothing for one mission alone must cost quite a bundle.

Grandma Tattie finished her *borscht* and reached for the last of her *pirozhki.*

The waiter appeared and began to gather empty dishes. "May I interest you ladies in dessert today? Our Russian honey cake is quite special. It consists of thin layers of honey-infused sponge cake, each layer separated by a rich sour cream filling. The cake absorbs moisture from the filling, resulting in a wonderful sweetness and mild tangy flavor."

"Oh, you had me at dessert." Grandma Tattie laughed. "Dasha?"

My mouth salivated like Pavlov's dog. "I wouldn't miss that for the world."

The waiter left to dispose of the dishes, and when he returned with our dessert plates, I don't think I uttered more than an "oh, yumm!" for about five minutes, while I demolished the cake.

Grandma Tattie smiled and reached for her purse. "Now, if you *are* planning a trip with Alex, I want you to listen to what he says and do what he asks of you. He'll keep you safe. Can you promise me that?"

I chuckled, happy and full of honey cake. "Sure. No problem." I'd say yes to anything while chewing that honey cake.

She paid the bill, and I noticed her stop at the dessert display case to take home two pieces of the honey cake. "Your mother loves this cake, but she rarely indulges. Maybe this will entice her. I'll give the second piece to your father."

She picked up the pink bakery box containing the cake pieces, and then turned to go. Unfortunately, I wasn't paying much attention and bumped into the back of Grandma Tattie when she stopped abruptly. As a result, I found myself staring at a woman sitting alone at a small table for two near the window. When the woman turned, I saw that she had an aura that surrounded her head and shoulders, announcing to the world that she was extraordinarily beautiful. It would be impossible to miss those bright amber eyes, nor the fact that she was smiling at Grandma Tattie.

Grandma stiffened and pushed the outside door open. When we reached the sidewalk, I stopped and put a hand on her arm, noting her pallor.

"Who was that lady, Grandma? Do you know her?"

Grandma Tattie's lips tightened and she closed her eyes. "Sin. I haven't heard that name in years. Her name is Sin Ryland, and she's a very dangerous woman."

I refused to let Grandma Tattie's uncharacteristically emotional announcement slide. That afternoon, after hearing her words and seeing the anguished look on my grandmother's face, I found it almost impossible to focus when I returned to work. Frustrated, I took off early and caught a cab out front of the building. I headed straight for home. Once there, I went from room to room, and for the first time, the details of our family life warmed my heart rather than stressed me out. Gigi was at soccer practice, according to the schedule on the refrigerator. I glanced at the clock and realized Mom must have driven her there and sat through practice. Sasha was working the afternoon shift at Araminta's Vintage Clothing, and Wednesday was Rosana's day off, so she'd left a casserole in the refrigerator. I'm ashamed to say I knew little about what Dad did as a corporate CEO, but whatever he did left me with enough time to drink tea in the kitchen with Grandma Tattie.

For once, I was glad we had the whole house to ourselves so I could get the lowdown on Sin. Grandma Tattie pushed her stool up to the counter and dunked her teabag several times before launching in.

"Sin came to the Duquette Ballet Company right about the time I retired from dancing to become a teacher to some of the newer girls. Right from the start, she was arrogant and condescending, and insisted she be given a lead part in our latest production of Swan Lake. It wasn't the company's policy to just hand over a star role like that for a new dancer, and an untried one at that. I told her she had to earn the part and gain the trust of the staff."

Grandma pushed the plate of Rosana's oatmeal cookies toward me.

"She went crazy, yelling and screaming because she couldn't have her way. She even used some very creative curse words, as well, things I've never been called before.

I picked up a cookie and smiled when I noticed it had chocolate chips in it instead of raisins. Rosana was the best baker, outside of those at Samovars, and even better, she was like one of the family.

I turned my attention back to Grandma. "So, was that the end of her temper tantrum?"

"Hardly. Every week, she came to my office and asked the same question. And every week, I gave her the same answer. She was eventually given the understudy role for the Black Swan, which I will admit she earned. She practiced and practiced, almost twenty-four hours a day."

"What happened that makes you call her 'dangerous'?"

Tillie chose that moment to announce her entrance with a resentful meow. Grandma put some food in Tillie's little pink dish and then straightened her back, an odd look on her face, as if despite all these years, summoning this information caused her great pain.

"One day, after a particularly brutal practice, I left the studio and saw two girls arguing at the end of the hallway. A dark-haired girl held something against the other girl's throat. I knew the dark-headed girl had to be Sin. I recognized the other girl as our lead, Ceara Donovan. She was a sweet, soft-spoken Irish-American girl, and she didn't deserve that kind of assault. At first I couldn't see what was happening, but when she screamed, I dropped everything and rushed down the hall."

"What was she doing?"

"Sin was holding a martial arts baton against Ceara's throat, then decided to aim for Ceara's right knee. When Sin saw me, she grinned. It was really strange. 'Sinovia! No!' I shouted. She must have been distracted for just that brief second, because she missed Ceara's knee, but whacked her thigh. I pulled her away and told Ceara to find the director. She limped away, but thankfully, obeyed. We struggled, and Sin managed to land a few blows on me as well, but I was able to protect myself."

My mouth fell open as I stared at my grandmother. "A martial arts baton?"

Grandma let a small smile show. "Isn't that the wildest thing? And at a ballet studio? It turns out Sin had quite a personal collection of small weapons in her locker, which the police found during their investigation."

"What happened to Ceara?"

"When the police arrived, Sin wasn't making any sense. She was spitting and practically frothing at the mouth." Grandma licked her lips and sipped more water. "We rescheduled the performance so Ceara's leg had plenty of time to heal. It was a deep bruise, but not broken, fortunately. Sin was convicted of assault, and did her time in a psychiatric facility. That's why I was so surprised to see her. I didn't realize she'd been released."

I grabbed onto the counter, feeling sick to my stomach. "That's absolutely horrible. You could have been seriously hurt! Or killed. She sounds like she belongs in jail."

Grandma Tattie pulled me up from my stool and opened her arms, embracing me for a moment. "I've tried to stay away from people like Sin and focus on my life with you girls and the baby ballerinas."

When she let go of me, her eyes sparked with determination. "I've heard rumors that Sin has relatives in the Middle East who were trained by their military to kill. That's why she's so dangerous. She could show up just about anywhere, at any time. And she knows way too many ways to kill."

I looked away so she wouldn't see tears gathering. "So, this wacko lady and her family could...what? Come after you?"

She shrugged. "Anything is possible with Sin."

I rubbed my temples, pondering what she'd said.

Seeing how upset I was becoming, Grandma Tattie changed the subject. "*Dashenka*, one last word on Alex. If you decide to accompany him on his mission, you must look out for each other as a team. But, you must also look out for yourself...for me. For our family."

I processed all this new information, trying to make order out of it. I felt like I was getting mixed messages. But that was Grandma Tattie. She must have her reasons.

Relieved to put Sin behind us for the moment, I said, "If the Time Menders are the good guys, as you suggest, then that means ATTO agents are the bad guys. How bad are they?"

I felt naive asking, but I needed details so I knew what I would be getting myself into. Grandma Tattie seemed to understand, because she took me in her arms once again.

"ATTO agents will bend the rules and shape their own laws. Sin may have the darkest heart of them all, but I wouldn't bet money on it. They will kill if it suits their purpose, and if it means they reach their goal faster. Rarely do they negotiate. Alex will drill this into your head: you must not let them capture you. If that happens, there are no guarantees we can find you, let alone rescue you."

My heart sank as I took all that in.

"And Dasha," Grandma Tattie continued, "at times, making the determination about who's the good guy, who is bad, will be a challenge. If you join BTM, you will come across people like Sin. You have good instincts, Dasha. Use them."

We had wandered as far as the living room, and I sank onto the couch, any thoughts of food vanished.

"*Bábushka*, what was the very last thing Sin said to you as she was taken away after the attack at the ballet studio?"

Grandma Tattie ran a hand down the side of her face. "She was black-balled in the ballet community. My guess is she is bi-polar and perhaps a bit of a psychopath. No one would consider taking her on, except ATTO, who saw her passion for hurting others as a skill in their book of tricks. She said I ruined her life by arranging for a car to hit her in a crosswalk. Which is absolutely ridiculous. In her misery, she said she would someday take her revenge on me. And my family."

I grabbed a pillow off the sofa and hugged it to my stomach. "With everything you've told me about Sin and ATTO, I don't know what to do," I finally said.

Exhausted, Grandma picked up Tillie and gave her a hug.

"I want you to say no. Stay here with me." She combed my hair back with her fingers. "You're my special one, Dasha. I want to keep you safe. But you're also a grownup now, so it's your decision about whether you want to go with Alex or not. As for Sin, just remember, if you ever run across her again, no matter what she says to you, you're to stay away from her. She is a master manipulator and a pathological liar. Never forget that."

I slumped back onto the sofa, more confused than ever. It occurred to me that being Grandma Tattie's favorite granddaughter might not be all it was cracked up to be.

Chapter 23

*"The Empress offers abundance, and material comfort,
sensuality and security, and emotional support.
(Tarot Card: The Empress)*

"We've had agents combing Russian Hill and the Richmond District for Rasputin the past two days," said Alex, as we stood in my backyard. It was another warm day, and he wiped the perspiration from his forehead.

"What do you think he's doing there?" I asked, my mind on filling the hummingbird feeder that hung strategically above grass-like clumps of reddish-orange crocosmia blossoms that the tiny birds adored.

"A BTM agent says he's a real talker. Talks to himself all the time. Kind of like checking on his own progress. He told a shopkeeper he plans on relocating here soon."

My heart jumped. Calmly, I finished with the birdfeeder and turned back to Alex. "Can he legally do that?"

"Not without the right papers."

I sat down at the long patio table and indicated Alex should sit. It was the hottest day of the summer so far, and I had opted for jean shorts and a white linen blouse over a blue tank top. It was not the most professional outfit I owned, but I'd had no idea Alex would drop by unannounced.

"I appreciate you taking the time to talk to me without much notice," he said. "I..." He paused as I crossed my bare legs and reached for the glass of lemonade Rosana had brought out moments ago.

I pointed at the glass I'd poured for him. "You look thirsty."

"You look amazing."

I smiled sweetly. "Focus, Alex. I'm sure there's a rule you're breaking with your eyes." I laughed. "Do you know where Grisha is right now? I don't recall you placing a tracking device on him."

Alex took a long sip of lemonade. "He doesn't wear a lot of clothes, and he seldom bathes. However, we got lucky last night. He stayed at a fleabag motel that had a pool. An agent tagged his left sandal inside the rubber. I don't know how long it will last, but it's all we've got." He watched Gigi and her friend, Rani, for a moment as they played fetch with Rani's Corgi, Zowie.

For a brief second, I wondered what Alex would say if I told him I talked to a ghost dog. And two ancestor ghosts who died in the 1906 earthquake.

"We really need to get going. We got word that Katya's meeting Rasputin tonight to exchange something."

"Do you think he's blackmailing her?"

Alex shrugged and chugged the rest of his lemonade. "Why don't you go in and change. Put on something you might wear inside a nice restaurant. If you don't have anything, I have a dress in the trunk—"

"I have nice clothes." Offended at his words, I rose from the table and handed him the rest of my lemonade. "I'll meet you on the porch in..." I glanced at my phone. "Twenty minutes."

He grinned. "Can't wait to see this."

I walked right by him, gently brushing his shoulder with mine. At that moment, I think we both knew we'd crossed some unspoken line.

Things were going well, so Grisha decided he had time for pleasure in addition to his ATTO business. He began exploring San Francisco on foot, and had been astonished to discover a part of San Francisco called Russian Hill. That day, he visited almost every shop, restaurant, and Russian Orthodox Church he came across. Who knew the United States of America would build and sustain a place that welcomed all Russian people?

When he stopped to speak to shopkeepers and restaurant owners, they were more than glad to exercise their Russian language skills to share the history of Russians in Grisha's soon-to-be newly adopted home. Everyone had an opinion or advice on where to live.

He had to admit he'd neither expected a welcome at the Russian churches nor received one. He wore only his dirty white gown, which now bore new stains from Bubba Gump's Shrimp Company. In truth, he'd never been ordained in the Church that supported the Czar, so he never received a rich red, brocaded priest's robe. He was an imposter, so it was just as well.

He paused at the bottom of the famed Russian Hill at Lombard Street. True enough, the street zig-zagged back and forth all the way to the top. He wanted to see the ocean view from there. Just one more thing to tell his three children and his long-suffering wife when he returned home.

Oh, right. He couldn't return to Russia. Not until he finished making money. Would people here be willing to be hypnotized and have their futures told? He should have asked Katya, whom he'd invited for breakfast in order to discuss his diary. From what he could tell, superstition was not an everyday thing here. People were too busy for fortunetellers. He had, however, managed to steal a twenty-dollar bill from an old lady at the grocery store, who left her handbag open and unattended while she talked to the produce person. He figured she deserved it if she was that naïve.

During his satisfying visit with Katya that morning, she'd shared pieces of a boxed white and pink candy called Good 'n Plenty. He had a new vice now and took one out of his pocket and popped it into his mouth. He then lifted the ragged hem of his priest's gown and started the long walk to the top. He realized right away how out of shape he'd become. Wheezing, he made it to the fifth switchback and paused to catch his breath. He smiled and waved at an old woman who swept the doorway of her small hair salon. She said something in Russian, but he didn't catch it. He smiled and waved again as if he'd heard just fine, and she returned to her sweeping.

He was glad he and Katya had come to a kind of understanding that morning. He'd ordered a tall stack of pancakes, and finished the entire breakfast that also featured sausage and eggs. It had been a celebration of sorts, but he reminded himself to start his diet the next day. That evening, Katya planned to meet him at the top of Lombard Street at a little bistro, and he smacked his lips at the thought of another delicious meal. He'd choose steak this time. He wanted to see it rare, blood filling the plate. He could never get enough meat with the war shortages back in Russia. If the restaurant didn't serve steak, Italian pasta always hit the spot.

By the time he reached the halfway point, Grisha was beginning to feel odd. Assuming it was heartburn, he revised his expectations for dinner. Californians seemed to consume tons of lettuce and salad greens. Perhaps he should eat more like that, at least twice a week. Maybe once was all he needed. He took pride in his strength, so seldom thought about the paunch he'd developed. When he felt his chest constrict with pain on the left side, he paused and placed his hand there, massaging gently.

He looked up and saw four more zigzags left to maneuver, certain he could make it. He was strong. At forty-seven, he was still young, or so he thought until now. Sure, he'd begun to lose some of his long, flowing hair, aging not a kind companion. He finally reached the top, still gripping his chest, a tight pressure making him lightheaded. He struggled for one breath, then two, and sat on the top step, gasping for air.

People stood in line to enter the restaurant. He could see Katya, who waved from her spot about ten people from the front. "Grisha, over here!"

He tried to smile, but his face felt frozen, his body weak. They'd had such a lovely breakfast together. Katya had explained her anger over her father's death. Grisha had admitted to spinning who did what in his diary. Katya just wanted to hear him say her father, Stepan, was not a bad man who sold out his community. But now, she appeared alarmed by his condition, and forfeited her place in line to come to his aid. Although Grisha wasn't sure if Katya believed his story, he decided it didn't matter if she was willing to help him now. A waitperson came with a glass of ice water, and she asked if Grisha was suffering heat stroke.

"That must be what this is," he said, ignoring the pain in his left arm.

"Stop here!" I yelled.

Alex pulled his car into a suddenly vacant parking spot about halfway up Lombard Street. "Are you sure?"

I checked Alex's phone tracker. "The little cursor stopped moving."

We both looked up at the top, and saw a crowd gathering around someone lying on the ground.

"Oh, my gosh, Alex. Is that Grisha? And Katya on his right, in the red dress?"

Alex pulled out mini binoculars and watched for several moments. He glanced back at her. "It is. We have two choices. Wait and deal with the police."

"What's the second choice?"

"Deal with Sin. She's still in the picture, whether Grisha or Katya know it or not. We can't take our eyes off her. Not for a minute."

My heart pounded. "This is not good. What do we do? We should go see how they're doing. Maybe it's going to be okay."

Alex calmly put away his binoculars. "It's not going to be okay if Rasputin is still alive. That's not even a Time Mender decision. It's the law of nature."

I looked at him, bewildered, and started to climb Lombard Street in my high heels and mini-skirt. When I reached the top, Katya was on the ground, holding Rasputin's head in her lap. The look of anguish on her face said it all—horror at his actions, sadness at his shortcomings. I don't know about her, but I felt bad for his poor wife. Katya turned to me with dry eyes, registering her shock.

While Katya had her head turned toward me, I helped her up so she didn't see Alex slip what I assumed was a fake I.D. into the leather pouch around Rasputin's waist. With his other hand, Alex removed the tracker device from the sandal, and dropped it into his pocket. I'd forgotten those items needed to be retrieved if we intended to avoid questioning, which I assume was the plan.

Alex knelt and touched two fingers to Grisha's pulse. He was in the process of smelling his breath just as an officer arrived on the scene.

"What have we got here?" asked the officer.

"It appears to be a heart attack," Alex responded, glancing at the crowd, hands on hips.

"Sir, is this man a family member? Acquaintance?"

"We barely knew him," said Alex. "He didn't speak much English, but I know he came from a Slavic country. He said his name was Oleg."

I paid attention to Alex's words, how much information he provided, and how much he didn't. That should keep the police busy for a few days before they gave up. The officer shuffled off to confer with colleagues, but seemed in no hurry with a dead body lying there.

"Katya," I said gently. "Were your questions about the diary answered to your satisfaction?"

She sniffed and lowered her head. "I don't know if he told me what he *thought* I wanted to hear. I just don't know.

Katya rose and took my arm. "I'm all alone here..."

The ambulance arrived. They quickly put Rasputin on a stretcher and took him to the nearest hospital. I turned to Alex.

"Who's going to tell the morgue they're dealing with Grigori Rasputin...who died almost a hundred years ago?"

Alex looked away, clearly uncomfortable. "These are the things I hate to explain. No one will believe us." The crowd was beginning to dissipate, and he sighed.

"Please don't leave me here alone," Katya pleaded.

"Why are you so frightened?" I asked, curious.

Katya looked from me to Alex and blinked. "Sin is the one who brought me here. She says she wants to mentor me...at ATTO. She thinks Rasputin told me where Anastasia is located."

"Has he?" Alex asked.

Katya shook her head no. "He never said a word. But Sin...I think she may try to force the information from me. And I haven't a clue. Do *you* know where Ana is?"

Alex stared at Katya, and I didn't like the look he gave her, hard and calculating.

I put an arm around Katya's shoulders and addressed Alex. "Will an agent claim the body so it can be disposed of quietly?"

"Yes," he answered. "That would be standard BTM protocol. I'll do that now." He walked on the other side of Katya as we descended the hill toward the car.

I realized I was starting to like Katya, and sincerely hoped he wouldn't use force to find out the answer to the million-dollar question.

Where is Ana Romanov?

Chapter 24

"This is a time when past errors or imbalances can be redressed.
You benefit from a fair system, provided you are accountable,
honest, and deserving."
(Tarot Card: Justice)

Sin didn't trust Alex. And Dasha was an unknown quantity. And she *really* wasn't fond of hospital morgues, which is where she found herself at St. Francis Hospital after hearing the news about Rasputin. She stayed out of Alex and Dasha's view as they spoke to a doctor, their footsteps echoing further down the hallway. If she was going to formulate a Plan B, she needed to be alone.

Sinovia Ryland, or "Sin," as she'd been called all her life, prided herself on her patience and persistence. She had more than enough of it now, as she stood with her hands behind her against a cold concrete wall and sniffed the antiseptic air. She saw her breath, and from across the room and into where the forensic doctors worked, she could almost feel the stainless steel tables with patients in various phases of decomposition. It felt as if she was experiencing that day at the ballet with Tatiana Marusov and Ceara Donovan all over again, the cold metal baton.

Sin blinked to regain her focus. *Don't you dare flake out on me, girly!*

For days, she hadn't heard from Rasputin, so she'd staked out local hospitals and morgues. Just in case. She knew she'd hit the jackpot when she saw the name "Oleg Slobotkin" in the obituary section of today's newspaper. It was a fake name assigned to the priest by ATTO several years ago to alert the Russian and American Secret Services of the physical demise of Grigori Rasputin. A man no one seemed able to kill.

She chuckled at the irony. The newspaper said he'd climbed all the way up Lombard Street, the fool. Now, with him dead and out of the picture, she'd have to coerce the information she wanted from Alex, Katya or Dasha, if Dasha even knew Ana's whereabouts. She'd put her money on Katya. And Katya had a huge grudge against the BTM. Sin had to make it so Katya couldn't walk away.

She seated herself on the cold, uncomfortable bench and reached for a scented handkerchief in her handbag then held it to her nose to avoid the smells of death.

There had been rumors that ATTO would offer a huge reward for anyone who knew Anastasia Romanov's location. As an active member of the Anti-Time Travelers Oversight, Sin knew that if she were to locate Ana, it was up to her to keep the flames of animosity bright against the family responsible for Katya's father's downfall.

Poor girl never even met her own father.

Normally aware of her immediate environment when she was on assignment, Sin felt the shock of surprise when she heard footsteps and then someone sat down on the plastic seat next to her. A girl wearing a long, flowing skirt with botanical flowers on a white background, and an embroidered lacy sage-colored peasant blouse. Sin immediately recognized the woman's old-fashioned lavender perfume and lowered her newspaper.

"Katya. Don't you look fetching. What are you doing here? I said *I'd* contact *you*."

Katya turned to glance at the open room where Rasputin lay. "I heard about...Grisha. I wanted to pay my respects."

"Where did you hear it?"

"Street people. They're saying—""He had a heart attack. But you were there when it happened, yes?"

Katya's naturally dark skin tone appeared a bit gray this morning as she nodded.

"Well, it looks like BTM wins this round. Let's go work on the next," said Sin.

"Aren't we going to ask Alex where Ana went?"

Sin hesitated and frowned. "You don't know?"

Katya held up her hand and crossed her heart. "I swear I do not."

"But if you remember something later, you'll tell me?"

"Definitely." Katya glanced around, coughing at the smells. "Can we leave this place now?"

Sin tried not to show her disappointment. Katya, she could beat. Alex was a whole other opponent. As a former administrator with the BTM, it only made sense that Dasha's grandmother had filled her granddaughter in with the latest information on the Anastasia assignment. It would be near impossible to get Tattie alone, but Sin held onto that as her final option, if necessary.

"You don't wish to stay here?" Sin rose gracefully. "That's okay, my dear. I've decided that you and I are going to host a party at my hotel tonight. Did you bring along anything with a bit more va-va-va-voom?"

Katya looked at her with huge hazel eyes, then down at her peasant clothes. "What does that mean, va-va-va-voom?"

Sin placed an arm around Katya's shoulder, making sure Alex and Dasha were busy with the doctor and wouldn't notice them leave. Then, she smiled and escorted Katya to the elevator up to the main lobby. "You are about to find out, tonight. My treat."

Two men, one on either side of the elevator doors, gave an imperceptible nod to Sin as she swept into the elevator like a flamboyant movie star, waving her feather boa.

As I listened to Alex talk while he went about his job, I paid particular attention to how he worded his questions to the doctor at St. Francis Hospital regarding Rasputin's death. It occurred to me how lucky I was to have him as my teacher for Time Mender duties. He had a way about him that was diplomatic, yet firm, and people generally responded well to him.

Normally, as civilians, we would never have been allowed access to the morgue, or to meet with the pathologist. But once Alex waved his BTM badge, we had his complete attention. The doctor said that from all appearances, Rasputin did indeed die from a heart attack.

The pungent smell of decay almost gagged me, despite the cold air circulating through the vents. Shiny stainless steel tables where autopsies were performed left behind a lingering disinfectant odor.

"I did find some evidence of calcified arteries. Did Mr. Slobotkin exhibit any other symptoms of heart disease? Did it run in his family?" the medical examiner inquired.

I started, then remembered the fake I.D. Alex had planted on Rasputin. I glanced at him to respond.

"I don't know, doctor. He was a visitor, so none of us really knew Mr. Slobotkin."

"Ah, that's unfortunate. Since it was a hot, humid day, and he *did* eat a big meal, then climb to the top of Lombard Street, I'm going to list a heart attack as cause of death, perhaps exacerbated by the heat and humidity. Does he have any next of kin here in the States?"

I felt the sweat gather on my forehead. I was right on the cusp of mentioning Rasputin's fascination with Good 'n Plentys, and asking if that could be a contributing factor. But Alex said nothing, and I trusted his instincts, so I remained silent. It did, however, plant a seed of doubt in my mind regarding Katya. How far could she be trusted?

We took the elevator back up to the main floor and parted ways, pleased to have a free afternoon. We'd been invited to a low-key get-together at Sin's hotel, but we didn't need to be there until 8:00 p.m. Katya would meet us there. Sin had told Alex over the phone that she had some "negotiating" to do, then laughed. When I asked Alex what she meant, he simply shrugged, unconcerned.

As the day progressed, I concentrated on what to wear. Sin liked costumes and dress-up, so I assumed she would wear something fashionable from the 1920s. I rushed over to Sasha's shop and found a dress that had made its debut in a Hollywood movie in 1936.

"Oh, you need this outfit!" said Sasha, fussing over the deep periwinkle dress that fell to my knees. "I'm sure I have earrings to match that color. Oh, and beads! We mustn't forget the beads." She grabbed three ropes of pearls, each in a different length, and practically strangled me as she threw them on me.

We headed for home and I started getting ready with Sasha's help. I'd had time for a quick 30-minute nap after the shopping trip, so I was feeling refreshed and ready to end this assignment as quickly as possible.

As Sasha finished pinning long, shiny strawberry blonde locks into place so sections framed my face, and then added the makeup, which I seldom wore, I noticed my hands start to tremble. The way I saw it, I had nothing to contribute in regard to Ana's whereabouts. Not really. We were down to Alex and Katya knowing something about Ana. If we hit rock bottom on that, would Sin start beating it out of us? After all, Grandma Tattie had told me that awful story about Sin hitting a fellow ballerina with a metal baton. She was no stranger to violence.

"Come on. Let's go downstairs and show Grandma Tattie your new outfit." Sasha put away her makeup case.

Five minutes later, we entered the living room and took our usual places on the couch and sectional lounge, where Sasha picked up Tillie so she could give her a good chin rub.

"Dasha, there's no point being nervous about tonight. My guess is that Alex and Sin will do all the talking. Think of yourself as eye candy for your date." Sasha patted me on the back and returned to caressing Tillie's long summer coat.

"Sasha's probably right," added Grandma Tattie. "If Sin mentioned the word negotiation, that must mean she already knows the location she's seeking. Alex will try to squeeze it out of her so you two can get to Ana first to warn her, if need be."

In the quiet afternoon, all I could hear was the grandfather clock at the bottom of the staircase. A shiver ran down my spine, and I had the strangest premonition that Sin knew almost nothing, and was toying with us. After all, she could simply be on a fishing expedition. I would have to be super careful about what I said in her presence.

Alex will be there. He'll take care of you.

I looked down and unconsciously pulled on the skirt of the vintage dress I'd purchased at Sasha's shop. Made in 1936, the periwinkle confection of a dress was daring and innocent at the same time.

"Don't pull on the fabric," Sasha warned. "Gee, I wonder what movie they used this dress in? What was popular in 1936, Grandma Tattie?"

Grandma Tattie set down her knitting project. "That's ten years before I was born, Sashenka. I could take a guess, I suppose."

Gigi beat them both by looking on the Internet. "I don't see mention or photo of a bright purple dress, Sasha, but the film that won the Best Picture Oscar was *The Great Ziegfeld* with William Powell and Myrna Loy."

"Good use of the Internet," Sasha joked. "What else came out in 1936?"

Gigi narrowed her eyes and squinted at a list. "*My Man Godfrey. Mr. Deeds Goes to Town...*"

Grandma Tattie picked up her knitting once more, whatever it was supposed to be...mittens? It was a luscious shade of mint green. "When will Alex be here to pick you up?"

I chewed on the end of a perfect deep rose nail. "Seven-thirty. What time is it now?"

"Stop that or you'll ruin your nails!" Sasha leaned close to check out my long chandelier earrings in silver and sleek gray pearls. "Those earrings look fabulous, don't you think, Grandma Tattie?"

"Yes, indeed. Why don't you girls run upstairs and pick out your lipstick, Dasha. That's the only thing I see missing on my lovely granddaughter." She glanced at the time. "Hurry, Alex is due any minute now."

We raced up to my room, where Sasha quickly tutored Gigi on what the colors of lipstick meant, just like flowers. She tried on all of them, while I stuck with *Starlight in Flight.* As I sat at my vanity, I pondered what kind of mood Alex would be in tonight. I didn't want to say anything and appear as if I had expectations for romance. It was a working date.

"So, has Alex kissed you yet?" Gigi managed to ask, the little squirt.

"Gigi, that's personal. You too, Sasha!"

"It's no big deal. I think it's healthy and means you're returning to the land of the living."

I sighed loudly. "How do I look?"

Sasha stood behind me so I could see the full effect in the mirror. She'd wound my long straight hair artfully around my head. As she did, the earrings tinkled.

"Just one last thing."

"What?"

Sasha adjusted the collar of the dress so it skimmed the tops of my breasts. "Perfect. Alex won't be able to resist you tonight."

I frowned and pulled the neckline up to a more comfortable position.

A knock on the door made my heart pound. Grandma Tattie stood there, holding out a note sealed in an envelope. As I stared at what was in her trembling hand, I felt as if my whole world was turning upside down. Where was Alex?

"What's that?" I asked, even though it was obvious.

"A messenger just brought this from Ms. Ryland's hotel. He said Alex isn't available to escort you tonight. You're to come alone."

I took the note and tore it open. I scanned the brief contents and looked at myself once more in the mirror.

"Is it from Sin?" asked Sasha. "Did she say why Alex isn't coming? And why can't you just postpone?"

"Oh, I don't like the sound of this," said Grandma Tattie. "I don't trust Sin one little bit. I can't let you go alone, Dasha."

I glanced at myself in the mirror and shook my head. "I have to go, Grandma Tattie. The note says there's something Sin wants us to know. And she's counting on me to be there. She said something about reward money. I have to find out what this is about." I grabbed my black purse and matching raincoat because I didn't have a sweater to go over the dress. "Tell Marcos he'll need to drive me to the Fairmont on Mason Street and escort me to and from Sin's suite. I won't be all alone then. Have him meet me in front with the car. We'll just have to be late."

"Are you absolutely sure, Dasha, my love?" Grandma Tattie fretted. "Remember not to say or do anything that will make Sin lose her temper. She's not in her right mind when she's upset." Grandma Tattie enveloped me in the circle of her arms.

"I promise."

"You be very, very careful, Dasha. You hear me? You know, I can throw on something decent and accompany you."

I gave her a quick hug. "I have to do this myself, Grandma Tattie. I owe Alex a rescue or two. Please don't worry about me."

I didn't give her time to argue as I hurried to my closet, grabbed my tote bag and threw in clean underwear, socks, sneakers, jeans and a T-shirt. And for good measure, the green-sequined evening gloves.

If Alex was in trouble somewhere, I was going to rescue him.

Chapter 25

*"Conflict is part of relationships, however, this also
implies ill intent behind the conflict. Ensure that you
or your partner are not manipulating the situation."*
(Tarot Card: Five of Swords)

I didn't use a driver very often, unless the weather was bad. It was Grandma Tattie's idea that showing up in my dad's dark blue Audi with a chauffeur may earn us some respect. As I sat in the back seat, planning what I would say to keep this meeting short and sweet, Marcos pulled out of our driveway and entered traffic on Market Street. After several blocks of silence, I gazed out the window and sighed loudly.

Marcos glanced in the rearview mirror. "You're usually a bit more talkative, Ms. Marusov. Is everything alright?"

The rich timbre of Marcos' voice broke through my distracted thoughts. We didn't have enough business for a permanent chauffeur, but Marcos was always glad to fill in when he could. As the son of Rosana, our cook, Marcos Vela was a quiet man, who had recently completed two tours of duty in Afghanistan. At twenty-eight, he did whatever odd job he could find while pursuing a master's degree in astronomy. Brilliant, bold, and beautiful. That's how Rosana proudly described her eldest son. And she was right to brag. He'd turned into a fine young man. He hadn't been around much since he'd graduated college and enlisted, so I didn't know him very well, but a certain calm presence about him reminded me of Sasha.

I looked into the rearview mirror and smiled. "Sorry, my mind was elsewhere. I'm a bit nervous. I'd feel better if Alex McKain was here."

Marcos nodded, his sparkling brown eyes appearing serious. "Your grandmother told me to stick to you like glue tonight. Are you expecting trouble?"

I thought about my suspicions for a moment before answering. "The person holding the costume party, Sinovia Ryland, is a bit of a mystery."

At the drop of her name, Marcos' dark brows rose a fraction for a brief moment before returning to normal.

"Did Grandma Tattie mention you needed to escort me both to and from the party?" I asked, to be sure of my return status.

"Yes, she did. Are you okay with that?"

My nose twitched. How could I say this without offending him? "I'm so used to Alex these days, but I guess something came up." I glanced out the window at the city lights. "Though if ever there was a back-up person I trusted, it would be you, Marcos."

He ducked his head. "Thank you, Ms. Marusov."

"Call me Dasha."

"Perhaps after the party is over and you are safe at home." We smiled at each other in the mirror.

We pulled up to the front entrance of the Fairmont, the nicest hotel located on Nob Hill, which had officially opened in 1907, a year after the earthquake. A valet rushed over to park the car, then Marcus offered me an arm, and we headed inside and straight for the elevators. I glanced at my watch, noting we were about thirty minutes late.

"Sorry if it took me some time to clean up," Marcos said, making conversation as he entered the elevator after me, and pushed the "penthouse" button.

"No need to apologize. Considering we gave you almost no notice, this fashionably late entrance should turn out just fine."

He nodded as the elevator ascended, stopping at the top floor. Slowly, the doors opened. We left the elevator and walked to the end of the hall, taking our time. When we stood before the penthouse suite, I patted my hair in place, then nodded at Marcos, butterflies flitting about in my stomach. At last, I gave him the OK signal, and he knocked firmly on the door.

Sin stopped to take one last look at the Fairmont's superb penthouse suite before answering the door. It was ridiculously big for any one person, but she preferred to live the rules of excess in everything she did.

Katya had arrived at the party alone, still insisting she knew nothing of Anastasia's whereabouts. However, Sin suspected she was waiting to see which way the wind blew for the reward money mentioned in Rasputin's diary. Sin smiled and ignored her, certain that money would be *hers*. She was the one who had sacrificed everything for her ballet career all those years ago. All because of Tatiana Marusov.

Before Sin's guests had arrived, she'd paced and stewed, while Katya had watched old episodes of *Dancing with the Stars* while shuffling her tarot cards and silently doing her own readings. Sin was convinced Katya was playing cat and mouse about Ana's whereabouts. She absolutely *must* know where Ana was hiding.

Sin had been in the middle of scolding her two hired men about the placement of a huge display case in the middle of the living room when she'd heard the firm knock on the front door.

She stopped one last time to check her hair and makeup in the hallway mirror before opening the penthouse door wide, while still giving orders over her shoulder to her two Farsi-speaking hired men, Faakhir and Haamid. Her cousin, Mitra, had done the catering, and had provided an amazing array of Persian appetizers and hors d'oeuvres that filled the buffet table. Sin waved a hand in dismissal at the men and pivoted to Dasha and Marcos in front of her.

"Greetings! Welcome, and please enter," she said, hoping she sounded formal and classy.

Dasha nodded. "I'm Dasha Marusov, Tatiana Marusov's granddaughter. I don't think we've officially met."

"Yes, of course," said Sin, not reaching to shake her hand. "Tatiana's eldest granddaughter." She studied Marcos. "I see you got my message about Alex."

Dasha frowned. "Yes. It was brief. Where is he? Is he alright?"

"He's fine. Some kind of business he had to deal with tonight. He may still show up. We shall see." She turned to Dasha's escort. "And *who* are *you*, handsome stranger?"

Dasha bristled and held onto Marcos' arm tightly. "This is Marcos Vela, a friend of the family. I asked him to fill in for Alex, so he's my guest," I said, daring her to flirt her way into Marcos' good graces.

"Well, welcome, Marcos. Help yourself to the appetizers." Glad to be able to speak to Dasha in private, Sin turned and regarded Dasha's outfit as Marcos headed for the buffet table. "Lovely dress. It looks so svelte and beautiful on you. Is the color of your dress blue or purple?"

Dasha looked down. "It's called periwinkle, after the flower." She straightened her shoulders as if preparing for a fight. "Forget the costumes. Where is Alex? I want to see him *now.*"

Sin ignored Dasha's outburst and turned around slowly so everyone could admire her floor-length, form-fitting, Egyptian-themed flapper dress in gold and black sequins over black knit material. A chunky gold charm bracelet jangled on her left wrist. Her dark hair and eyelids sparkled with gold glitter. Sin clearly didn't mind preening in front of strangers.

"Now, do I look like Cleopatra, or not?"

Sin giggled and chose an hors d'oeuvre from a waiter. "Here's a little tidbit about me to break the ice. When I turned eight, I began trick-or-treating dressed as Queen Cleopatra. I did that for seven years in a row. I wonder what that says about me?"

"That you were obsessed with Cleopatra?" said Marcos, who had returned with stuffed grape leaves. "But, who really cares? Bring Alex to the party. We're not going anywhere without him."

Dasha gave him a grateful smile.

"I see you're a take-charge kind of guy, Marcos. Why don't you tell us what you know about my latest acquisition? That will kill some time while we're waiting for the last of the hors d'oeuvres." She posed in front of the display case placed in the middle of the huge living room, drawing everyone's attention. Inside the hard acrylic display case, sat an ancient, curved sword, resting on a fake tree branch.

Dasha gasped. "Is that a real scimitar?

"Oh, it's real, and worth a lot of money. That sword was given to my grandfather in payment of a debt." Sin smiled. "Would you like to test the blade?"

"I don't know about Dasha, but may I?" Marcos inquired, then sat his plate onto a nearby table. "I know a little about these blades, but I've never seen one up close." He stood and took a few steps toward the sword.

Sin asked Haamid to hold the sword after removing it from the display case. Marcos appeared confident, in contrast to Dasha, who was sure her face had turned chalk white at this turnabout.

Marcos reached out and gently caressed the blade, a small smile on his face. "A scimitar is a curved blade first used around the 9th century among soldiers in a region called Khurasan. Scimitars were lightweight compared to other medieval swords at the time."

"Why the curved blade?" asked Katya, coming to take a look.

Marcos gave a rueful smile. "It seems that Nomadic horsemen discovered a curved edge worked better for slashing opponents while riding a horse."

"Figures," muttered Dasha. "Where is this place, Khurasan?"

"Northeastern Iran, parts of Afghanistan, and southern portions of Central Asia. The name, Khorasan, is Persian, and means 'where the sun arrives from' or 'the Eastern Province.' Persia is the name for Ancient Iran."

"Very impressive," purred Sin, her hand on Marcos' shoulder. "My father and grandfather are Iranian, so I grew up with these stories."

Katya cleared her throat. "Mmm, aren't the stories kind of...violent?"

A loud knock at the door caused everyone to freeze. Before Sin could answer the door, a security guard stepped inside using a key card. "Pardon my barging in, Ms. Ryland, but this man and this woman claim they were abducted and attacked in this hotel."

Alex stood in the doorway, holding up Grandma Tattie, whose face was wan, yet she stood upright. Alex sported a new black eye and blood ran down his arm.

"Alex, what happened?" Dasha rushed over to the two, shocked at the blood beginning to pool on the marble floor.

His good eye quickly scanned the room and landed on a scowling Faahrik. "Sin's hired hand has four daggers hidden on his body. I would think one would be more than enough if the man's aim were better."

"Grandma Tattie, did he hurt you?" I asked, visually taking inventory.

"I'm fine. Nothing a nap won't cure. Now, Alex McKain, you're smaking this harder than it has to be. We need to treat your wounds."

Alex lapsed into silence while Grandma Tattie wiped up the blood.

"Why are you here, Grandma Tattie?" Dasha asked.

Grandma Tattie finished her task and turned to give Sin the "evil eye." "Because that woman was afraid to be alone with me for a simple conversation. Instead, she decided to kidnap me instead of *invite me*, rather than you."

"You are such a filthy liar." Sin's voice was husky, her eyes flashing.

"You know, Sin, in all these years, I don't think I've ever heard you speak the truth. And we all know why we're here. You're desperate, aren't you?"

I heard the emergency vehicles racing up Nob Hill. When Alex whispered something to Grandma Tattie, Sin must have known what was coming. She grabbed the scimitar from Haamid and brandished it from atop the coffee table.

"Everyone, stay away from me! I will not go back to that place!"

When the security guard drew his gun, my stomach dropped to the floor like a deadweight elevator.

Afterward, Marcos took a step toward Sin, who leaped across the room and accidentally slashed a drape in the process.

"You're wrong about me, Tatiana. You never believed in me." Grandma Tattie just shook her head.

"If you want to know Anastasia's whereabouts, why go to all this trouble? Why not just ask the cards," suggested Katya.

I quickly caught on to what Katya was doing. If she could calm Sin long enough to get the police to race upstairs and overpower her, we'd be okay. Sin handed the scimitar to Haamid, who watched everyone's movements with suspicious eyes.

"Is that what your tarot cards tell you? A person's whereabouts?" Sin grabbed the deck that Katya had been working with earlier. "Okay then, Miss Know-it-All, pick a card. Ask the question. Let us hear the answer."

For a brief moment, Katya grimaced as she stared down at the cards.

"Is Anastasia Romanov alive? If so, where can we find her?"

Katya chose a card. Her face turned a chalky color. She set the card on the coffee table, face up. "The Five of Cups. Oh, this is bad news." She covered her mouth with her hand and began a rocking motion.

"Fool! What does that mean?" Sin demanded.

Katya looked up, her eyes haunted. "Loss. Leaving. Sorrow."

At that moment, three police officers burst through the door. Plenty of time for Sin to grab onto the ballet slipper on her charm bracelet and reach out for Katya. In a matter of seconds, a red mist appeared, and the two women vanished.

Chapter 26

Katya noticed two things she found odd upon her return to Russia. First of all, the ride through time was much bumpier. The second item was the sound of Tchaikovsky's *Swan Lake,* blaring from a modern CD player in the corner of a huge ballroom. Not a modern ballroom, but a ballroom from *1918.*

The jolt of her body and the anxiety that followed her rough landing, caused her to stand up slowly. As she shook out the bumps and kinks, she saw Sin and froze, every muscle drained, Katya's body poised to flee. Had Sin really been slashing the air with a Persian sword at the Fairmont just moments ago? Or had that been a dream? And what did Sin mean she didn't want to be sent back *there*? Where was "*there*?" Katya had heard rumors that Sin had been put away in a mental institution. Now, she was beginning to believe it may be true. She shuddered as she forced back the panic. She just needed to stay calm long enough to find a way out of this mess.

To soothe herself, Katya breathed in and out through her nose, relieved to see no sign of the curved blade sword.

As if none of that had happened at the Fairmont, Sin straightened her dress, then glanced around to get her bearings. When she recognized the music, her eyes darted from corner to corner of the huge ballroom. "Whoever brought that music back in time is in big trouble."

"How is that possible?" Katya whispered.

Sin's flawless face formed a grimace. "We've got another fool to handle."

Katya followed as Sin headed toward the front door. This crowd was much larger, and most people were either drinking or dancing to this new kind of music. Impatient, Sin shoved people out of her way. As much as Katya was terrified by what Sin might do, Katya feared being left in a strange place all by herself. She should have brought Dima. Surely there must be someone she could trust to help her get away.

She caught up to Sin, and feigned cooperation. "Do you know who you're looking for? And where are we? Is this the same ballroom as before, where Dasha was dancing with Prince Ilya?"

Sin put her hands over her ears as if focused on the visual details. "This is the same house, but different residents live here now."

Katya's eyes grew huge. "How can you tell?"

Sin pointed to a banner tacked to the wall near the staircase. It took up most of the wall and was painted the faded red and yellow colors of the new Soviet Union. It read:

> Home of Vadim Kurbatov
> Minister of the Treasury
> Union of Soviet Socialist Republics

"I've heard the name Vadim Kurbatov before. He's an up-and-comer in Soviet politics," said Sin, gazing across the room to where the new minister stood with his beautiful wife, Valentina, in a green flapper gown.

"What happened to the previous owner of this house?" Katya asked.

"Oh, as the men always say, don't worry your pretty little head about that." Sin placed a cigarette in a holder and lit it. "Besides, no one cares, anyway."

Katya had indeed heard that phrase about women minding their own business, and it irritated her to no end. But fortunately, at that moment she spotted Prince Ilya across the room. "I would like to greet Prince Ilya before we leave. He and Dima really really hit it off the last time we met."

"So, why didn't you bring Dima with you to the Fairmont?" Sin gave her a sly glance.

"I needed time alone." She looked across the way and caught Prince Ilya's eye. "I'll be right back. I'll ask if he's seen Ana."

"Be discreet!"

Katya nodded and hurried across the room. The relief she felt once she was no longer in Sin's view was like a blast of fresh air. When she reached Prince Ilya, the first thing he did was give her a quick kiss on both cheeks, while she grabbed his arms.

"Miss me, dear Katya?"

"Oh, sorry," she said, letting go and taking a step back. "I didn't mean to do that."

"I don't mind. Is something wrong?"

She wrung her hands and debated how much to say about her dilemma. She took a quick glance over her shoulder. "It's just that I'm helping someone find someone. And we're way behind."

"That doesn't tell me much, but what can I do?"

When next she looked, Sin stood only a few feet away, her expression fierce, her eyes flashing. Katya had no doubt what her fate would be if she didn't cooperate.

"Katya," the Prince said, taking her hands. "You're shaking. Have you asked Dima to help you? He's here."

"Dima's here? Are you sure?" But how did he get here without her?

"He's filling in for another man as a bartender. Over there," he said, indicating the direction with his chin.

She didn't think about it, she just reacted. "Come dance with me until we're at the bar. I don't want anyone to follow me." She pulled the prince onto the dance floor just as a lively tune caused the younger women to scream and rush the floor with anyone on two feet.

"Oh, dear," said Katya. "All these people."

Instead, she put a hand on the bar to get Dima's attention. "What's today's date?" she asked.

Katya barely recognized him. His long black hair was slicked back, and the buttons on his white shirt were open, starting at his chest. An emerald green vest fit snugly to showcase his muscles. Out of the corner of his mouth dangled a cigarette, the ash about to fall on the temporary bar.

Katya stood there, unable to speak.

"You said you were in a hurry," said the prince, tapping her shoulder. "Tell Dima what the problem is. I'm sure he can help."

"What's today's date?" she asked, instead.

Dima set aside his cigarette in a full ash tray. "Why do you care?"

Katya darted a glance over her shoulder, but in this crush of people, she couldn't find Sin. If she was to escape, Katya had to keep track of her at all times, but when could she get away?

"Please?" she said in a small voice. "Don't you remember me, Dima?"

He shrugged, but didn't answer her question. Instead, he walked slowly to pick up a used newspaper, then returned just as slowly to show her the front page.

August 19, 1918. The same day she left. But if she had barely been gone one day, why did Dima look so different?

Someone turned up the music, and she could hear everyone throughout the room commenting on the new artist. Katya was no music expert, but she seemed to recall Dasha's sister, Sasha, playing what she called a CD from a movie. Imagine, music cast to a story! This song was called *Footloose*, and every toe in the house was tapping to the rhythm. She wanted to dance to the song, just like everyone else, but if Sin's attention was elsewhere, it was probably the best time for Katya to escape.

"Dima, are you the guilty party who brought the boombox back?"

Katya froze when she heard that voice behind her. Her muscles wouldn't work. Her brain wasn't working so well, either. She looked Prince Ilya in the eyes and moved her chin just the slightest bit.

Please ask Sin to dance!

Prince Ilya's dark eyes grew large, but he nodded as though he'd heard her plea. When he turned to face Sin, her amber gaze locked onto his. She smiled, and Katya had to admit, she looked amazing in her gold-and-black gown and strappy flat shoes. "Katya, please introduce me to your friend."

Katya's heart pounded to the song's lively beat. "Sinovia Ryland, this is Prince Ilya of Caldaran. Prince Ilya, Sin."

He seemed to know his current role, as she held out her hand. He kissed the back of it and escorted her to the dance floor, with a last encouraging look at Katya.

Katya stood rooted to the spot as long as she dared. She scuttled around the other side of the bar and grabbed Dima by the hand. "Come with me! We don't have much time. I see you got a job. I'm sorry I left you behind."

"What are you talking about? I don't know you, lady. And yes, I do have a job to do."

They stared at each other for a long moment, and then Dima turned on his booted heel and returned to the bar, singing along with the words to *Footloose*.

Katya shuddered from head to toe. By herself, she was no good to anyone. What was she supposed to do now?

Dasha waited for the police to leave Sin's penthouse at The Fairmont. By midnight, Alex's injuries had healed, and Dasha had asked Marcos to take her grandmother home. Before Grandma Tattie left, she smiled at Marcos and nodded to me, eyebrows raised, but I had no interest. Besides, Alex was the one who made my heart beat so loudly that I thought the whole world could hear it. I needed to have a talk with Grandma Tattie. No doubt Marcos would make someone a fine husband, but with Sin and Katya vanishing into the red mist (and what was that all about?), I had to go after them before something terrible happened.

Alex took me home in a taxi. I sighed as we stood on the front porch.

"I know you don't want to wait until tomorrow to search for Katya and Sin, but we need to spend time with your grandmother to find out what she knows about Ana before we go." Alex's blue eyes softened as they focused on mine.

I shrugged, confused. "Isn't Katya in danger?"

He surprised me by pulling me into his arms and capturing my lips as if they were the grand prize in a dating game show. At first, I gently resisted, hands on his chest. I'd promised Grandma Tattie to keep my worklife separate. Moments passed, then, he gently pushed me away, and I could see the reluctance in his eyes, as if he fought the same battle I did.

"You know your grandmother was a Time Mender at one point in her life, right?" he said.

"Sure. She told us everything. Why?"

He held onto my shoulders. "She didn't tell you *everything*. She's been the Acting BTM Director for four months while a search is being conducted for a permanent director. Tatiana Marusova is known the world over, and she has a lot of secrets and tips to share. She might even have something to share with us before we leave. Something that may save our lives. Let's let her rest, then ask in the morning. I don't think Sin or Katya will go flying off, either. And as for Rasputin, for all we know, he's still alive."

I grimaced. "But we saw him at the morgue."

"He has a way of defying the laws of nature."

The sun had disappeared, leaving a cool breeze that made me shiver. When he let go of me, I felt the loss of his warm and gentle hands.

"In the meantime, we need to find Sin and Katya, but time travel isn't precise. That's why we sometimes have to bend the rules to get to the right place or risk getting lost in space, as it were."

"Then why do it?"

"Because some things can't be left uncorrected," came Grandma Tattie's voice from where she stood behind the screen door, arms folded across her chest. After a pause, she opened the screen and said, "You might as well come inside, both of you. In the morning, I'll fill you in on the latest with Anastasia so you can get an early start before the others are up." She indicated the stairs with her hand. "Alex, you might as well share Dasha's room. She's got her own bathroom, and I'm guessing you won't be able to sleep tonight, anyway." At the top of the stairs, she turned and shook her finger. "But no funny business. You've got two, young impressionable sisters. I don't want them using you as an excuse. You hear me?"

"I promise." I tried hard not to laugh. "What about Sasha?"

"Sasha is an old soul. She's good at making her own decisions."

Alex saluted neatly. "On my honor, I will behave myself."

An hour later, after Tattie's de-briefing, Alex fell asleep, his arms around me. I cherished the way his skin smelled like the waves, the sea, and the sky. Minutes later, I fell asleep next to him.

Three hours later, Tattie awakened us, then Alex's staff assistant dropped by with a packed duffle bag. I packed my own, wanting at least a couple of things that were comfortable. We then climbed the stairs to the attic. Alex and Tattie spoke quietly in the attic corner, and for once, I didn't want to hear what they were saying. Rather than tired, I felt revved up when I thought we might actually find Sin and Katya, then save Ana and her baby, once Grandma Tattie told Alex where to look. If all went well, we would close this case that same day.

When they were done speaking, Grandma Tattie came over and handed me the green-sequined evening glove. "Did Alex discuss your 'home talisman'?"

I raised a brow.

"The evening glove, as you know, responds only to you. Sin has that gold charm bracelet with a ballet slipper. The home talisman is what gets us as close to where we need to be, in one try. Without that talisman, it's hard to say where we'll land. Always keep that with you, because if you lose it, you can't return home."

"Did you consider stealing Sin's talisman to stop her from wandering?"

"We did discuss that," said Alex, glancing at Grandma Tattie. "But we'll keep that as a last defense."

"Why a last defense? Why not a first attack?" I countered.

Alex shrugged.

"We don't want to kill anyone, Dasha, and that's the only way Sin would part with it," said Grandma Tattie. "But these rogue wanderers are doing us no good. If anything, it disturbs the balance in the world."

I picked up one of the *matryoshka* dolls, and ran my fingers down its smooth wooden sides.

"It's time to go now," said my grandmother with a smile. "You will find Ana and Misha in Chicago. Alex will know where to locate them." She hesitated. "Have you changed your mind, Dasha?"

"No. I haven't. I need to do this to keep our family alive, and to make sure Ana and her baby live."

Grandma Tattie agreed, then turned to Alex. "You take care of my little Dashenka, yes?"

"Absolutely, *bábushka.*"

Alex took my hand and put the evening glove on it. He leaned in for a quick kiss, counted to three, and with a puff of air, we were in motion.

Chapter 27

"A powerful symbol of hope, this card shows that you are destined to be with someone. It's time to find a soul mate."
(Tarot Card: The Star)

I held onto Alex's hand and felt the air whoosh out of my lungs as we traveled through space. I gasped for breath, squeezing his arm until I thought I couldn't breathe. The air was fresh, but cold, everything silent as a tomb as we whirled and spun for what felt like forever. Finally, we slowed and were unceremoniously dumped onto a hard floor. I groaned and opened my eyes. To my astonishment, four pairs of eyes stared at us where we sat. They appeared to be kitchen staff in an Italian restaurant, based on the heavenly aromas I detected coming from the kitchen. However, what alarmed me most was that they were gagged and tied up, their eyes radiating fear as they all looked to the dining room door.

Alex acted quickly by removing their gags and untying three men and one woman, their white uniforms splattered with what I hoped was tomato sauce.

"What's going on here? Are you in charge?" Alex asked the man wearing the chef's hat.

The chef rubbed his wrists and glanced toward the dining room door. "Yes, I'm Head Chef Dante Pollitti. What's happening is that Enzo Calvani and his men like to eat lunch here."

"But they scare away all our customers," said the woman. "Unless they want us to serve something special, they tie us up while they're here because they don't want us to alert anyone." She appeared to be young, maybe around eighteen, but a spark of anger flashed in her dark eyes.

"Mind if I ask, who is Enzo Calvani?" Alex asked in a calm voice, standing so he could peek out the swinging door into the dining room.

One of the other cooks guffawed. "You been livin' on the moon, buddy? He's a mastermind, the biggest gangster in America."

I felt the color drain from my face, but hesitated to say anything. Why hadn't Grandma Tattie warned me? Once we'd finished untying their ropes, I happened to see Alex glance at his watch, a reminder that time was not on our side.

"My name is Dasha. This is Alex. Could you please tell us the name of this restaurant, and where we are in Chicago?"

The girl popped a piece of gum into her mouth, appearing unaffected by Enzo Calvani's presence in the dining room. "I'm Ardith Jones, kitchen assistant. You're on the south side at Vincente's Italian Restaurant. Hey, how come you don't have any snow on you?"

Alex had turned his back so they wouldn't see him fiddling with a setting on his watch. But at the word "snow", he patted his watch and faced the group once more. "What do you mean, snow?"

"Haven't you heard the news? Up to four inches by midnight. You two will freeze," said the third man, the one I thought of as Mr. Negativsky. "By the way, I'm J.J."

I looked down at my boring tan lightweight trench coat. Though not as warm as a wool coat, I figured it was better than nothing. Alex, on the other hand, wore a men's camel wool coat, tailored to fit. I'd noted his clothing in the past, but I just realized at that moment that Alex was a clothes horse.

"Always good to know the weather when you travel," Alex said as he looked more closely at the kitchen. "Is there a door that leads to the outside from here? I hate to say it, but we're kind of in a big hurry."

"There's a door over there," said Ardith, pointing to the far corner. "Are you two Federal Agents? Is that how you snuck in so quietly?"

"Something like that," Alex mumbled. "Why don't you folks follow us out and get to safety?"

They all looked at each other, like it had never occurred to them to escape.

Finally, the chef replied, "These visits happen all the time. I think we're better off if we stay right here. They'll trust us more if we *don't* leave through that door."

All three nodded in agreement.

"He leaves us a good bonus for our trouble," said the head chef.

"There may be a lookout posted in the alley behind us. I hope you know karate," said J.J.

"Thanks for the tip." Alex tightened the cinch on my coat belt and turned me toward the door. "Are there buses or trolleys running?"

"Not in this snow," said Chef Dante. "Maybe after the snowplow comes through."

Alex frowned. "What about taxis?"

"You'd be lucky to find one."

I had this terrible sinking sensation that we were too late, or wouldn't make it in time because of the weather. Grandma Tattie warned us we had until noon the next day. If Ana and her child were killed, we Marusovs would cease to exist.

"Let's get going," I said. "Thanks, everyone. Carry on." I smiled at the kitchen staff, who no longer appeared quite so helpless. In fact, they looked like they were enjoying the attention...and the anticipated bonus.

Alex checked the back door that opened onto an alley. He signaled for me to follow, but not to talk. The alley was clear, yet just as we reached the corner of the building, shots were fired inside. I grabbed Alex, who already had his own gun in hand. I hadn't known he carried a weapon.

"Why do you have a gun?" I whispered.

Alex placed a finger on my lips to quiet me. "Because I knew we may run into gangsters, and Tattie thought it was a good idea...especially if I'm to protect her granddaughter."

I didn't know what to say to that last part, but I did wonder why the BTM would ask Grandma Tattie to be their acting director. Did she really have that much experience as an agent? It made me angry that she had put herself in harm's way. It also made me sad she'd kept that secret about a threat to our family for so long. I relaxed against Alex's chest, my cheek appreciating the fine, soft wool of his coat. I shivered and heard my stomach growl.

"I'm freezing. What are we going to do? The clock is ticking."

"I'm thinking. There's no chance in hell that if we walk we can beat Sin and Katya to Ana's home. It's unfortunate we landed here in winter. Chicago is already a big city of over two million people without having to worry about the cold."

"Seems like a good place for Ana and Misha to hide in plain sight."

Alex looked down and stared at my lips. "I was off on the landing by quite a bit. I'm sorry."

"I can't let you take all the blame. You told me that time travel isn't always precise. Let's come up with a plan, anyway. I need you to be strong, Alex."

I kissed his cold nose, and he smiled back at me.

I heard a man's gruff voice nearby. "Where you two lovebirds headed?"

We stepped apart at the same moment, and I don't know about Alex, but I felt awkward in front of this stranger who had caught us in an intimate moment.

I waved a hand in the air and feigned a casualness I didn't feel, rather than admit my stomach was in turmoil from his abrupt approach. Had he heard me say *time travel* out loud?

"Oh, we're in a hurry to meet up with some friends. If taxis aren't running, do you have any idea how we can get there on time?" I turned to Alex. "Where are we headed...dear?"

I turned back to the tough-looking old man, his black horn-rimmed glasses thick, but his eyes alert. "I'm Enzo Calvani. Perhaps I can give you two a ride to your destination? My driver is quite good despite these road conditions. It could save you considerable time, if that's a concern."

Alex glanced at me, and I knew he was silently cursing me for telling a stranger our dilemma, let alone a known gangster. I purposely said nothing about the people we were to meet at our destination.

My teeth started chattering, and I eyed Alex's warm coat with longing.

"We're only a few blocks from Marshall Fields, my dear," said Enzo, who must have seen me shiver. "Why don't we stop there so you can get a warm winter coat, like your friend here. Then, you can be on your way to meet up with your friends. It won't take long. I promise. Alex and I will make sure of that, won't we?"

Alex swallowed, nodding. "Sure. You need a warm coat."

I placed a hand on Alex's arm. "Oh, I promise to be in and out of the department store in ten minutes."

"You better be. It's your family's demise, if not." He muttered the words so only I could hear, but they bothered me. Like I would rather shop than save my family. There was still so much Alex didn't know about me.

"Mr. Calvani, I'm Daria, and as you know, this is Alex, my fiancé. We'll take advantage of your kind offer for a ride, but once

I'm better prepared for this weather, we won't impose on your time any further."

"Call me Enzo. And this is my driver, Giuseppe. We'll get the heat turned up in no time."

They helped me into the back seat of what must be a luxury car in the 1920s. I'd seen several cars drive by, but this was one of the few with a permanent roof, instead of a convertible.

I huddled next to Alex, while Enzo sat up front with the driver. For some reason, I suspected Alex was still angry with me, but anticipating a more comfortable afternoon ahead of me, I didn't care.

Despite very little traffic flowing on this frigid day, it still took almost an hour to get to the well-known department store. I knew what I wanted, so we hopped out and raced inside, Alex and Enzo savoring the warm store.

I showed them my first choice. It was a deep burgundy full-length coat that would keep me warm from head to toe. The pockets were generous, and the double-breasted extra buttons made an elegant statement. *Now comes the hard part.* I had no money with me, nor a credit card, because they could all be traced. I looked up at Alex and blinked. I knew he carried cash from other trips, but he hadn't offered to exchange any before we left San Francisco.

"What do you think of this?" I whirled around, modeling like a pro.

"Burgundy? Don't you think that will draw attention?"

"Ah, Alex, your fiancée is a beautiful woman. Why should she not stand out for her greatest admirer?" Enzo grinned.

My greatest admirer? Had Enzo caught those looks Alex had been sending my way every few seconds?

Alex glanced at his watch. I knew I was under ten minutes, so I pursed my lips.

"Why don't you let me pay for this? It's no burden, and you do look so very sophisticated." Enzo fingered the fabric. "Very well made. This should last a long time. Please, may I make this a gift?"

"No!" Alex and I responded at the same time. I felt my cheeks burn red-hot. I hadn't wanted to come across as rude, but I didn't want to owe a gangster for anything. Surely, that would be frowned upon by the BTM, no matter how nice he seemed.

"Mr. Calvani...Enzo, thank you so much for your offer, but I just met you. You've been so kind and generous, and we thank you for that." I almost admitted how important the car ride had been. Before I could say more, Alex took over.

"Let's pay for it and get going," said Alex, rushing me to a store clerk. Until we got to the counter, I hadn't realized he'd walked behind me, picking up other items he thought I should have: a warm wool beret, mittens, a scarf with black, burgundy, and gold squares. By the time he pulled open his wallet, I had quite a haul.

I touched his sleeve. "I will repay you—"

"Not necessary if we're to be wed soon, is it...*dear*?"

He grinned, picked up all my purchases, and we walked out to the street with Enzo.

I had asked the clerk to cut off the purchase tags, and wore my coat out of the store. I did the same with the extra items Alex had picked up, bless him, so the only items I needed to carry were a cobalt blue cashmere sweater and gold hoop earrings.

We said a pleasant goodbye to Enzo, and he accepted our request to walk the rest of the way. Alex named a nearby hotel as our final destination. I knew he didn't want Enzo to know where we ended up, so I hadn't pressured him to accept another ride. Which was fortuitous, because we walked right by a shoe store that sold good quality winter boots. Alex insisted I try on a pair.

"You could fall on the ice and twist your ankle, jeopardizing the rest of the mission," he said.

Five minutes later, I walked out of the store wearing a new pair of burgundy short boots with three buttons.

"I *will* repay you," I said once again as we started a brisk walk.

"I told you, you don't need to worry about it."

"But I do worry. I should have known to pack a warm coat."

"That's silly. When we left San Francisco, it was August."

I let that sink in. "Still. You're very generous, Alex McKain." I patted my hands to stay warm. "Do you know what kind of car that was? It seemed quite fancy, and rode so smoothly, despite the slushy streets."

"Umm. A Pierce Arrow, I believe. And yeah it's fancy, but not as nice as my cherry red Malibu."

"That's true." I waited a beat. "When we get back home, would you take me for a long ride up and down the coast with the top down. Maybe into wine country?"

A small smile appeared. "That's a possibility."

I liked the sound of my boots on the sidewalk where the snow was melting from the sun's unexpected appearance. So much for the weather report. For once, since we'd arrived in 1920s Chicago, I felt maybe Lady Luck would blow *my* way.

I placed my hand on Alex's elbow. For several blocks, we strolled arm in arm, happy and content. And for a brief time, I was able to forget all about what was coming.

But I knew only too well, some things in life are impossible to anticipate.

Chapter 28

"Under this influence, your intuitive powers
heighten, and you may find yourself tuning in to
people from the past – who magically reappear."
(Tarot Card: The Wheel of Fortune)

"How many more blocks?" I asked, feeling a blister from my new boots.

We were making our way up Michigan Avenue in search of the hotel Grandma Tattie had indicated Ana and Misha would be staying for one night to celebrate his thirtieth birthday. With the sun's appearance, more people were out and about, and the sidewalk seemed easier to manage as the ice melted.

Alex hadn't told me the name of the hotel nor spoken more than a few words since we parted ways with Enzo, so I had no idea what was going through his mind. He glanced at his watch for the hundredth time and focused on walking straight ahead.

"You know, it might help if I knew what we were looking for," I said.

"We need to find the Palmer House. You'll know it when you see it." He pressed his lips into a thin line. "You might be interested to know it's where the brownie dessert was invented for a Columbian World Expo."

"No kidding? Tell me more."

Alex peered over my shoulder to see through the window of a shop. "It has an interesting history, especially in its later incarnations as an example of Classical French Beaux-Arts architecture. Also, it was the first hotel in Chicago to be equipped with electric lights, telephones, and elevators."

Then he filled me in on the fires it had suffered over the years, including the first, which burned the new hotel to the ground only thirteen days after its grand opening. "Did you learn that in school, Professor McKain?" I teased.

I enjoyed watching his face turn red. "Uh, I read some articles about Chicago architecture not too long ago."

I almost blurted out, "Is this what you went to college for?" but he quelled that question with a "look," so I remained silent.

For the time being, I had to satisfy myself with the thought we were nearly done with this mission. With the weather improving, Alex was almost certain he saw Sin and Katya up ahead of us. People were so bundled up, it would be hard to identify them in winter clothes, however.

"If I'd known it was this far, I might have suggested we try a trolley car. I know they're not exactly fast, and they stop at every stop, but it's better than walking." I paused on a street bench just long enough to loosen my boot and dislodge a small stone.

Alex sat down beside me to pour through a paper map in place of his phone, which wouldn't work here. It gave a whole new meaning to "urgent" when we had no cell service, and it certainly didn't help that Alex appeared to be one of those guys who couldn't ask for directions.

"There's a store over there," I said, pointing across the street. "Maybe we can ask a local the quickest way to our destination?"

Alex sighed and refolded his map, replacing it in his inside coat pocket. "You don't trust me, do you? I thought we were past that."

"I *do* trust you. It's just that Ana could be dead and here we are wasting time. Plus, I don't want to take another step with my feet bleeding like this."

"Let me see."

"No, I'm—"

He pulled my ankle up onto his lap, removed the boot, and inspected my heel for about ten seconds.

"I don't suppose you brought a Band-Aid with you?" he asked.

"Of course not. Besides, a Band-Aid wouldn't have helped the last time, when I was hit on the head with a bayonet. BTM should make a list of what to bring, no matter where you go."

"You and your lists," Alex said, massaging my foot. "They have all kinds of lists, I'm sure."

"Alex, we're in a hurry. We shouldn't be attracting attention." I gave a long sigh. "For all we know, this could be considered lewd behavior, in this time period."

"You're right. Do you have something you can wrap around that foot?"

It never failed that as soon as we made a plan or a decision, someone local noticed us. A police officer, probably on a routine foot patrol, saw us on the bench. It wouldn't have been so bad, but I was wearing a long skirt, which Alex had hiked up to get a good look at my ankle. As the officer approached, I forced a welcoming smile and decided to distract him with the truth.

"Hello, Officer. My new boots are giving me blisters, and we still have several blocks to walk, don't we, sweetheart?"

The patrolman had his Billy club out, tapping the palm of his hand thoughtfully. "Is this your husband, ma'am?"

"Why—"

"Yes, sir. That's me," Alex replied with an adorably flummoxed expression.

"You can't be flashing your wife's legs in public like that, even if she does have blisters on her feet. Where are you headed?"

Finally. Alex would ask for directions. I reached into my bag for a cotton handkerchief I could use to wrap around my heel. Meanwhile, I scanned the wide boulevard for signs of Sin or Katya, when I saw a hard-top sedan come careening around the corner, and spied the taxi sign. I started to hold my hand out to flag it. But customers had already engaged the driver. As they swept by, I saw two women's faces looking right at me, and my heart stopped. *Katya and Sin.*

Alex and the policeman were talking about the Chicago Cubs baseball team that year, and I had no idea when that would wind down. We had to try and beat Sin and Katya to the hotel, so I didn't care how clumsy I appeared. I grabbed my bag and raced to the signal, calling out, "Meet you there!" to Alex. I hoped he would forgive me.

Right as the light turned green, a big green sedan came bearing down on me, screeching to a halt just inches from my new boots. My heart pounded as I recognized Enzo Calvani. He wore a Fedora, and put it to good use as he stepped outside the car and pulled the hat down to hide half his face from the policeman.

"Dasha!" Alex called, running after me. "Are you alright?"

I glanced at Enzo, and felt some sort of connection between us, although I'd never met him before today. He reached out of the car and put a hand on my shoulder, his face showing his concern.

"Miss Marusov, I'm so sorry. Giuseppe was in a hurry, and he didn't see you until the last minute. Please let us give you a ride, and no arguing this time."

I exchanged a look with Alex, who had regained his composure. His eyes darted from the policeman to Enzo, then down at a piece of paper in Enzo's hand.

Enzo gave us no time to consider our options. Instead, he gathered us quickly into the back seat of his flashy Pierce Arrow, while Giuseppe hit the gas and made a quick left turn. My heart skipped a beat as Enzo lifted heavy canvas bags of what I could only assume was money, and stashed them out of our way.

Alex gave the bags a quick glance before pulling me to his side to make room for more bags on the seat next to me.

"Alex, are we—?"

"I think so, yes."

Somehow, we'd become part of a bank robbery, and all I could think was my sterling reputation as a "good girl" was now ripped to shreds.

"Enzo, we so appreciate your help, but we have to get out at the next intersection to meet our friends at the Palmer House." Alex's voice was calm, but firm, his hand on the door, as if he would jump, if necessary.

I leaned my hand on the car window, my mouth dropping open at my first sight of the hotel Alex had mentioned earlier as one of the oldest and finest hotels in Chicago.

"And you're certain this is where the brownie dessert was invented?"

"I told you the whole history of how it burned down in the Chicago fire, and was rebuilt, only to burn again, and that's what you remember?" said Alex with a chuckle.

Enzo barked in laughter.

"Giuseppe, pull around to the underground parking at the Palmer House. "We'll switch cars there, and no one will know where we've been. Isn't that right, Alex and Dasha?"

Alex caught his meaning right away, but of course, I had to use my vivid imagination. Was he suggesting we disappear and never mention he was there? Or that we knew for a fact he was part of a bank robbery, which meant we were too, but Enzo wouldn't tell anyone.

Giuseppe pulled into the parking structure and found a remote spot where the dark-colored car would blend in with the shadows of the late afternoon. Alex was out the door in seconds, pulling me and our bags out and dropping them on the cement.

Enzo regarded the two of us. "Miss Marusov, I want you to know that your grandmother Tatiana once did me a big favor. It kept me out of prison. That same night, she also risked her own life to save my little white terrier, Luigi, from being hit by a car. It was a long time ago, but I never forgot. I owe her two big favors. Can you young people forget you ever saw me today, and never mention anything about those bags to the police?"

I reached for Alex's hand, and we shared a long look. His brows rose slightly, and for once, I thought I could read his mind. I looked down and nodded my head.

"I'll be sure to mention your name to Grandma Tattie next time I see her," I said in a husky voice.

"You're a classy lady, miss." He looked across the garage and waved. "I see Giuseppe has found us another mode of transportation. I must go now." He handed me a slip of paper with a Chicago phone number. "If you need anything, give me a call. I guess I'm a sucker for a beautiful dame in distress. That favor will be free."

He waved as Giuseppe drove up in a black sedan nowhere near as posh as the Pierce Arrow. They took off with a screech of tires and disappeared from sight.

"I don't want us anywhere near here when that car is discovered," Alex said, indicating the Pierce Arrow. "Let's go up to the lobby." He strode toward the elevator, and I followed, still trying to process everything.

"I wonder how he knew Grandma Tattie."

He shifted his duffle bag into his other hand. "You'll have to ask her."

"I guess I'm going to have to write down all these questions. I'll never remember them." She untied the handkerchief around her right heel and leaned against the railing as the elevator crept up to the lobby.

The door opened with a ding, and Alex seemed to relax, because he smiled for the first time that day. "And here's The Palmer House.

When I walked through the doors, I opened my mouth, in awe as I breathed in the elegance, the rich tapestries and the gold-gilded picture frames on the walls. Above me was a painted ceiling and ornate chandeliers, while the floors were tastefully tiled and the furniture upholstered in velour. I inhaled the enticing smell of old books and aged cognac. Prior to this, I'd never stayed in a place this posh (Dad and Grandma Tattie preferred a medium-priced utilitarian hotel with a decent pool to entertain us girls).

"I don't see anyone we know. Are you sure this is the right place?"

Alex set his duffle on the floor. "This is where your grandmother told me to go. Let's just hope we've beaten Sin and Katya to the punch."

"What a day this has been, and we're not even halfway through our twenty-four-hour window."

Alex looked like he'd been thrown into a pit with a lion, his nice, neat clothes rumpled and soiled. He drew in a deep breath and gazed at me with admiration, maybe even love?

"I need to do something. I'll be back in a few minutes. Don't you dare take off without me," I warned.

"I'll be here...sweetheart."

"Don't you—"

"Just hurry up. Then, once we find Ana and make sure Sin and Katya can't hurt her ever again, we'll grab some food."

"Now you're talking," Alex said.

"Ever since we arrived, I've smelled deep-dish pizza. That's what I want, and then I'll be satisfied."

His little smirk appeared. "Too bad it wasn't invented until 1943."

"Don't rain on my parade."

"I wouldn't dream of it."

As I walked to the nearest restroom, I wondered what our encounter with Sin and Katya would be like. I no longer felt like the naïve and trusting girl I'd been at the beginning of this adventure, but then, I wasn't lost anymore either, I realized.

And these people, good or bad, were an important part of my journey. But why? That was the real question.

Chapter 29

"This is a card of greed, temptation, and materialism. To change the situation, you will need to think laterally and use a little cunning. It's never worth confronting the problem."
(Tarot Card: The Devil)

It wasn't every day a friend asked me to carry a gun. Reluctantly, I tucked the small pistol Alex handed me into my waistband, then exited the ladies' room. As I surveyed the massive lobby, my heart raced.

"Stay in one spot where Alex can find you," I mumbled to myself. "Remain calm. Remain alert." Maybe Alex *had* provided some good lessons, after all.

As I waited for him, I took stock of the deluxe hotel. According to the brochures, The Palmer House was busy year-round with guests coming and going from all over the world. Seeing the opulence, I felt like my eyes were opened wide. Mom and Grandma Tattie had lived this life in San Francisco. How had I never realized that Grandma Tattie and my mom were part of the BTM? I was beginning to think I'd sleepwalked through life, not even paying attention. And it wasn't about the bling. It was more like I could *see* the history, the struggles of our ancestors, and the horrors they lived through to get to this day.

But it would all be wiped out if we couldn't save Anastasia.

I'd been waiting about ten minutes when I finally spotted Alex approaching me from the reservation desk. His eyes scanned the lobby quickly, which meant he expected to find Sin and Katya there. He walked loosely, his hand holding his long coat open partway, but not enough to reveal the pistol he'd tucked into his waistband.

"The front desk says no one by the name of Ana or Misha has checked in today. They could have used different names. We have no way of knowing."

"Did you ask if anyone else had inquired about them today, and then describe Sin and Katya to the concierge?"

"Yeah. No luck."

I'd learned that when Alex was in "stealth" mode, he didn't smile or talk much. I'd made up my mind to not take it personally, but appreciated his trying to smooth things over in between. Still, I put my hands in my coat pockets, trying not to show how nervous the gun Alex insisted I carry made me.

I was contemplating what we should do next when Alex glanced over his left shoulder, then whirled and grabbed me by the arm and pulled me toward the revolving doors.

"I just caught a glimpse of Sin and Katya. Ana and Misha may have changed plans and are doing the tourist thing out on the town instead. It's Sin and Katya we need to track. Come on, let's follow them."

"Alex?"

"No questions. Remain silent. I don't want to spook them."

I felt like a little girl who'd just been scolded, and I growled. I was a professional. I didn't have to take this. Why had Grandma Tattie chosen *me* for this mission anyway, and with so little training? Whose fault was that?

We stepped outside onto the curb, and at a wave from Alex, the valet whistled a taxicab. The roads were better, but still slick. I assumed the slush would freeze overnight and make the roads even slicker tomorrow. As I trailed Alex, I prayed silently for more sun to scare off the gloom and dry the streets.

We got into the back seat of the taxicab, huddled together against the cold. Interestingly enough, passengers in the 1920s had glass windows that opened and closed, but the driver did not. Our driver was smoking a cigar, so it was just as well.

"Hey, buddy, I'll pay extra if you keep up with the two ladies walking toward Michigan Avenue," Alex told the driver. "But stay at a discrete distance."

"You got it!" said the driver, clearly up for the challenge and bonus.

I still had no clue what Alex would do when we caught up with them, and he wasn't soliciting ideas. If this was the way he went about his business, I would rather stay home.

The two ladies walked arm in arm as they crossed Wabash Avenue and continued another block to S. Michigan Avenue. There, they took a right, passing in front of the Art Institute of Chicago, its two lions guarding the entrance just like the two huge lions in front of the New York Public Library. I had never been inside either, but as we drove by slowly in traffic, I made a mental note to make time. I should take Sasha there. She'd love it. Books and cats. Cats and books.

Even though I hadn't been away from home for long, I missed my sisters, parents, and grandmother with a searing intensity. I had a sudden desire to talk to Alex, whether he wanted to or not. If it was our "work" he didn't want strangers hearing, I was fine with that. Anything to distract me from what may be coming.

"Do you have any siblings, Alex?"

For a moment, I thought he wouldn't answer, his eyes focused on the two women, but then he turned and smiled. "I've been surly today, haven't I?"

I pressed his arm. "Not so bad."

Cars in the 1920s didn't have seatbelts, so he put an arm around my shoulders and leaned close to whisper. "Follow my lead. I'm not mad, just focused on the job. But I'm very aware you're sitting right here." He nudged my thigh with his and gave me a smoldering look that left no doubt he noticed me as a woman.

"Siblings?" I repeated.

He settled back into his seat and watched the driver glance at him in the rearview mirror. "I have a stepbrother and stepsister, but they're a lot younger than me." He shrugged. "Unfortunately, I don't know them well. I left home at seventeen, when Jack was just learning to walk."

"Are your mother and stepfather still alive?"

He grimaced and glanced out the window. "Sure. Though they separated a while back. My stepdad runs the ranch, and Mom is here, in Chicago. She runs a business."

"Here? Oh, Alex, can we plan a visit with her? You could catch up."

His brows formed a deep vee as he gazed at where the two women had stopped to admire a street seller's wares just seconds ago.

"Driver, let us out here."

The driver pulled over to the curb, and Alex opened the car door. He helped me out, and then shoved a bunch of dollar bills at the driver. The driver thanked him, his lips curling into a smile at the big tip, then he raced off.

"What did you see?" I asked, concerned.

"Those two women. They're coming back this way. Try not to stare."

Although dressed similar to Katya in her long gray sweater coat, and Sin in her stylish wool coat from the 1920s era, I realized right away these were not our targets.

"Alex, those aren't—"

"Don't say it. And don't stare when they pass by."

He took a firm hold of my arm and turned so we both faced a display in a store window. I willed them to keep going, but when I saw their images behind us in the glass, I gasped just as Alex pulled me to the left, away from the woman on the right, who now held a gun...pointed at me. When we turned back to face them, my heart sank.

"Sin told us you wouldn't come quietly. In fact, she made us a bet. Maybe we can make this more interesting."

Up close, the taller woman with plain brown hair looked nothing like Sin. The other woman, upon closer inspection, was part African American, but her complexion was much rougher than that of Katya, her build not nearly as gaunt.

The tall woman, clearly the one in charge, forced us away from the wall, then signaled a man loitering a block away. He ran toward us, and all I remember after that was the rapid exchange of a language not quite Russian. My best guess was Polish, since I'd heard quite a bit of it around the neighborhood and recognized more and more words. But then the tall brunette pulled something from her pocket I'd hoped I'd never see again. I quickly grabbed Alex's lapel and cried out, "no!", felt the pinch of a syringe, then melted onto the sidewalk with sun-warmed slush for company.

I woke up cranky and annoyed, wanting to bite someone's head off. Mainly Alex's for allowing this to happen...again. As I came to, I heard voices in the background that sounded far away.

"I told you we'd draw too much attention if we did that in broad daylight."

I opened one eye a crack and recognized the woman in the long sweater coat.

"Well, we're here now."

The woman glanced at the wind-up watch on her wrist. There were days when I would have killed to have one of those wind-up watches so I could avoid little round batteries rolling around the floor of my bedroom, but this wasn't one of them.

"Boss said to keep them occupied until noon tomorrow. We'll need to move them, though."

I had so many questions for Alex as he came around. At least, we weren't tied up this time. Plus, we seemed to be inside a house with a large oriental area rug in navy blue and red, that covered a bare floor. As I looked around at the sparse furnishings, which included two cheap dining chairs in black faux leather, a small table, and a small two-shelf bookcase against the wall, it came to me in a rush where we were being held.

"Where in the hell are we?" Alex muttered. "A panic room?"

I'd heard about rooms like this, though I didn't know anyone wealthy or famous enough to need a place of refuge or security during a home invasion. "Whose place is this?" I asked.

"You see, Vernice. I knew they'd ask too many questions," said the brunette, turning her back.

"You weren't supposed to use my name, Pauline. Now, look at what you did."

"We can forget your names," I said eagerly. "Just let us loose. We have a crucial deadline at noon tomorrow. We have to save the life of a—"

"It's super important," Alex cut in. He glanced at his watch, then looked up at me. "I'm sorry. I thought this part would be a piece of cake, but I didn't anticipate so many conflicts."

I should have considered Alex's words as music to my ears. He'd admitted he didn't always plan everything right the first time around.

But I was growing impatient at our lack of a warm welcome to Chicago. "I'm not staying here while family members are beaten like criminals just because of their last name. If it's money you want, we—"

"What's your family's name?" asked the inquisitive Pauline.

"You wouldn't believe me if I told you. Now, what do you want? Who hired you?"

Vernice sat on a bench next to the wall and rested her booted feet on a box. "Wait a minute. We're asking the questions here."

"We have an emergency to deal with," Alex said, his voice rising. "We have to get out of here *now*. We've done nothing to break the law. If you don't let us go, we will have to report you to the police."

"Oh, we don't want nothin' to do with the police," said Pauline.

The lock on the door to the panic room began to jiggle. We remained silent, waiting. At the last minute, a uniformed police officer shoved the door open, followed by one Miss Sin Ryland, dressed like a queen, as usual. She looked at us with those unnatural eyes of hers.

"Oh, officers, just like I told you, these four are in it together. When I came home, I noticed the living room and bedroom were missing several valuable items. If they haven't fenced them yet, you should find them among these four individuals."

I'm not a violent person by nature, but at that moment, I wanted to punch Sin right between the eyes. Alex's face had turned red, and I knew he was struggling to stay calm.

"Officers, we are *not* burglars," Alex said. "We just met these two ladies, and they drugged us, then had their cohort help move us here."

"What's a cohort?" asked Vernice.

I felt so much better now that Alex had returned to fighting mode. "Cohort means partner or accomplice. There was a man waiting about a block away who came at their signal. He had a dark complexion, but spoke...what?" He looked at me. "Polish, would you guess?"

"Yes. I think so."

"He also wore a red plaid shirt and blue jacket. His pants had holes in the knees, and he looked like he hadn't eaten in a while."

Both officers stared at Alex, the perfect witness.

"I'll bet you memorized that," laughed Pauline. "Why don't you look inside the girl's duffle bag and see if there's anything that doesn't belong there."

"What did you plant?" Alex hissed at Sin.

The officer in charge opened my gray duffle bag, and sitting on top was something wrapped in a piece of blue silk. The same cobalt blue as my new cashmere sweater, which Alex bought for me. I changed into it for more warmth back at the Palmer House, and was glad I'd done so.

The second officer picked up the piece and unwrapped it to find an elaborate watch on a thick gold chain with ceramic beads done in blue, yellow and black. I gasped. "That's *not* my watch! In fact, I've never seen it before."

"You're not going to allow them to smooth-talk their way out of this theft, are you?" Vernice demanded. "That's got to be worth a pretty penny."

"How would you know that unless you had it assessed?" Alex stated calmly as the police officers handcuffed all four of them and marched them to a waiting paddy wagon, similar in size to the Pierce Arrow.

I was fuming and didn't want anyone near me. "My mother is going to be devastated if I'm put in prison...again. Grandma Tattie won't be happy, either. I went to Stanford, for heaven's sake."

I ignored the girls and turned away when, suddenly, Sin stuck her head inside the back.

"Not so proud now, eh, Dasha Marusov?"

Other than Pauline raising her head, neither woman said a word when hearing my surname. I was desperately hoping they didn't know our secret—that Anastasia Romanov was my great-great grandmother.

Chapter 30

*"It's time for communicating and expressing your
ideas and desires. Let go of procrastination."*
(Tarot Card: The Magician)

I hadn't expected to be spending any time inside the Chicago Police Station, let alone a jail cell. But listening to what suspects said, and interpreting their body language as they lied outright to the police was extremely enlightening. Alex tried to maintain his calm while pleading our case from behind bars. In the meantime, I spent my time in that same cell watching Sin on a bench directly across from us, outside the cell, legs crossed, as she waited to give her statement. She dangled her left foot every few minutes, along with her left wrist, where her charm bracelet jangled loudly, giving me a headache. She wore a smug expression and made a point to wave her cigarette smoke my way. I was dying to smack her.

Alex glanced at his watch, then at me. I didn't need to be reminded how quickly we were running out of time. Twelve hours and counting.

I was surprised that Katya was nowhere to be found. Rising from the bench, I placed my hands on the bars that separated us and motioned Sin over with my finger. I didn't want the entire department to hear what I had to say.

Sin grinned and sashayed over to me. "Hey, Dasha. How's the view from in there?"

"It's rather limited, if you know what I mean, but I have heard 'victims' such as yourself making deals with the cops. Tell me, Sin, why do you hate us so much? What have we ever done to you?"

She threw back her head and laughed a throaty laugh. "Don't you know the tale of *Swan Lake*?"

I shrugged.

"I'd be happy to tell you."

Fortunately, Alex had the gift of gab, so he kept the officer occupied while I did what I could with Sin. I shook my head and smiled. "No, thanks. I've heard the *true* version of *Swan Lake*. I'll stick with that one so I can avoid what passes for your vivid imagination."

"Why, you little... You're just as narrow-minded and snobbish as your grandmother."

I gave a sharp inhale, determined to leave my grandmother out of it, if possible. "All I want to know is what you have planned for Katya and Ana."

"As far as I'm concerned, Ana's family made an unholy alliance with Grisha. Anastasia is the Devil." She dropped her cigarette on the cement floor and ground it out with her shoe.

My stomach flooded with a familiar sense of dread. "How did you know that Ana and Misha would be staying at the Palmer House tonight?"

Sin ran a hand through her straight hair, displaying her tapered blood-red fingernails. "We intercepted a note that said they decided to celebrate her husband's thirtieth birthday in Chicago. Her husband, Misha, has stayed at that hotel several times, so I guess he wanted to show her that he could support her in a lavish lifestyle." She saw my surprise and laughed again. "What's the matter? Are you in a hurry, little swan?"

I stiffened, clenching my fists. "We both have a deadline tomorrow, and one of us will certainly die if Alex and I can't save Ana. Help us. We can make things right for you, Sin."

Sin sashayed back to the bench, where she put away her pack of cigarettes and lighter into her pouch. Then the smirk returned as she leaned down to straighten the back seam of her nylon, taking her time.

"Can you take me back to when I was eighteen and a promising prima ballerina under your grandmother's tutelage? Can you undo the car accident that messed up my knee so I'd never dance again? It's all your grandmother's fault! She orchestrated both events to get rid of me. She's the one who's evil, not me!"

Sin's voice had increased in volume, her words coming faster and faster, while her eyes flitted around the police department, coming to rest on Dasha. "No, I'm wrong. It's you! It's *you* who ruined my life. I don't care if it's you *or* Tattie. You both represent the same thing. Evil. Aristocracy. Corruption."

Everyone had stopped talking, their eyes on Sin. She glanced over her shoulder, then lowered her voice. "That's why I am sending Katya to end Anastasia's life. If she dies, you cease to exist. The world will be back in order once again, and I will get to be the prima ballerina. Don't you see? It's so simple." She spread her arms wide, as if she were an angel instead of the devil.

A commotion at the front entrance grabbed our attention when a loud alarm went off to indicate a fire. It set off a series of electric bells that were impossible to ignore.

"Hey!" a police sergeant called out. "We just installed that thing. Why's it going off now?"

"Everyone, secure your suspects, then evacuate the premises." The Chief of Police came rushing from a back room and grabbed his coat from a coat tree in the corner that was filled to overflowing with winter coats and jackets. Seconds later, the coat rack was empty, and the chaos set in.

"We'll burn up in here! Let us out!" one suspect shouted.

The suspects began shoving their way toward the entrance, some even jumping over others to get out. A tide of fear spread like gulls in a feeding frenzy on the shores of Lake Michigan.

While the human tide quickly formed a haphazard flow to the outside, no one but I noticed the calm, distinguished older man enter the station. Perhaps what set him apart was the wide smile visible beneath the brim of his Fedora.

"Enz...I mean Uncle Guido!" I almost blew it when I started to say his name, but a sharp pinch from Alex stopped me in time.

Enzo wound his way around the desks, stopping briefly to pick up an object wrapped in blue silk from the desk of the officer who'd arrested us and one of the first to evacuate the building. He grabbed the key to the cell and let us out, pointing to the back of the office.

"How did you know we were here?" Alex inquired.

"I've got eyes all over this city, bambino," Enzo said with a chuckle.

"Thank goodness," I said, grabbing my coat.

As the door shut behind us, I saw Enzo slip the blue silk into his pocket. When I turned around, he winked, and the next time I looked, he was gone.

When we stepped outside, Alex and his eagle eyes caught sight of Sin making a run for the subway stop across the street. He grabbed me by the hand as we dashed in between cars on Michigan Avenue, cars honking, people yelling. As most folks were returning home from work, we descended into the underground to a sea of stressed-out Chicagoans of every age and ethnicity converging on the city and suburbs in all directions.

Alex held my hand tightly as we looked in both directions for Sin. But to my surprise, I saw Ana, instead, and caught a glimpse of Misha beside her, holding a child, ready to board a subway train north. Sin must have seen them as well, because she and Katya squeezed into one of the last cars.

"We have to make that train," Alex warned. "Otherwise, we'll lose them in this crowd. Go!" The doors of the train car were in the process of closing, but Alex didn't let that stop him. He managed to insert his fingers and pried the doors apart, then yanked me inside after him.

Disgruntled commuters gave us dirty looks for delaying the train. Alex ignored them and watched through the door window, determined to see where Sin and Ana disembarked.

Standing behind Alex, I leaned forward and whispered. "Do you know where they're going?"

His brow furrowed in concentration as the train gathered speed, only to coast to a stop at the first station. "I might have an idea, but I don't want to jinx it. Can you bear with me?"

"Of course."

"Hey, outta the way! Gettin' off here," a man said as he shoved his way forward.

Alex stepped back with a sigh. At the next stop, two seats became available, and Alex indicated I should occupy one. A very pregnant lady was relieved when he offered her the other seat on the aisle. I hadn't had a good look when Misha cradled the child, so I couldn't help but wonder how big Ana's child was now. Was the toddler dark, like Misha, or darkish-blonde, like Ana?

Four more stops took us almost to the end of the line. From my window seat, I saw what I hoped was Anastasia's wild, frizzy hair from the back. She and Misha walked toward the exit. I signaled Alex and silently wished the pregnant lady well. Then we rushed up the stairs to the street and found ourselves in a lovely tree-lined suburb called Maple Grove. As we looked around for Ana and Misha, I couldn't help thinking this was exactly the kind of place I hoped they could go to raise their family and live an ordinary life. Despite the snow that still covered much of the landscape, it wasn't hard to imagine trees in bloom come spring.

"You keep an eye out for Ana and Misha. I'll watch for Sin and Katya."

Although Alex was once again giving me orders, now that we were off the hot, crowded, smelly train and inhaling fresh air, I didn't care. Perhaps because of the unending mad dashes, Alex held onto my hand as we walked briskly in the direction of downtown. Maybe he'd forgotten he even held it. Every once in a while, I'd glance at his face, but he was enjoying his stealth mode too much to notice me. I couldn't blame him. We'd come so far.

The noise of a toddler throwing a tantrum jangled my nerves, and I automatically covered my ears as Misha and Ana paused in front of a store window. The little boy in Misha's arms kicked and screamed until Misha put him down.

Alex stopped and turned to face me, as if we were tourists. "Remember, your grandmother said to stay in the background. No interaction, unless necessary."

He arranged my wool hat so it partially hid my face, and then patted my hair into place, before peeking to see what Misha and Ana were doing. If they recognized us, their reaction was subtle. Ana scooped up the boy, then she and Misha ducked into a family shoe store.

"Maybe the boy just wanted new shoes," I mumbled.

"I don't know. Let's go shoe shopping and find out."

Before we could head for the door, a black Ford Model T pulled into a parking spot in front of a furniture store to the right of the shoe store. I recognized the fashionable hat and long wool coat with the rabbit fur collar of the woman driving. *Sin Ryland*. She lifted something from the back seat and turned to Katya, who'd added a scarf tied around her head. But as the pair exited the car, I noticed that Katya still wore the black party dress and long wool sweater from before. Her legs were bare, and her shoes thin-soled. I couldn't believe she wasn't shivering.

I placed a hand on Alex's arm. "Wait. I don't think they've spotted us yet."

He opened a map and pretended to be looking for something as Sin and Katya entered the shoe store. "Give them two minutes, and then we'll go inside and see what's what."

"I have a bad feeling about this. The fact that they knew exactly where Ana and Misha would be is too much of a coincidence."

"You may be right. Let's go."

Alex opened the door to the shoe store, and a white flash dashed past us to the street, followed by a little red-haired boy.

Ana, who'd been looking for snow boots for her boy, dropped a boot onto the concrete floor with a thud. "William!" she screamed, then ran after the boy and dog.

From the corner of my eye, I saw Sin and Katya trying on short boots nearby.

Misha had been having a quiet conversation with a young man a few years younger than him, who had the same dark hair and bright blue eyes. When he saw Alex and me, Misha blinked and hurried out the door after Ana.

"I can't let anything happen to that dog," said the young man who'd been conversing with Misha. He turned to Alex. "I've been taking care of him while my brother and his family are out of town. William will be crushed if anything happens to that little escape monster." He locked his cash register and pointed at a sign in the window. "I'm Spencer. Could you please put up that sign that says I'll be back in fifteen minutes?" he asked Alex, a complete stranger, then headed out with a leash and collar.

Alex rushed over and picked up a business card near the register on the counter. He held it up. "I think that was Misha's younger brother, Spencer Morgan. I've heard Misha talk about him once or twice."

"They could almost be twins."

"You may be right. Let's go."

But before I could make a move for the door, Katya threw on her slippers and rushed out the door, with Sin close behind, leaving me and Alex alone in the store.

"Hurry! We have to follow them," I said.

Alex tossed the business card onto the counter, then we raced out the door.

From the front seat of her convertible, I saw Sin check her scarf in the rearview mirror while Katya finished putting on her old shoes. "Oh, let's *do* join the hunt," said Sin. "We could have a little white dog *and* a whiney red-haired boy for dinner."

Katya made a strange face. "That's not funny."

Though Sin had the advantage of the car, we could change focus quickly. We followed her car for only two blocks, then she parked and got out.

"What is she holding?" Alex asked, squinting.

"It's shaped like either a trombone...or a Persian Sword."

Alex regarded me as we ran after her. "Damn. If she hurts anyone..."

"She's taking that path, the one to the right, with the sign that says, Maple Grove City Park."

I picked up the hem of my coat and took off, using my long legs to my advantage. Behind me, I could hear Alex's boots on the stone walkway that led to the first clearing we came upon, ringed by oak and maple trees stripped of their leaves from the last snowstorm. Ahead of me, Katya's back was to me as she reached into her pocket and pulled out a gun. Ana and Misha took refuge behind a picnic table while other families screamed in terror and scattered, when suddenly, William broke free of their grasp and climbed onto the picnic table to hug his squirmy pup that had leaped onto it.

When Alex reached me, he pulled me to the side. It was then I realized Katya held a pistol aimed at Ana.

"Stay here," he said, directing me to hide behind a tree.

"No, Alex. I need to make this right."

"Dash, no!"

I moved directly into Katya's line of fire. "Katya, what do you plan to do with that gun? Did Sin talk you into this? She's not stable, you know."

"You shut up, Little Miss Perfect!" Sin called out from her spot to the left.

What I'd thought was a Persian sword, turned out to be a shotgun, which Sin pointed at me now. "You think you can stop this, but it's been simmering for a long time. There's no going back."

I narrowed my eyes and stepped closer to Katya. "If this is how you think you'll get your revenge, Katya, you're wrong."

"Don't listen to her," Sin interrupted. "She's a nobody. If you kill Ana, your life will be yours again. Your father's life will be avenged." Sin's voice sounded almost soothing. Perhaps she'd learned a thing or two about hypnosis from Rasputin, because that was the effect she was having on Katya.

Ana climbed on top of the picnic table to grab her son, then cradled her toddler while she kept her back toward Katya—Ana the ultimate protective mother. Meanwhile, Misha tried to grab a hold of the West Highland Terrier, or Westie, as they were called, a lively little thing, who William clearly adored.

On silent feet, Alex moved close enough to reach out and touch my shoulder. He whispered, "Keep her talking while I decide what to do with Sin."

Sin, indeed.

I wanted to tell him he didn't have to save everybody, but I knew it would be wasted breath. Alex was an old-fashioned kind of hero. However, I had my own ideas. I wanted no one to get hurt, and to talk through our problems. Naive as that may be, I still preferred to avoid any violence.

"Leave me be," said Katya in a perfectly calm voice. "I'm following through on a promise I made to my mother. I mean to keep it."

"Keeping your promise won't solve anything, Katya. It only repeats history."

She turned her head toward me. For some reason, the little Westie took that as a sign to wiggle his way out of the dangerous spotlight. He leaped over the picnic table bench, and took off the way they'd come in the direction of the parking lot, his little legs pumping as fast as they would go.

Ana snapped William up in her arms and climbed down off of the picnic table, Misha coming to join them, collar and leash in hand. Ana held William protectively as we all watched Sin lift her gun and aim for the little family.

"No, you don't, Sin!" I yelled, then dove into the mud to bring Sin down.

A wild shot went off, and I heard the dog squeal. Furious, I knocked Sin to the ground, horrified to see Finley just lying there.

William pushed his way out of his mother's arms and ran as fast as he could to cradle the dog. Ana and Misha didn't hesitate a second, as they raced to join their boy on the ground, which was still partially covered with snow in places where the sun hadn't exposed its warm rays.

Alex helped the family wrap a blanket around the dog. I felt sick inside, thinking of William's little white dog. Little boys shouldn't lose their best companions like that.

But Sin wasn't finished. She stood up, then lifted her shotgun once more and aimed it straight at Ana's heart. I leapt into the air and we came down with a crash. I wrestled briefly with her, finally taking the gun from her. I don't know if it was adrenaline or what, but I looked her in the eye, and could see she was scared.

"I wasn't really going to kill Ana," she said. "Katya, we're still friends, right?"

"You're *crazy*. I don't want to be anything like you," Katya said, dropping her pistol in a snowbank.

"Good girl," I said, pulling my gun from my waistband and pointing it at Sin. "Now come here and sit, where we can see you."

Families were returning to the park one by one, but as I looked at Finley, I said, "Has anyone called the police yet?"

"I did," said the father of twin girls. "They're on their way."

"Daddy, look at the little doggy. What's wrong with him?" one of the twins whispered.

I felt relief that I'd saved Ana's life, but as I kept the gun trained on Sin, I had to fight the tears that flowed nonstop down my cheeks. I'd always been sympathetic toward animals. Perhaps even more so than Sasha, the Kitty Queen, who'd seen her share of injured and lost cats.

Now that I had the tears under control, Alex stood watch over Sin so that I could go comfort William. I walked over and put a hand on Finley's little head. Blood smeared the dog's white coat, but I couldn't tell where the wound was coming from.

"William, what's your dog's name?"

"Finney."

"Finley," said Ana, doing a better job than me at fighting back tears.

Finley's little tail wagged at the sound of his name. I patted his head gently and he licked my hand.

One time clock had ended, with hours to spare. We had very little time to save the pup. I stood in the middle of the crowd that soon surrounded Ana, Misha and William, while Ana tried to hide her face with her long hair. Maybe, for this one event, I could help.

I brushed aside my own tears. "Does anyone have a car so we can transport Finley to the vet? We may still be able to save him in time."

"I'd be happy to drive you both to the vet," came a man's rich baritone that sounded so familiar. "My car's just over there."

My heart danced with joy to hear that voice. I was beginning to think Enzo Calvani was a leprechaun. My own private leprechaun. He grinned and told Finley what a good dog he was, but I felt like he included me in that greeting, and I knew then and there that everything would be all right.

Chapter 31

*"Look at your patterns to previous relationships and see what your
current love, or prospective new partner, can offer you that is
different and ultimately fulfilling."*
(Tarot Card: The Lovers)

The veterinary hospital was small, so we took turns occupying the ancient aqua vinyl seats. In one corner, Misha, Ana and William waited to hear the fate of their little Westie, Finley. William had finally stopped crying, and sat quietly sucking his thumb on his mother's lap. Misha's brother, Spencer, was also there, taking the rest of the day off from his shoe store manager position. Once she heard the news, Misha's older sister, Geraldine, arrived with home-cooked fried chicken and potato salad. Enzo stood near a back wall the whole time, not saying a word.

The vet was a young female, Dr. Josephine Barnshaw, which, for some reason, made me very happy. I loved seeing more women enter and excel in professions previously open only to men. I suspect Spencer had a bit of a crush on Josephine, or Dr. Jo, as everyone called her. I happened to think Dr. Jo and Spencer would make a handsome couple, if they ever got over their shyness and spoke to each other.

As I leaned against the wall and watched these wonderfully "ordinary" people go about their daily lives, I wondered how my story would end. I knew I had to do some serious thinking before Alex and I talked, so I stepped outside for a quick breath of fresh air. Enzo silently followed.

We'd received the good news that Finley had a flesh injury, and would make a full recovery. That was a good reason to celebrate with fried chicken.

"Can I ask you a question, Enzo?"

"Of course, my dear." He sat on a wooden bench in front of the vet's office and pulled out a cigar.

I never would have thought a Chicago mobster named Enzo Calvani would be my fairy godmother, but life is full of surprises. I wanted to know what some of those surprises might be.

"Why have you helped me and Alex so many times the past few days? I mean, we're complete strangers, and we've no doubt kept you away from your business responsibilities." I didn't mention being tied up in Vincente's Italian Restaurant the first time we learned of Enzo. That seemed so long ago now.

He nodded at my question and clipped the end of the cigar, taking his time to light it.

"I first met your Grandmother Tatiana at a dance when she was eighteen." He puffed on his cigar and gazed at Main Street as a better-late-than-never snowplow cleared up the muck. "She sure was a looker, tall and willowy, with the most graceful way of moving. She told me she was a ballet dancer."

"Did she say why she was in Chicago?"

He shook his head and blew a smoke ring. "Tatiana was a very private person. I got the impression she'd left San Francisco because of some trouble. It might have had something to do with a guy her parents had chosen for her to marry. She had relatives here, so she stayed the summer to give her time to simmer down." He closed his eyes briefly. "She always smelled like lilacs when she danced. It didn't take me long to fall for her. Eventually, I asked her to marry me. She knew my line of work, and I think that bothered her, though she seldom said anything. Tatiana was a good girl, but she had an independent streak."

Shocked by this description of my grandmother, I nonetheless waited, expecting some other revelation. When he didn't resume the story, I cleared my throat. "What was her response to your proposal?"

Enzo shrugged and put his cigar out, sticking it in a coat pocket for later. "She was gone the next day. Just like that. Never even said goodbye."

I tried to summon a recollection of what my grandmother was doing at that age from the stories I'd heard over the years, but I couldn't recall her revealing any big event in her life back then.

"I'm sorry she didn't respond. It must have been shortly after she returned that she started her dancing career at the Duquette Ballet Academy. She worked so hard to get there. Dancers are obsessed, so please don't take it personally, Mr. Calvani."

"Who did she marry? Some rich guy in San Francisco?"

I hesitated, sensing he was still wounded by the past slight. I didn't want to make him feel worse by mentioning my grandfather, or the fact that my dad had inherited millions of dollars from his father..

"Grandma Tattie's first husband died young from a long illness. She married a kind Irishman, who also died in 1997. She's been a widow for a long time now. She raised my father, and keeps me and my sisters out of trouble."

Enzo nodded quietly. "So, she had a good life."

"The best."

He stood and inhaled the cold, clean air. I heard the front door of Dr. Jo's office open, and Misha stepped out, gently holding a much livelier Finley, while Ana carried William...my great grandfather.

I glanced around to see if anyone lurked nearby, seeking to take another potshot at Ana. Enzo stepped down from the porch steps. As he did, I felt the slightest weight fall into my coat pocket.

But when I turned, he was nowhere to be seen. I felt inside my pocket and pulled out a silk cloth that contained a watch pendant on a gold chain. The pendant was large—perhaps three inches tall and two inches wide. If you held it at arms' length, you could make out the shape of a spotted cat. Its cat eyes were emerald green, rimmed in gold. I smiled, but why had Enzo given it to me? I shrugged and promised myself I'd deal with it later. Meanwhile, I couldn't help wondering if I would ever see Enzo again.

For now, I turned and focused on Ana. I was struck by how closely she and William resembled each other with their reddish-blond curls that would plague Ana for many years. Her son's blue eyes didn't miss a thing, especially where food was concerned. I saw nothing of Misha in William, but then, the whole DNA thing could be such a fluke.

"Finney going to play soon!" crowed William, clapping his hands together.

Ana smiled and kissed his chubby cheek. "Now, remember what Dr. Jo said. You have to be gentle until Finley is ready to play. Can you do that?"

"I can!"

She put him down, and he climbed into the back seat, Finley resting comfortably on his lap. I was so relieved with how everything had turned out, but it was starting to sink in that it was over. No more Sin. No reason to perpetually be peering over my shoulder.

I placed a hand on Ana's arm and drew her aside, hoping for a few final words. I could see Misha, William, and Spencer, anxious to be on their way.

"I know you're in a hurry, but—"

"You saved my life, Dasha. Thanks to you, I have my own family to cherish and love. You and Alex experienced some pretty horrible treatment because I couldn't decide whether to live or die. I just wish I'd known about the Time Menders sooner. I could have saved us all some time. I'll never forget your kindness and your patience."

She leaned forward and hugged me tightly, then stepped back.

"Where will you go?" I covered my mouth with my hand. "Oh! That's classified information, isn't it? What will you do? Oh, darn! What *can* I ask you? I want to visualize you and your family living in some place with four seasons. With people who don't judge you by your name. A place where you can explore and discover all kinds of new possibilities for who you want to be and what you want to do."

"When you think of me in that perfect environment, call me...Erika, okay?" She paused, as though filled with emotion. "And thank you most of all for giving me back my life, Dasha Marusova. I hope *your* life is full of peace and family, as well. Perhaps Alex will be a part of that family?"

My cheeks warmed at the mention of Alex. I'd been so busy speaking with the Grand Duchess that I'd all but forgotten Alex, who stood at the top of the stairs, arms crossed and wearing a doubtful expression. I would think of something to get his mind off what she said later, when we were alone. At last.

Erika gripped my arm gently. "I have to go. If you truly need to get in touch with us, use the timepiece that Mr. Calvani slipped in your pocket. He says it will take you wherever you want to go, even without talismans from home. Just think about the time, the place and the person, and you'll be there."

"How did you know about the watch?" I asked, retrieving it from my pocket.

Ana laughed, the sound a relief after so much tragedy in her life. "Funny story, that. Mr. Calvani was asking your grandmother to marry him, and had just taken her hand when both of them were whisked off to Russia on a mission."

"But Enzo's not part of BTM—"

"No, it was a simple accident. She got him back safely, but while he was there, he saved my brother from a fall, so I gave him the watch as a token of my appreciation. It was an old family heirloom. Now, it's yours, and I couldn't be happier."

Ana placed the locket over my neck and set the clasp. "I was worried I'd be dead and buried, along with that watch. It's impossible to miss, don't you think?" She winked.

I fingered one of the jeweled eyes of the cat. A watery smile curved my lips. "I kind of like it."

"Then, my job is done."

I didn't want to keep her any longer. She kissed me on both cheeks, then walked over to Spencer's car.

"Maybe I'll meet your two sisters one day," said Erika.

I laughed and nodded. "Maybe. They would love to meet you, I'm sure. Thanks for everything."

Misha stepped forward. "Thanks, Alex and Dasha. You made it so we can be together as a family. Now we won't have to worry about who's on our tail. But what will happen to Sin?"

I sobered and looked down at my feet. "She's been taken into custody. I don't think she'll get away with staying in a mental hospital this time. There were too many witnesses."

"And Katya? What happened to her?" asked Erika from the back seat.

I had to shrug at that. "I'm hoping she went home to Russia, and will stay there. I have a feeling she's not so hot-headed anymore."

"And if she is?" Alex quietly came to stand beside me.

"I guess we'll have to look in on her and see how she's doing. Don't you think BTM will make that decision?"

"Probably." We waved as the new family took off. I didn't know if Spencer was taking them to a big city, or to his home in Maple Grove. But it occurred to me, I should let go. I could start making my own plans and decisions about my life. And it didn't feel so scary anymore.

I held out my hand to Alex and started walking.

Epilogue

"This card denotes triumph, completion, and reward for your efforts. It also signifies deep joy and happiness, and now you can really feel you deserved success. Life feels balanced, too, as work, relationships, finances, and domestic affairs run smoothly."
(Tarot Card: The World)

Eight Months Later
Present Day

I sat in our living room with my parents, sisters, and Grandma Tattie on a beautiful summer's evening, the windows open to let in a cool breeze off the Pacific Ocean. Both Rosana, the cook, and Carita, the house cleaner, had been given the day off with pay.

Today happened to be Grandma Tattie's eightieth birthday, and even though she wasn't one to groan and complain about her "old lady" pains, I could tell she was tired but happy to have all us there. While Sasha, our Baking Queen, had put together a gorgeous three-layer red velvet cake with vanilla buttercream frosting, Grandma wanted things low-key in terms of presents. And usually, what Grandma Tattie wanted, Grandma Tattie got.

"What's the use in buying me some fancy piece of crystal, when I'll just have to turn around and give it back to you when I die? That's just plain silly."

Eight months had come and gone since our return from Chicago. By now, Tattie had broken the news about the family time travel business. The fact that Mom had known all along and Dad did not had caused a few days of tension, but eventually Dad gave in, muttering, "I always knew there was something screwy going on around here."

They weren't happy with the idea of me taking off every now and then, but I reassured them the current missions would be light and easy, usually completed in a day. I also started training in martial arts and had signed up for a brush-up course in world history, and an advanced course in Russian conversation, so I was already feeling better prepared. I hadn't seen Alex all this time, not since his appointment as Director of the Bureau of Time Menders. Though I had no doubt he was extremely busy, I pushed back any disappointment and forged ahead with my own plans, hoping we could reconnect at some point.

I'd been thinking of Grandma Tattie, and I wanted to ask if she'd had anything to do with Sin's car accident. According to Sin, my grandmother had been responsible for the accident that ruined her ballet career. But the more I thought about it, the more I realized my grandmother would never do anything like that unless it meant saving countless lives. Maybe I was starting to think like a true Time Mender.

We'd been enjoying our cake when the doorbell rang. Gigi jumped up and returned a minute later, reading an envelope. The handwriting had faded, the paper soaked at some point, then dried, and was now impossible to read.

"It must be a birthday card for Grandma Tattie," said Gigi, handing it to her.

Grandmother held it up to the light and shook her head. "I can't read the return address or a postmark."

"Maybe it's one of those lost letters from a back room of the post office," suggested Gigi.

"I don't think that would happen, Geej," said Sasha, taking the card and turning it over. "Though I'm pretty sure that's your name on the front, Grandma Tattie. You should open it."

"I agree," said a male voice behind me. Alex stepped into the living room and waved. "Sorry. Someone forgot to close the front door." He glanced at Gigi, who turned a pretty pink.

"Ooops. Sorry, Mom."

"You're just asking for us to be robbed someday," muttered Dad, waving Alex in.

"Oh, do come in and have some of my birthday cake, Alex," Grandma Tattie said. "The girls were just asking about you."

"We were? That was about three weeks ago." I made room on the leather sofa, but Alex opted to sit in a side chair. I decided to act cool, like I didn't care. I was so tired of those on-again, off-again, romantic games. If he wanted to talk to me, all he had to do was say so. Besides, Brendon was back in town after his world tour. He had called, and we talked for a while. He did sound a bit more mature, and I had no doubt the experience had been good for him. But he wasn't Alex.

Since then, in between studying and training, I had worked a lot of hours at the foundation. I'd felt a renewed sense of purpose and obligation to those women who had no homes and no way out of a difficult situation. I was currently trying to talk a famous Russian folksinger into playing at our next fundraiser, but it was hard getting a hold of him with the distance and communication problems.

With my mind back on work, I'd all but forgotten about the envelope. However, Grandma Tattie hadn't. She slit it open and pulled out a card. It was indeed a birthday card, an old-fashioned one at that. At the same time, a piece of paper fell out.

Grandma held up the paper so she could read it out loud. "This is a check for your foundation in the sum of $100,000." She handed it to Mom. "Am I reading that correctly?"

Mom's eyes grew large. "It is indeed for $100,000. Who is it from?" She turned the check over and over, but the name was no clearer.

"We can take it to a bank to make sure it's still valid," Grandma Tattie said, "but I have a feeling it's from the BTM's 'Mysterious Benefactor'. Just last week, Melinda in Accounting told me she has received two $50,000 checks a year on a regular basis from Enzo Calvani to be kept anonymous until his death. He made arrangements for $50,000 of that to help and train BTM operatives, and $25,000 goes to the Foundation. Starting this year, however, another $25,000 will go to support my neediest ballet babies. This is the first time money has been sent directly to me."

"He was a smart man," Alex commented.

Grandma Tattie held the check near her nose and I wondered if she could smell cigar smoke after all these years.

"Enzo Calvani was a tough gangster, but a kind man with a big heart." I felt my voice tremble. "He was kind of a crazy uncle, but he treated us like family." I was going to say something about how he stopped his getaway car during a bank robbery to take us to the Palmer House in Chicago, but as if Alex read my mind, he gave me a grouchy look that stopped me. "And he did all that because of you, Grandma Tattie."

"Maybe he set it up to have those checks continue automatically until the money runs out," said Dad, already turning back to the evening newspaper.

"That would be my guess." Alex agreed. "Would you excuse Dasha and me for a few minutes? I'd like to talk to her about a different subject."

"Of course. Go on, Dasha." Mom was suddenly the matchmaker, and although I didn't like it, I walked outside to watch the sun go down from the front porch, hoping this wouldn't take long.

We closed the front door after us and sat on the porch swing. Alex pulled something out of his pocket, and unwrapped the watch timepiece—the one Enzo had dropped in my pocket. I recognized it right away by the saucy expression on what appeared to be a spotted jungle cat's face.

"I thought you gave that to your research team. Didn't they find anything out about it?"

"The team did some controlled experiments. It does do what Ana—I mean, *Erika* said it would. The person wearing the necklace can travel to any place, time, or person, with just a few words. Because of its cat-like shape, we're calling it 'The Cat Master', for short."

"How *cat*-chy."

He ignored my pun. "We've found two other cat necklaces similar to it, so far, which you need to see. Each cat has a slightly different look and includes different jewels and gemstones." He handed The Cat Master to me, along with the other two, which made my fingers tingle. I took the pieces and turned them over, squinting at the writing.

"Where were the other necklaces found?"

Alex hesitated long enough for me to catch that knowing smile of his. "The Pinkertons were hired by the family of the woman who owned the two originally. A treasure diver found these two necklaces near the sunken ship at the bottom of Lake Michigan after a heist some years back." He indicated the necklaces I held. "They want you to hold onto the original one that Ana gave Enzo."

"Me? I can't accept it. Give it to that woman's family, the one who the other two necklaces belong to."

Alex chuckled. "You don't get to pick and choose who gets to keep the necklace, nor do you get to choose your missions, my lady. Besides, the woman who owned them is no longer living, and apparently she had no heirs. But there's someone out there who wants this Cat Master and the two others really badly, so that's why I need your help."

I thought about it. "Are you asking me to join you on another dangerous assignment? Wait...who does this cat necklace impact? Who's messing with history?"

"That's what I'm hoping to discover, which is why I'm going undercover with the Pinkertons. And I want you to come and pose as my bride...so we can find out together."

Acknowledgments

I was catching up with my email one day, and I came across something unusual. I don't recall the exact details, but it seems I received a message that invited me to "pick a card." Oh boy! So, I chose a card, and then forgot all about it – until the next day, when I received a message from a "Madame Esmeralda," tarot reader. She said, "I've been concerned since I read your card yesterday. I feel you are not living the life you were meant to live." My first reaction was, "Well, of course not!" I don't remember which card I drew. I don't recall if she was trying to sell me a complete tarot reading (which seems likely, since that was her business). Those words somehow freaked me out, at least a little. I quickly buried the email and tried not to think about it. "If I'm not living the life I was meant to, then whose life is it?"

From there, Dasha's story bubbled to the surface. This was a "first," in several regards. It's the first major character I've written from a first-person point of view. I had no idea how freeing that could be. The memories (including the Russian language) came rushing back. The sights, the sounds of balalaika music, the smell of rich and earthy Russian food, and, oh yeah, the Cold War.

The second thing, and maybe more important, is that as a former librarian, I'm a keeper of lists. Lists that go on and on. But this story came so fast, I had a hard time keeping up with the thorough outline I had started. So, I decided to take the plunge and become a "pantser," one of those renegade writers who don't use outlines at all. They just write by the seat of their pants. And I felt free, to a point.

All this is to say I want to thank Carol Craig, writer – friend – editor, and founder of the Editing Gallery, who had the patience and sense of humor to endure my lists. Without your compass, I'd be in Siberia about now, stuck in a swamp (do they have swamps in Siberia?). Thank you for liking my story and always encouraging me to the end. What more could I ask for as a writer?

I also want to thank Elaine Stec, whom we met all those years ago in our first critique group. I appreciate your opinions and ideas, and only wish we could see more of you. Thanks for the details regarding working in a morgue. I'm going to hold onto the ideas I didn't use this time, and save them for the *next* book. Oh, boy! I'm sure they will be useful.

Since the story started out with tarot cards, I must thank Joni Herbst for sharing her tarot history and wisdom. I have a long way to go to call myself an expert, but at least, by the end of the story, I had a good idea how to handle the chapter content with the tarot meanings above many chapter headings. Thank you, thank you, thank you!

As always, a huge thanks to my brother, David for keeping my computer humming along, and working with the newsletter. You are the best.

This novel was a joy to write, and I thank you, the reader, for choosing to read my first novel in what may be a new series. I wish you many giggles and laugh-out-loud moments along the way.

Author's Notes

The Main Character

I've always been fascinated with the story of Anastasia and the last Russian royal family, and what became of them. It took a while, but Russian forensics finally caught up and admitted that one of the two graves where the Romanov family is buried contained the remains of Anastasia. Always a curious person, I wondered what may have happened if she had survived and escaped Russia. What would her death mean to any possible descendants? From those thoughts came the Time Menders, with Dasha Marusov and her family, and Grandma Tattie (Tatiana) leading the way to "fix" those glitches in time and offer a happy ending, instead.

A Cast of Thousands

Since I ended up with over sixty named characters (Leo Tolstoy, look out!), I created a *Master Character List* of all characters mentioned in *The Time Menders*, even if they didn't appear "on stage." I hope you find this useful. It will also appear on my website (see below).

Russian Vocabulary

I also prepared a basic Russian vocabulary list, so you don't need to make a major purchase of a Russian dictionary. I'm happy to have discovered that even 40+ years after taking high school and college Russian classes, I still remember a few words. Usually food-related words. ☺

Tarot

I am no tarot card expert, but being a good librarian, I consulted several books that were particularly helpful for a beginner. Among them, my favorites were:

- Jones, Ruby. *The Heart's Compass; navigating love and relationships through tarot.*

- Dean, Liz. *The Ultimate Guide to Tarot.*

Both these books placed an emphasis on the thorny world of relationships (career, partner, and love), and the path to true love, which is right where I wanted my focus for the novel to be. My interpretations are my own, so please forgive any major deviations. I selected what I felt were close tarot matches with the contents of a particular chapter regarding Dasha and Alex only, because it was Dasha's story to tell.

Rasputin's Death

Grigori Rasputin managed to use his priestly hypnotic eyes to lull the ladies at court, and, in particular, influence Tsarina Alexandra regarding the health of her only son and heir, Alexei, who suffered from hemophilia. When Nicholas II left for war, he left Alexandra in charge of the country. She made the mistake of keeping company with Rasputin, who loudly bragged about his ability to control Nicholas II and Alexandra. Vicious rumors spread about his relationship with the tsarina. By 1916, his power and influence waned, and the Russian people lost all respect for the Romanov government. On the eve of December 30, 1916, Rasputin was murdered. Legend has it he ate tea cakes laced with cyanide; imbibed three glasses of poisoned Madeira wine with no signs of distress; was shot in the chest, but suddenly jumped up and attacked his assassin, chasing him outside; and, finally, wrapped in a cloth, his body was dropped into the Little Neva River. It would seem he was quite the superman. When the official surgeon gave his autopsy report, he stated that his death was caused by a single bullet fired into the head at close range.

Consequently, when it came time to get "Grisha" Rasputin out of the way permanently in my story, I chose the tourist route. He found Bubba Gump Shrimp in San Francisco, totally overate, and decided to climb Lombard Street for exercise. Dying on the spot of a heart attack at the top of the street and being placed in a grave with the fake name Oleg Slobotkin on the headstone so no one would be the wiser that he was the real Rasputin, his presence was wiped from time. I mean, the guy was evil.

If you enjoyed this book, I'd love to hear from you. I will be placing extra 'free' materials on my website, as mentioned above and noted below, and will keep you posted on the next book in the series. While you're at it, sign up for my newsletter so you can hear all the news hot off the press!

Thank you, readers. You make my day. :)

Laine Stambaugh
(10/06/2025)
laine@lainestambaugh.com

Master Character List
The Time Menders

(as of: 10/28/2025)

BTM = Bureau of Time Menders (Good Guys)
vs.
ATTO = Anti-Time Travel Oversight (Bad Guys)

NOTE: Not all characters appear "on stage." Some are in the background and mentioned for backstory purposes. Names in BOLD and ALL CAPS are major characters. The following list is by character's first name.

ALEX McKAIN: Senior Agent for the BTM, originally from Texas in 1886, and a former Texas Ranger and Pinkerton Operative. *(ALLY & HERO).*

Alexandra (**SASHA**) Marusov: Sasha's birth name. Dasha's middle sister. See also: Sasha.

Amanda Corbin: Dasha's college roommate.

Anastasia Romanov: Youngest of the four daughters of Nicholas II & Alexandra; also known as Ana. See also: Annie Marist.

Annie Marist: The aka for Anastasia after she escapes Russia.

Ardith Jones: Kitchen assistant at Vincente's Italian Restaurant in 1920s Chicago.

Barnshaw, Dr. Josephine: Veterinarian in Maple Grove.

Beacham, Dr. Shawn: ER doctor who sews Dasha's stitches in present day.

Ben Mikoyan: Dalton's best friend in college.

Brendon Alessio: Lead singer for his band, All Souls Day, which appears at the Foundation fundraiser.

Ceara Donovan: Lead ballet dancer for 'Swan Lake' when Grandma Tattie taught at the fictitious Duquette Ballet.

Chef Dante: Head Chef at Vincente's, Enzo's favorite Italian restaurant in 1920s Chicago.

Clark Meadows: Dasha's first kiss (at 12).

Dalton Fairfax: Dasha's college boyfriend/fiancé, killed in a freak wrestling accident her senior year.

Daria Marusov: Dasha's birth name; see also: Dasha.

DASHA MARUSOV: Dasha is diminutive for Daria. Eldest Marusov sister. (***PROTAGONIST & HEROINE).***

Dianna: Young server who spills champagne at the fundraiser. Dasha steps in when her supervisor (Alex) gives her a bad time.

Dima: Diminutive for Dimitri; Madame Peshkova's (Katya's) bodyguard.

Enzo Calvani: Fictitious 1920s Chicago gangster who befriends Dasha and Alex.

Faakhir: Sin's Evil Henchman #1.

Geraldine Morgan: Older sister of Michael (Misha) and Spencer Morgan; lives in Maple Grove.

Gigi Marusov: Dasha's nickname for youngest sister, see also: Grace Gabrielle.

Grace Gabrielle: Birth name for Dasha's youngest sister. See also: Gigi Marusov.

Grandma Tattie: Dasha's grandmother on her father's side; Dasha gave her the nickname 'Tattie' when very small. see also: Tatiana Marusov) (*ALLY*).

Grigori (Rasputin; see also: Grisha; Rasputin).

Grisha: He depends on Sin to help him escape death in 1916, then forces Katya to alter a time travel potion so he can keep ahead of the authorities. (*ANTAGONIST*).

Ilya, Prince of Caldoran: Dasha's dance partner in 1918 Moscow; a penniless prince looking for a beautiful woman with money in exchange for a title.

Irisa Marusov: Dasha's mother and CEO of the Heart-Held Women's Shelter Foundation. Married to Pyotr (Pete) Marusov.

J.J.: kitchen assistant at Vincente's Italian Restaurant in 1920s Chicago.

Jan: Irisa's personal assistant at the Heart-Held Foundation.

Katya: Diminutive for Ekaterina; see also: Madame Peshkova. Her goal is revenge against Tsar Nicholas Romanov, his Russian nobles, and all of the Romanov family, who covered up a food stampede-turned-tragedy when her father was killed on the day she was born—the day Nicholas II was crowned. (*ANTAGONIST, SHAPESHIFTER*)

Lillian: Works in Marketing at the Heart-Held Foundation with Irisa.

Lissa Carter: BTM staff member who provides clothes for Dasha in 1818.

Madame Peshkova: Katya's tarot card fortune telling persona inherited from her mother and enhanced with Dima's Aunt Oksana's skills.

Madame Rushinsky: Neighbor of Katya & Dima; supposedly a witch, but a good Seamstress.

Marcos Vela: Son of Rosana, the family cook. He recently returned from Afghanistan, and does odd jobs, such as chauffeuring the sisters and Grandma Tattie while working on a master's degree. (*ALLY*).

Maria Rasputin: Eldest daughter of Grigori Rasputin; opportunist.

Marya: Russian for 'Mary'; servant who looks after Rasputin's apartment in 1918.

Michael Morgan: BTM agent; undercover teacher (Misha) for Romanov children; elopes with Anastasia.

Melinda: works in the Heart-Held Foundation Accounting Department.

Misha: Agent for the BTM. See also: Michael Morgan.

Nesya: Dima's little sister, killed in the Khotynka Field Stampede.

Nicolai: Ghost of Dasha's ancestor killed in 1906 earthquake.

Oksana, Aunt (Dima's aunt; acts as Katya's guardian when her mother dies from fever and enhances her tarot card interpretation.

Oleg Slobotkin: false name used for Rasputin's Death Certificate.

Pauline: hired by Sin to lock Dasha and Alex Pavel Miliutin: Dima's neighbor and friend.

Pyotr (Pete) Marusov: Dasha's father and Irisa's husband; CEO of Marusov Technologies.

Rani Goldman: Gigi's best friend.

Rosana: Cook for Dasha's family. Mother of Marcos Vela.

Sam Garrity: Brendon Alessio's manager.

Sinovia (Sin) Ryland: Former professional ballet dancer out to destroy Dasha's whole family because she was injured when Grandma Tattie was a ballet instructor, and never danced again. (*ANTAGONIST/, VILLAIN*).

Spencer Morgan: The younger brother of Michael Morgan.

Stepan Peshkov: Katya's father, killed at the Khotynka Field stampede the day she was born and Nicholas II was crowned.

Svetlana: one of the "straw hat girls" trying to confuse Rasputin at the National Museum and buy Dasha some time.

Tatiana Marusov: Dasha's grandmother; former professional ballet dancer, teacher, and Time Mender Agent. Later, appointed Interim Director of BTM.

Tessa: Ghost dog that Tatiana adored. Died when Tatiana was 17.

Varvara Rasputin: youngest daughter of Grigori Rasputin.

Vasya : Ghost of Dasha's ancestor killed in 1906 earthquake.

Zoya Peshkova (aka: Madame Peshkova). Katya's mother and fortune teller.

ANIMAL CHARACTERS:

Finley: William Morgan's (son of Ana and Misha) West Highland Terrier. Was accidentally shot during struggle.

Tessa: Grandma Tattie's King Charles Cavalier Spaniel, now a Ghost Dog that died of old age @ 12 in 1959, when Tattie was 13.

Tillie: Sasha's white cat. Came in as a stray. Also loves Grandma Tattie.

Russian Words & Phrases from The Time Menders

(10/06/2025)

NOTE 1:
I am using the Library of Congress Russian Romanization Table for Transliteration.

NOTE 2:
I do not have access to a Russian alphabet keyboard, but this should still work, as Russian is very phonetic. Accents are mine, to help in pronunciation.

RUSSIAN	ENGLISH
(Transliterated from Cyrillic to Roman alphabet)	*Words*
A-mer-i-kánt-sy	American
Pí-vo	Beer
Mal-chick	Boy
Zaí-ka	Bunny
Kósh-ka	Cat
Dyé-ti	Children
Vuh-kús-nye	Delicious
Chort	Devil
Plá-tye	Dress (n.)
O-deh-vát-sah	To get dressed (v.)
Ó-tyets	Father
Iz-vi-nyat	To Forgive; pardon (v.)
Gos-po-dín	Gentleman, Sir, Mister
Po-dá-ruk	Gift
Dé-voch-ka	Girl
Grát-si-ya	Grace
Dé-dush-ka	Grandfather
Vnúch-ka	Granddaughter
Bá-bush-ka	Grandmother
Prá-ded	Great-Grandfather
Pra-bá-bush-ka	Great-Grandmother
Gos-po-zhá	Madam
Ma-try-ósh-ka	Matryoshka (nesting doll)
Mát	Mother
Ma-tyúsh-ka	Mother (nun)
Nyét	No
Ko-néch-no	Of course; certainly
Lyu-bí-mets	Pet, favorite
Pi-rosh-kí	Pie, with meat or vegetables
Svin-yá	Pig
Po-zhál-u-ysta	Please
Kar-tó-fell	Potato

	Phrases
Gós-po-di	Good lord! Good heavens!
Dó-bro-ye útro	Good morning
Pri-der-zhí-tye lo-shad-yey!	Hold your horses!
Ó-tyel Av-ró-a	Hotel Aurora
S-ból-shim u-do-vóls-tvyem	I'd love to!
Pro-stí-tye	I'm sorry
Bó-zhe moi, Slá-va Bó-gu	My God! Thank God!
Mo-yá Lyu-bóv	My love
Za-kús-ka	Snack or bite, appetizer
Spa-sí-bo	Thank you
Vo-dá	Water
Hren zná-yet	Who knows?
Dá	Yes

About the Author

LAINE STAMBAUGH earned a Bachelor's Degree in Russian Studies, a Master's Degree in Linguistics (the scientific study of language), and a Master's Degree in Library Science. Her love of language and culture led her to a satisfying career in academic libraries, where she served as acquisitions librarian and as library human resources director for twenty-nine years. *The Time Menders* is her fourth novel. She is the author of *The Heartstone Trilogy*, historical fiction that takes place during the 11th and 12th century in Scotland and Orkney.